THE DARK GONDOLA

Further Titles by Virginia Coffman from Severn House

The Royles Series

BOOK ONE: THE ROYLES
BOOK TWO: DANGEROUS LOYALTIES
BOOK THREE: THE PRINCESS ROYAL

The Moura Series

MOURA
THE BECKONING
THE DARK GONDOLA
THE VICAR OF MOURA
THE VAMPIRE OF MOURA

Miscellaneous Titles

THE CANDIDATE'S WIFE
HYDE PLACE
THE JEWELLED DARKNESS
LOMBARD CAVALCADE
LOMBARD HEIRESS
ONE MAN TOO MANY
THE ORCHID TREE
PACIFIC CAVALCADE
THE RICHEST GIRL IN THE WORLD
TANA MAGUIRE
THE VENETIAN MASQUE

THE
DARK GONDOLA

Virginia Coffman

This title first published in Great Britain 1995 by
SEVERN HOUSE PUBLISHERS LTD of
9–15 High Street, Sutton, Surrey SM1 1DF.
First published in hardcover format in the USA 1995 by
SEVERN HOUSE PUBLISHERS INC of
425 Park Avenue, New York, NY 10022.

Copyright © 1968, 1994 by Virginia Coffman

All rights reserved. The moral rights of the author have been asserted.

British Library Cataloguing in Publication Data
Coffman, Virginia
  Dark Gondola
  I. Title
  813.54 [F]

ISBN 0-7278-4750-3

All situations in this publication are fictitious and
any resemblance to living persons is purely coincidental.

Typeset by Hewer Text Composition Services, Edinburgh.
Printed and bound in Great Britain by
Hartnolls Ltd, Bodmin, Cornwall.

I

IT WAS a great, dark stretch of unknown water we reached by nightfall and I glanced out of the coach window, searching in vain for the fabled floating city of Venice. The coffin-faced coachman looked back and down at me from his high perch, surprising me by the flash of white canine teeth in a frightful grin.

"We are at journey's end, Signorina. A gondola carries you from the quai."

Journey's end being a desolate, swampy shoreline, black as a peat bog, I thought it a bad thing entirely, this arriving in the night at an unknown destination, to face an unknown employer. But having made the long, tedious trip, first by channel packet, and then the public Accommodation Coach, all the way from my last housekeeping post in the west of Ireland, I was in no position to retrace my steps tonight. I could only hope my prospective employer, Mrs. Elvira Huddle, an English resident in Venice, would provide the ferrying across the lagoon that she promised in her letters to me.

I raised the window again, closing out briefly the foul stench of the night air, while I tried to make myself presentable to my new employer in such wardrobe as I had worn during this last ten hour ride. Before pulling my warm, cape-shawl up over my shoulders, I shook wrinkles out of my dusty green worsted skirts and re-tied the ribbons of my bonnet under one ear. I then started to descend from the coach, hoping for the best. I thought for a little while that the saturnine coachman would let me make the sizable leap to the muddy ground without aid, but at the last second he let down the steps and I descended like a lady and not the upper servant he had doubtless, and very properly, categorized me.

Widowed two years previous in 1818 at the age of twenty-one, I had returned to the sort of post I held before my marriage and by a concentration on my work for the normal sixteen hours a day, I had managed to bury my grief. The offer of this new post in the Venice of magic myth and story had seemed especially welcome to me as I was leaving a post on my foggy native coast of Ireland. My very first employer, an Englishwoman, obligingly made most of the arrangements, but the post seemed less attractive now, although the coachman pointed out the nearest signs of Venice, the flicker of torches and lanterns far out upon the cold waters and interspersed by huddled masses of centures' old palazzos.

"I regret, Signorina, I must go about. You comprehend? For the sake of the team which must be stabled. But you see? A gondola sweeps this way. For the Signorina, without doubt."

Since he had dropped off his young postillion at the last posting house on the mainland, he had to get down my portmanteau and bandbox from the roof himself, and this gave me an opportunity to look about, to see that there really was some sort of conveyance scuttling toward us over the waters, a slender cockleshell boat like an aborigine's canoe, painted all black, as dark as the lagoon itself. A liveried man, leaning forward in a curious stance at the stern of the boat, was making good time with a long, substantial oar, more like a sweep. A hooded lamp on the bow of the gondola gave off glints of surprising richness from the exterior of the boat, surprising because Mrs. Huddle's correspondence with me had suggested a woman more than careful of her funds, unlikely to send a gondola with bright silver trappings, merely to fetch a housekeeper from the Accommodation Coach.

"The boxes of the Signorina," announced the coachman with a flourish, dropping my cloth portmanteau to the ground. Before I could stop him, this was followed by my bandbox, with me wincing to see the delicate green ribbons trail in the mud. I rushed about, rescuing my property barely in time to avoid the big carriage wheels as the coachman gave his team the office to start. His circling turn caused the horses' hooves to ring upon the stones of the quai and the sound trailed eerily over the waters. A moment later I was enshrouded by the misty dark.

"I'll be finding that black gondola more than welcome," I thought, however sinister it might look from this distance. I moved across the time-worn stones, avoiding little pools of fresh spring rain, until I stepped into one up to my ankle, just as I reached what apparently was a big, black and white striped mooring pole. Another step would have sent me reeling over into the slimy waters below. As I rubbed my ankle and instep briskly, using the mooring pole to keep my balance, the shadowed gondola came within sight of me, headed for the mooring pole.

Details within the gondola began to materialize out of the surrounding dark, and I noticed that there were several figures in the waist of the little boat. Strange figures. Or perhaps, only the silhouettes seemed strange as the distance closed between us. I thought they must be churchmen enveloped in cassocks or capes, but as the gondola's lantern slowly illuminated the details of the three figures, there appeared to be a frightening similarity about these phantoms. There were no faces visible, only a macabre, inexplicable blackness where the faces should have been.

I snatched my hand away from the mooring pole and jumped back, hoping the odd creatures would not notice me. The sight of those three chilled me to the bone, so like to Death they were.

But there was no escape from their notice. The gondolier hooked in close, tied up at the mooring pole and the three black-clad creatures began to climb out upon the quai. While I watched, curious as well as apprehensive, I saw a human hand, male but effete, I thought, with a huge emerald sparkling on one finger as it caught the lantern-light. The strange trio spoke among themselves about the time of the return and then, as the man with the emerald stepped away from the gondolier, leaving one of his companions to give orders, I began to understand the weird absence of faces.

This was the month before Lent, and Venice was in carnival. The faceless creatures merely wore masks.

While the third of the trio talked to the gondolier, the others caught sight of me and both started a little, exchanging quick, uneasy glances. It would appear that I, Anne Wicklow, standing there silent and motionless in the dark, had frightened these weird figures. The idea did much to restore my confidence. As those who knew me in the past would testify, although a perfect repository of fears of ghosts and the Unknown, I was reasonably competent otherwise. I felt that I owed both my fears and my competence to my Irish heritage.

"Good God!" muttered the black-clad masquerader who had first seen me, speaking in Italian, "Are you real, Signorina, or an apparition from the netherworld?"

"Not from the netherworld, I hope, Signore," I replied, and bobbed a quick, respectful curtsey, trusting that the hems of my skirts would not be stained with muddy water. "I am from Ireland."

"The same thing, eh, Giacomo?"

His friend laughed and I could see the mask blow outward with the spurt of breathy laughter. He turned his head and called to the third figure who was dealing with the gondolier. "Ketta, My Angel, you had better look to your beauty. You have acquired a rival."

Although such a compliment is good to hear when one has reached twenty-three and can no longer be called a "young woman." I suspected the remark had been made in the spirit of a pinprick to the beauteous "Ketta" rather than as flattery to me. I was amused but kept a sober, respectful face; for they obviously thought me a lady and not a hired housekeeper. It would be embarrassing if I allowed them to continue in ignorance and they might react either frigidly or too familiarly. Neither alternative was pleasant. I thought my best chance to escape this awkwardness would be by explaining my dilemma to the mysterious lady they called "Ketta." I took a few steps forward again, to the mooring pole. The lady's grace and elegance were revealed by her movements even under the black cloak, mask and tricorn hat, and I curtsyed again before addressing her in my bad Italian. This was flavored with the French which had been my husband's native language.

"Signora, if you please, is this a general mooring place for private gondolas from Venice?"

"For some of them. Why do you ask, my dear?" The lady's light eyes sparkled through her mask and I was relieved at her pleasant manner. She guessed my dilemma almost before I could explain, and she went on, "I see. You are to be taken up by someone. But then..." Her shrewd eyes looked me over. Except for the short years of my marriage to an aristocrat, I was always careful not to dress above my station, which would have been a habit particularly annoying to any female who employed me. "You are not a guest? A governess, I daresay."

"The housekeeper," I explained; for a housekeeper's place, in my experience, is as far above the power of a governess as it is beneath her in social position, and I would never trade my idependent state as the highest servant in a household for that of a governess, the most dependent person to be included in the gentility.

"Come, Ketta! They will have drunk all the Champagne in Mestri," called one of the two masked men while the other studied me, obviously having heard me explain my position.

"Yes, yes," said the lady impatiently. "A moment yet. The poor child cannot be allowed to remain here until someone comes for her. It is not the Canareggio, after all. Where are you employed? Perhaps I can tell you where your employer's boat will dock." She looked toward her companions and made as if to join them. I knew I was in her way and that she was probably bored with this little problem which was not of her making.

I said quickly, "If your gondolier might know of the dock or the quai, you need not trouble, Signora."

Relieved to be free of the matter, the lady set her black tricorn hat more securely over deep auburn hair that was heavily curled all around her neck and blew in the night air across the mask that concealed her face.

"Very well, then. Filippo—" to her gondolier, "do the young woman any service you may. . . . I am coming, Giacomo. Don't be so irritable." She had already passed me when she asked casually, "What did you say your employer's name was?"

"She is an English lady. Mrs. Elvira Huddle."

It was not a prepossessing name, lacking both splendor and money, and I knew that the moment I uttered it the lady called "Ketta" would lose her last shred of interest in me and my problems. To my astonishment, she swung around so abruptly I caught the flash of jeweled garments beneath the wide cloak. At the same time the gondolier, by his manner of address to her, told me something of the Lady Ketta's importance and explained her bejeweled clothing.

"As Your Highness wishes. Will there be time for me to take the young woman to the Huddle Palazzo before Your Highness and the Signori return from Mestri?"

So the lady called "Ketta" was a princess! What was even more surprising, she began, quite suddenly, to show a new interest in my affairs.

"A moment, Filippo. Perhaps I may . . ." She raised her black velvet mask and I noted that despite her age—she must be nearing forty—she was a woman of scintillating, if imperious beauty. Her manner of ironic humor may have contributed to this beauty. Certainly it softened what I suspected was a native arrogance. She motioned to her two companions. "My carriage will be here at any moment. Tell my man to take you to the casino."

"And you, Ketta?" asked the man with the emerald.

"Perhaps later. I'll play the Samaritan and deliver Elvira's housekeeper to the old witch."

While I was pleased at her unexpected company, the

Princess' sudden interest was most mysterious, and what is more, I did not above half like her description of my prospective mistress. I considered my surroundings, the dripping spring night and my weird companions, the unknown destiny that beckoned to me from those lantern lights across the lagoon, and I tried to be grateful for this sudden, overwhelming attention. I said nothing, neither question nor thanks, until the lady motioned me to the edge of the quai.

"Your boxes. You have them? Filippo! Come and take the boxes of the young woman."

But I had already lifted my portmanteau over within reach of the gondolier and one of the Princess' masked male friends threw my bandbox down to Filippo who caught it deftly and set it under the covered metallic bow of the glossy black craft. I wanted to step down into the gondola as easily as the Princess had stepped up and out; so I looked over the situation with care, calculating how great a leap would land me on my feet in the waist of the boat, with no loss of dignity or broken bones. Out of the corners of my eyes I saw the two masked men turn to watch me and was sure they smiled, expecting to witness my awkward descent to the gondola. Although I confess the effort was considerable, I managed to step down and into the little swaying craft without providing my audience with their entertainment. It was all a matter of careful balance, I discovered. The regal lady who had mysteriously chosen to escort a mere servant to her place of employment, stepped down beside me with enviable ease.

"I am Catana, the Princess da Rimini," she introduced herself as she buried her mask in a pocket of her cloak. "And you, my dear?"

"Anne Wicklow, Your Highness," I said, neglecting to give her my married state and name. My husband had been executed as a Bonapartist in Restoration France, and I was warned that his name would be my death warrant, in French-oriented Italy.

The Princess looked at me sharply. I wondered at her extraordinary curiosity about the affairs of my employer, and I did not feel wholly at my ease with her.

"Wicklow . . . One wonders at the tongue that encompasses these English names."

"I am Irish," I corrected her and added her title, to soften my abruptness.

She gave the word to shove off, paying no attention to her cavaliers on the quai who waved, and being ignored by her indifferent back, they turned toward what I supposed must be the approaching carriage that took them to their revels in Mestri. Had they not behaved so very like the Princess' paid cicisbeos, or platonic lovers, I would have thought the two black-clad creatures sinister indeed, with their all-encompassing cloacks lashed by the mist, and their flesh, except the hands, picturesquely concealed. I hoped I would not see many more such phantoms in Venice, although I had heard that every male in the City of Canals dressed in somewhat similar fashion, during this season. But then, I had heard a great deal of idle and absurd gossip about the city.

"So you are Irish," the Princess mused as the gondolier sent us scuttling over the gleaming waters. "How curious! Elvira Huddle pays as little as may be to her servants, and to be at the expense of hiring a girl—you are little more—from that far away island of yours, it is almost as if she did not wish a local resident to have the freedom of her house."

I wondered if my employer merely felt the need of a housekeeper who would not pry or show inordinate curiosity. If all Venetians were like the Princess da Rimini, they were certainly prying.

"There may be a simple explanation, Highness. Mrs. Huddle probably prefers to give her orders in English. Then too, she is acquainted with my first employer, the mistress of a Young Ladies' Academy in England."

Filippo, the gondolier, surprised me by putting in, with a rasping voice very like his face, "The *Inglesi* is needed for the wedding, doubtless. After that, like the last female, she will not be missed."

I looked up but saw that he was speaking to the Princess as though I could not hear. He probably thought I did not understand his distinctive dialect. One thing came to me very clearly, this mention of

The Last One, who would not be missed. I had a flashing thought that almost anything could be done to a foreign woman like myself, so far from her native heath, and with no acquaintance in Italy. I assured myself that I, personally, would not be endangered. I was used to fending for myself. But . . . if I were less self-reliant, there were endless dangers in a city like Venice, with its remnants of maritime power, its easy access to the Turkish ports of the Levant. Servant girls, country girls, seamstresses, governesses, all are grist for the White Slave trade that I know is vigorously carried on between the Christian and the Muslim countries of the Mediterranean, even during these enlightened times of the Nineteenth Centruy.

Remote as such a danger might be, the idea was chilling. When the gondolier and the Princess glanced at me, I pretended to shiver at the wind-blown mist that penetrated my shawl and crept in under the brim of my bonnet. A life of intermittent danger had given me this devious approach to strangers. Long ago, I learned never to let others know the extent of my own knowledge. In this case, it was my understanding of the gondolier's dialect. To put them off any suspicion, I said vaguely,

"Pardon, but you speak of an Inglesi? If you recall, I am Irish." And I changed the subject with a lightness that I hoped would convince them. "Is Your Highness familiar with my employer's household?"

My seeming ignorance of the gondolier's remark appeared to reassure my two companions. It was their very reassurance which kept me on my guard, though the Princess obligingly sketched a little portrait in words of Elvira Huddle's household. The gondolier, balancing on his sweep in that odd, forward stance, guided us nearer to the winking lights of Venice, while the Princess spoke.

"As to my dislike of Elvira, I shall say nothing further on that article. We are friends, after all." I thought this a curious way to speak of a friend, but was careful not to smile. "In any case, her son, Bartrum, is very precious to her, and as he is betrothed to a young—

person of mysterious antecedents, Elvira despises her amazingly. You may find the household a bitter one."

Naturally, I inquired as the young lady's "mysterious antecedents" and the Princess smiled.

"A figure of speech. I am well acquainted with little Julie Sanson's guardian. It is he who provides the mystery. But then . . . I take a notorious delight in sinister characters. Do I not, Filippo?"

The man flushed so noticeably I wondered whether she referred to him also with that sharp witticism.

"As Your Highness says." The gondola headed out of the lagoon and into a canal no wider than a Dublin alley, between forbidding walls unbreached by windows for thirty feet above the dirty canal waters. The walls themselves appeared dark and wet with mold, especially close to the water where the landing steps were heavily scummed. There was a stench of rotting food, decaying vegetation that seemed oppressive, though I was far from unused to such alley smells.

It was different, however, when we reached the Grand Canal.

"The Palazzo of the Signora Huddle is in the Rio del Cavallo, Filippo. Beyond the Rialto Bridge."

We were much too short a time in the wide, stately Grand Canal with its lamps at every mooring pole, illuminating such delicate, lacy palace facades as I had only dreamed of heretofore. The waters were alive with the laughter of masqueraders in gondolas that glided past. There were even songs, and the pleasant tinkle of mandolinas everywhere, despite the weather. This was beginning to be the Venice of romance.

But then, with a curious, high-pitched and birdlike call, Filippo shifted one foot slightly and maneuvered his sweep so that we turned and cut across the main stream of traffic toward a narrow and very dark canal, once more between high walls. So quiet was it, after the gaiety of the Grand Canal that we could hear the waters lapping everywhere around us, as if sucking at our graceful gondola, trying to draw us down into those murky depths.

"There. You see the Huddle place. Gloomy old prison," the Princess remarked and pointed out a heavily shadowed corner beyond us, where another canal opened into ours. Along the sharp, square corner formed by the two canals, the mooring lamps were unlighted, but by our own gondola light we were able to make out an untended little garden on the junction of the two canals, and beside it, the square, dark, empty-looking palazzo of Elvira Huddle. We could scarcely see a light showing behind the shutters of the high iron-grilled windows. There were probably three and a half stories here, but they looked as ugly and forbidding as any house which is not lived in. Surely, an odd condition for a home in which the wedding of two people is to be celebrated.

The Princess, in her imperious way, provided an explanation now: "You see what a miser your employer is. Not even lights, my dear Anne. If you wish to hold a place in Elvira's affections, I suggest you spend as little as possible upon the household."

I smiled, pretending I considered her advice lightly humorous. But as Filippo guided us to the mooring pole and then managed to hold the gondola steady while I climbed out, I liked even less what I saw from the level of the slippery stone quai.

The gondola shoved off. "Go with God. Or is is the Devil, Anne Wicklow?" the Princess called across the intervening waters. "Break into Elvira's pockets and invite me to the betrothal ball."

Laughing, I promised to do so. I had begun to appreciate her lively manner. It had a definite effect upon my own spirits, which were starting to flag as I stood there staring at the pathetic little garden with its stone benches and massive centuries' old urns that cast grotesque shadows against the walls of the palazzo. There was an aspect or a mood about the garden that made me think of graveyards in Ireland with their weird old Gaelic crosses to haunt the lone observer.

I shrugged off such thoughts, angry at the weak impressionability which had gripped me for a minute or two. Then, with my portmanteau and my bandbox, I made my way across the garden, over the stone walk, among the sad gray urns to the door of the palazzo. There was an iron grillwork behind which the window in the door had been sealed up. The massive iron knocker still was in use, however, and I rapped on the door, harder and more anxiously than I had intended.

I was uncomfortably aware of the silence that succeeded the noisy clang of the iron knocker. I had not expected an immediate welcome. There was, after all, only one light visible, and that high in the mansion. I stepped back to make a more careful study of that particular light, to see if it moved downward, but found myself touching one of those great, cold, funeral urns that were large enough to hold an assassin or two but which, undoubtedly, held only dirt and debris of months, perhaps years. Hearing the scratch of gravel behind me, I swung around rapidly, susceptible to almost any horror.

By the vague light from the misty night sky, I could make out nothing in the garden beyond the formal position of each untended, half-dead plant or hedge, each huge urn and the stone benches now speckled with rain, until a lengthy, soft, almost boneless thing rubbed across my ankle.

The ghostly thing was unmistakably a cat, lean and starved enough to be a wraith, and the poor creature gazed up at me with every tooth gleaming.

II

THE METALLIC click of a door-bolt being thrown back made me aware that the garden door of Mrs. Huddle's palazzo was opening. I looked that way in time to hear an irritable female voice demand, surprisingly in English,

"So you've arrived at last; is it? You made a deal of noise, Miss."

In the circumstances, I felt that her shrill complaint had a deal of effrontery. But as I approached the doorway, the uncomfortable suspicion grew that this tousled old woman, grotesquely lighted by a single, flickering candle in her hand, was my employer.

"I am the new housekeeper. From Miss Nutting's Academy in Richmond, Surrey. I understood I was to have been met at the quai near the post-house. However, I was fortunate enough to—"

She interrupted me as successfully with her piercing black eyes as with the brusque: "That was my son's doing. He had some notion of sending a gondola to fetch you. But you'll find his memory is faulty at best. . . . Come along. Miss. You've kept me burning candle-ends until all hours."

All hopes of the future were cut up at this proof of my worst suspicions. The gaunt, small woman with her graying witch locks and her sharp-cut Roman profile was Elvira Huddle. With a quick wave of the candlestick, she motioned me and my luggage inside the narrow, damp passage and then slammed the door shut. I saw the scrawny, gray cat barely leap out of the doorway and into the nearest garden urn to avoid being crushed. The urn was taller than I, who am accounted a tall woman, and the cat's leap was very creditable. I wondered briefly what anyone would have cause to admire about those dreary, enormous urns that mounted guard out there.

"Accursed cats!" the woman muttered as she shoved the bolt into place on the door. "They are the scourge of Venice."

"But you do have a problem with rats here?" I suggested, supposing that a city built on pilings over the water would appreciate its feline population.

Mrs. Huddle looked around at me as though I had said something incivil, but I was busy debating whether I should take the dark, seeping ground floor passage to the back of the house, or mount the steps behind my prospective employer, on the threadbare carpeting.

"I'll be quit of those cats, or die for it."

She did not pursue her suspicions of my manner, but motioned me to the stairs before her, and followed close behind me, rather like a wardress escorting her prisoner. The higher I mounted those steps, the less I liked this foreshadowing of our relationship.

There was a certain relief in the knowledge that my quarters would, at least, be above the water line. We did not stop as we reached the first floor, but took another flight of steps over another strip of well-worn carpet, having caught the barest revealing glimpse of a sombre series of rooms, one opening into another as far as the canal on the east side of the palazzo. This view cutting through the width of the building was revealed by a single, low-burning candle on a tabaret near the balcony doors, a glow that winked in the thick dark like a mischievous eye.

Thinking of my miserly employer I wondered as we climbed to the second floor just how I was to transform a dusty, dark house scarcely more comfortable than a prison, and certainly far from the palazzo its exterior suggested. Matters were not improved by the flicker and quiver of the candle in Mrs. Huddle's hand, which hinted that the wick had burned down to its frayed ends.

"Beelzebub!" muttered my employer, nursing along what remained of our only illumination. "So much for that candlemaker. Mark me, Miss, no more candles are to be purchased from the Rio Bianco shop."

I felt there would be little point in my reminding her that a candle, whether purchased from the Rio Bianco or another shop, would not provide an eternal light. In any case, the shrewd woman managed to nurse the flame until we reached my room on the second floor, three stories above the quai and the stone garden. We stepped into a second floor corridor, dark as the rest of the mansion until Mrs. Huddle's flickering candle provided the briefest trail of light, and she opened a door nearby.

I found myself in a very tolerable room, or one that would have been pleasant, if I had not found it necessary to fumble in the dark among the substantial articles of furniture.

"I have ordered Cobb to remove to smaller quarters at the far end of this story," said Mrs. Huddle briskly.

I felt, uneasily, that it would be a poor beginning to my regime here if I put someone else out of his quarters and said so.

"Nonsense! Cobb is only the butler. You must make yourself his superior. The room is yours, and do not let me hear any absurd rambles about it between the two of you. We will discuss your duties tomorrow. You arise early, I trust."

"That's the way of it, M'am. But—" She was actually leaving the room, and me, in the dark.

"Well?" She looked back crossly. For an instant I remembered the first time I saw such a woman, at the French chateau of the man I adored and subsequently married. To me, the sharp face with its black eyes and implacable countenance was just such as would have appeared at the foot of the guillotine during the brief but bloody French Reign of Terror. True, Elvira Huddle was reputed to be English, but the spirit, I thought, was equally cold blooded.

"Please let me put a candle to your light."

She looked more than a little disgusted and let me know it as she applied the tip of her carefully guarded candle-end to a fairly heavy candle in its holder on what proved to be a bedstand.

"I say it to your head, Anne Wicklow, there'll be no wastage here, or back you go, no matter what notions Bartrum may have. Do not let the candle burn after you have found your way around the room." And she left me, closing the door with some force but leaving me blessedly alone.

Wishing now that I had eaten a larger luncheon at the post house that day, I set about unpacking and placing my brief property, which long years of travel had abbreviated to necessities that could double in usage, plus the few luxuries I allowed myself, and which gave cheer to each new lodging. Among these luxuries were my splendid silver framed miniature of my husband, and a number of items of personal apparel re-purchased and re-furbished frequently, such as my choice of both green and lilac ribbons and shawls to prevent my ever looking like the established grim, haughty figure of a housekeeper. I set the portmanteau before the open door of the mahogany armoire and hung my gowns on pegs inside the big, dark cupboard. I untied the ribbons of the bonnet I wore and set it beside my lilac bonnet on the shelf above the drawers on the right side of the armoire. By the time I had rubbed and put away my two pairs of morocco street and dress slippers, along with stockings and petticoats, I had worked up an appetite that was not likely to be satisfied in this house, tonight or any other night.

I am an Irishwoman in more than name. My appetite is that of my ancestors, not to be satisfied by sleep or such absurdities as mental determination. Although it was scarcely eight o'clock in the night, I hesitated to ring for a maid to bring me a pot of tea, since the household was run so parsimoniously there might be a rule about retiring at sunset. And it would be clumsy of me to wander about the ground floor alone, searching for the stillroom.

I glanced around the room, considering the dusty mahogany and Chinese furniture, the unshuttered window that opened upon the garden far below, and the likelihood of my having the same food problem at dawn when, in well-regulated households, I might expect to be served a proper tray of tea. It seemed clear that I must put a certain routine into effect at once if I was to have the management of this sadly neglected house. It even took me some little time to locate the worn, petit-point worked bell-pull which hung behind the end of the huge armoire, of all the absurd places. I was about to give it a stiff tug, but one glance at the top of the petit-point strip showed me the danger of that. The whole thing was so frayed it would come down in my hands at any minute.

I gave a couple of gentle tugs, hoping for the best, wondering at the same time how my predecessor, Mr. Cobb, the butler, had managed. The room was masculine, the Chinese teak furnishings, along with the mahogany. I could well imagine Mr. Cobb's enthusiasm for the woman who had usurped his place. It would require considerable persuasive and diplomatic power.

I opened the door and looked out into the passage, which I now noted with surprise was a wide, interior salon, beautifully tiled, somewhat vacant of furniture. Only a pair of cerule chairs and a Chinese fretwork table relieved the almost sinister empty look of the salon. Sinister, I thought, because, just for a moment, I had the notion that in spite of the room's emptiness, I was being observed from some corner, some point of vantage that I knew nothing about.

"Is anyone here?" I called in a voice I found so near to a whisper I was forced to clear my throat and repeat the question. Even then, I strongly misliked the odd, hollow traveling sound of my voice through the salon and beyond, probably to a balcony over the opposite canal. I could not see the balcony itself. The doors were closed and their small diamond panes of glass reflected only the single gleam of light, repeated many times, from the candle in my room. Or was it Mr. Cobb's room still?

As I stepped back inside, leaving the door ajar, I saw almost immediately that some part of Mr. Cobb's property, as I supposed, had been left behind him. It was a curious, cylindrical object, the length of my arm, and it was propped against the wall beneath the window which overlooked the garden. I crossed the room, took up the curious cylinder, saw that it could be compressed upon itself, and suddenly recalled seeing one on the Channel Packet. A ship's mate had raised the cylinder to his eye and studied the foggy waters.

"A spyglass! Now, why should a butler find it necessary to spy upon the neighborhood?"

I put the spyglass to my eye and directed it downward at the ghostly urns, the misty stone benches, and then at the lean cat who curled up on top of one dirt-filled urn. He was following the system I might be forced to resort to myself. He was trying to dull the edge of hunger by sleep. I understood his frustration perfectly.

The high urn cast a shadow and I glanced up. The sky overhead had begun to clear. A sprinkle of stars appeared, almost directly over the Grand Canal which I could make out in a winding southerly direction from the palazzo. The noise and music and carnival activity were blunted at this distance. My attention was caught then by the lengthening of that shadow behind the urn. It was a definite motion, not to be explained by any rapid cloud movement overhead. I brought the spyglass to bear upon the urn and the great shadow behind it.

Something seemed to be there waiting and hidden,

or perhaps stalking. I could not make it out distinctly. The creature appeared much too tall, too powerful to be a female. Suddenly, the man looked upward toward the wall of the building, and I saw a stern, powerful, rather heavy face, the flesh briefly caught by the scudding clouds overhead. The eyes seemed dark and luminous, but it may have been the mere reaction of the light from the heavens. It was my own reaction to these eyes that made me aware of the impropriety of spying. I backed into the room hastily, more embarrassed at having been caught watching the stranger than from any fancied fear for myself. The truth is, it all happened so quickly I had not yet thought of danger, or of the sinister implications in that silent, ominous figure skulking in the shadows. But I took a couple of steps backward before I had occasion to know what terror was. I walked back into an obstacle that had not been there three minutes before. Stifling a cowardly scream, I swung around.

A small, neat man with a not unintelligent face, was standing in the middle of my bedchamber, so close to me I seemed to read my own reflection in his clear, cold eyes.

"Madam? May I trouble you for my property?"

Still a bit shaken, I looked so confused he smiled faintly. It was a careful, measured smile. I had a notion he used it for pre-conceived occasions.

"Your property? I have only just arrived, Sir. You'll be Mr. Cobb, I make no doubt."

"Precisely. And you? Miss Wicklow, of course. They had not told me you were so very— Hm." Then he held out his hand. "If you please?"

I looked around, trying to discover what it was precisely that he had come for and found the spyglass being slipped gently through my hand.

I apologized, at which Mr. Cobb said gently, "How beautifully you Irish blush, Miss Anne! It was worth the inconvenience—" he caressed the spyglass "—merely to see you color up so fetchingly. Are you well provided? You must bespeak any little comforts you lack."

I was about to dismiss this offer with indifferent politeness, when my famished condition got the better of me and I asked if I might possibly have tea served, with some small addition, a slice of buttered bread, perhaps.

He glanced out the window quickly and I was aware of two oddities. First, he assuredly was interested in the view of the garden—with, perhaps, its hidden watcher, and second, that he could see nothing from this far inside the room. Although I pretended not to notice the direction of his interest, he must have guessed I knew, and told me with the utmost graciousness, "I shall attend to it myself, at once, Miss Anne. One of the maids will still be at work."

I thanked him, beginning to find the cold, precise little man less unpleasant. But when he had gone with his spyglass, I did wonder. I intended to make constructive use of the moments when he brought me my tray. Perhaps I could discover why I had been led, so far, under such false pretenses. From the entire attitude of my employer, I was not here at her wish. And clearly, she had little need of a housekeeper in a house which was scarcely lived in at all.

I washed at a footed pewter bowl that was badly scratched, and I scrubbed dry all the area of flesh that I could reach, with a well-worn, beautiful lace-edged linen towel.

It was not Mr. Cobb who brought me my tray shortly after nine o'clock. A pretty young Italian girl arrived, pouting that her work, and I, kept her from the carnival and the evening on the Grand Canal.

"What a pity!" I said, and decided abruptly to satisfy both her wishes and my own curiosity. I went to my netting bag and took out some of the coins for which I had exchanged English money at the port of Genoa. I jingled what totaled roughly three *scudi*, her wages for a fortnight, and I offered them to her "so that we shall become acquainted. Then too," I added, "there may be other nights when a tray is desired and we must be prepared to serve. All of us."

The meal was worth the three scudi: a hot chocolate pitcher full of strong tea, pieces of several interesting breads, including the fruited and sugared dessert cakes, and even an apple, at exactly the ripe stage. I looked up as she stood there staring at the coins in her palm.

"Signorina! Such a riches! Is it for me? A month's wages?"

Well then, I hadn't known that, but Mrs. Huddle's great care with money should have warned me. I smiled and began to pour.

"What will you do with the money?"

"Go to Florian's, of course. That is in the square of San Marco."

"Why will you go there? To see your sweetheart?"

She grinned, a big, red, toothy grin. "Not so, Signorina. To catch one. Maybe I will make the Signore jealous."

"The signore?" Not the cold-eyed, self-contained Mr. Cobb!

"Yes, yes. The Signore Bartrum. So handsome!" She rolled her big eyes. "He looks at me sometimes. I can tell. And once, he kissed me when I took him wine to his bedchamber. If it wasn't for the Signore Bartrum, I would never stay in this hideous place. It is full of horrors and the biggest horror is that old—"

Again I thought of the butler, but she added: "miser" and I knew that my employer was included in her blanket denunciation. I could scarcely blame her, but if any order was to be maintained here, we must, all of us, show our mistress at least a modicum of respect.

"Thank you for tray, at any rate," I said quickly. "We had better not discuss our employer; don't you agree?"

She frowned over her shoulder into the deep darkness beyond my room.

"Maria-Elisa used to say that. But you see what happened to her. Elisa was First Parlormaid, you know."

I could not but ask, "What *did* happen to her?"

"Like me, she was mad for Signore Bartrum. And then she committed the dreadful sin."

"Which dreadful sin?"

"Suicide. So they say."

I began to be uneasy again. "But why do they say— if she died, do they not know how she died?"

Barbarita seemed to have heard something out in the gloomy salon beyond my door. She lowered her voice.

"They do believe she threw herself over one of the balconies and drowned in the San Georgio canal. But it is not known for a certainty. You see, we could never find her body."

I shuddered. "But perhaps the body was carried out to the Grand Canal."

"Perhaps. Mr. Cobb believes so. But the servants think . . . Well, bodies are usually found in San Georgio. They are not washed so far away." While I digested this grisly little tale, Barbarita appeared to think she had gone too far, or perhaps only she was afraid of being heard by someone out in the salon beyond us. I wondered briefly where the silent-footed Mr. Cobb was at this minute. "You understand, Signorina, Elisa may have run away, because she was unhappy. Dear Bartrum—The Signore," she corrected herself, "was about to become betrothed to Julie Sanson. As if a betrothal, or even a marriage need stop the Signore Bartrum if he cast his eyes my way!"

It was hard to believe that the harsh, witchlike Elvira Huddle could have produced a son who had such devastating effect upon all the household females. I was curious to see the irresistable Bartrum. But meanwhile, the disappearance, or suicide of the missing parlormaid troubled me, although I cannot admit to surprise. So many odd and disquieting things had formed my mood from the moment I stepped out of the Accommodation Coach at the quai's edge.

The girl watched me pour tea and take a strengthening sip. Then she leaned forward, presenting a bosomy sight in her loose black bodice, saying in a hoarse whisper, "Did you know the Signora Huddle was once a keeper in a madhouse?"

Before I could reply to this non-sequitur, the girl swung around and left me. I heard her feet pattering over the tiles of the salon and wondered how she could move through this complex mansion in almost complete darkness, with so little effort and so little uneasiness. Or was she genuinely uneasy? It was difficult to guess from her volatile, gossipy personality.

It occurred to me that the Elvira Huddle I had met was precisely the sort of woman I might expect to discover in charge of helpless inmates in a madhouse. Finishing my dinner while several delicious breads still remained on the tray to tantalize me, I recalled Mrs. Huddle's mention of Bartrum, her son. There had been the hint that the gentleman might have been responsible for the hiring of a foreign-born Irish housekeeper. Perhaps, too, it was something about young Bartrum that the Princess and her gondolier had called "sinister." Unlikely, though. I began to recall that the sinister character had some connection with Bartrum's betrothed, Julie Sanson.

All of this should not be my concern, I reminded myself. I got up and shot the bolt on my door. Then I poured more water into the pewter bowl from the exquisite, though chipped glass amphora, and washed my body, then combed and brushed out my hair and dressed for bed. The bed itself was oppressive, though uncurtained. The high headboard and foot posts were carved out of a blackened wood, like the little Chinese table in the salon. They gleamed in the candlelight despite the dust that coated them

Just before scrambling up into the bed, I decided the room's coat of dust was too much to breathe after the foggy Atlantic coasts of Ireland and the Surrey winter at Miss Nutting's Academy. I went to the window and gave the latch a hard stiff jolt to open it, knowing in what horror these Latin countries held a breath of fresh air. To my surprise the window gave very easily. Someone, undoubtedly Mr. Cobb, must often have opened the window. An open window would give his precious spyglass much better leverage, and bring the object of his attention closer as well.

The screeching sound of the window being pushed outward so abruptly filled the air above the desolate garden and I was not too surprised when a cloaked and masked man, looking as if he had newly stepped from the masquers in the Grand Canal, came out of the darkness behind the huge stone urn and looked up at me. He was big, I thought. Tall and powerful. Frighteningly so when I remembered how long he must have been standing there, secretive and watchful.

And then an even more puzzling thing occurred. I

made out a faint blinking light, so quickly vanishing, in fact, that I barely had time to see that it was caused by the starlight falling upon a metal object near me, a few windows away. It was Mr. Cobb's spyglass, projecting a little way out of the window, and pointed downward. So he had not given up his Peeping Tom activities!

Meanwhile, the overpowering figure in shadows below was staring up, studying me in my thin night-rail. What shocked me more was the fact that the man had as clear a view of my own flesh as that view I myself vaguely deplored when displayed by the maid Barbarita. I hurriedly drew in my head, but left the window ajar. I gave Mr. Cobb over, mentally, to the mysterious waiting man. The two might make what they liked out of their mutual spying.

I had already gotten into the comfortable bed and was determined to throw off all disturbing sleep-interfering thoughts, when the mysterious suicide of the parlormaid, Maria-Elisa, crept into my mind.

What a curious business it all was! I had half a mind to leave the palazzo tomorrow. Still, it would be very like the reading of but half a romance, the hearing of scarcely half a Franchetti score. I wanted very much to know why these curious things had happened and continued to happen.

There were no more human sounds or disturbances outside for several hours. Meanwhile, I went to sleep. But not, unfortunately, for the night.

III

I WAS awakened very soon by an unfamiliar sound, one of those peculiar things that occur to me when I sleep the first night in a strange house. I thought the weird cry must be a night bird, but soon remembered that I had heard it before, when Princess Ketta's gondolier made his interesting turns from one canal into another. The call came again and I thought it sounded so close there must be a gondola tying up at a mooring pole of Mrs. Huddle's palazzo.

I glanced at the little gold clock I treasured from my husband. It was a trifle before ten o'clock. Exceedingly curious to know whether our silent powerful man in the garden had been awaiting this gondola, I got out of bed and pattered to the window, becoming aware of the clammy dampness of the Venetian night. I saw the gondola light at once, as well as the slim young man who leaped to the quai and waved his thanks to the gondolier who, obviously, was not in service to this household. It was so like the miserly Mrs. Huddle to own this great, empty palazzo and nothing else that would make the living in it comfortable. From his face and what I guessed about the figure of the young man who had just left the gondola, I felt that he was the handsome Bartrum Huddle so much sought after by the parlormaids of the household.

In my effort to see the young man, I had neglected to watch the big, silent, interesting man in the garden. I saw now that he was still there and had begun to move out into the starlight, obviously to cut off the young man's exit into the palazzo. This quick though silent movement of the watcher in his huge, windblown cloak, caused the gray cat to leap up from his place in the dirt-filled urn and peer out over the top. Poor creature! I wished I could get some food to him. He looked hopeful for a few seconds, then stretched his attenuated shape still further and curled up to sleep once more on the high-piled earth in the urn. What a fondness he had for that gigantic urn! It was a matter for wonder to me.

Meanwhile, Mr. Bartrum had cried out in a musical English voice: "What the deuce!" upon being confronted by the big, dark man. "Really, Sir, I'd no notion you'd be visiting Mother. But why skulk about in the garden? Come inside and I'll pour you a stirrup cup. The gondola's rented. You're welcome to take it off my hands."

"I am not ready to leave yet," said the big dark man in a low voice that yet had great power.

I meant to make some disturbance if there should be a violent move from him, but it began to seem that this would not progress beyond the obvious attempts of young Master Bartrum to be conciliatory.

"Word of honor, Sir!" He took off his mask and waved it as he punctuated his remarks. "I love your ward. Enchanting little creature. Wouldn't dream of taking an ungentlemanly advantage. You needn't have come here to escort her home, you know. I'd never dream of bringing her here without your consent." He added engenuously, "Awfully sorry if you don't approve our betrothal. Mama does."

This seemed to me rather amusing effrontery and I waited expectantly for the reaction of the big, caped man. I couldn't make out what he said, but I saw Mr. Bartrum cower a second before trying to placate the man.

"Frightfully sorry, dear boy . . . I mean . . . Sir. But I assure you, I am most eligible. Cut quite a dash with the nabobs of Venice, you know. And Mother's not precisely a pauper. When she's gone, I shall be quite the thing. Rich as a Doge."

Again, I heard the voice of the dark man, deep and haunting, painful to me with its resemblance to my husband's. Perhaps the resemblance lay only in the faintly French intonation; perhaps in the resonance, or something else. Something I would understand only after—and if—I myself met Julie Sanson's mysterious guardian.

The strange man said, "Your mother and I are old acquaintances. You can tell me nothing of Elvira Huddle. I warn you—"

The flash of light from a window beyond my own attracted the two men at the same time that it caught my eye. A night breeze had swept away the clouds overhead, and starlight gleamed on the barrel of a spyglass. I assumed it was in the hands of the butler, Mr. Cobb, and I left the window, realizing I had behaved no better than the inquisitive Cobb, always supposing it was he who held that spyglass to his eye.

I heard the mysterious Frenchman call to the gondolier, and after a little silence, the gondolier's voice made the sound now familiar to me which was the directional warning as he moved out into canal traffic with the big, dark man. A few forgotten words came to my mind. I could not recall at first where I had heard them: "*I take a notorious delight in sinister characters. . . . A person of mysterious antecedents. . . . It is Julie's guardian who provides the mystery. . . .*"

I suspected I had just seen Princess Ketta's *Sinister Character*. I would never forget that voice speaking so quietly, yet with such deadly power to Mr. Bartrum on the quai.

I heard young Bartrum call out, "Ahoy, Cobb! You, up there, spying again?"

Then the butler's voice, near me from a window further along, obsequious, yet never quite humble:

"No, Master Bartrum. Merely considering how best to capture that cat. Your mother has instructed me to wring its neck or slit its gullet."

This was a horrid thing entirely. Before it could occur to me that my interference was improper, I took my caped coat from the armoire and fastening it securely over my bedgown, I stepped into my day shoes and hurried out through the salon which lay so unexpectedly beyond my door. My eyes, from being used to the semi-darkness of the garden below my window, now found surprising help in the occasional starlight that filtered across the floor from the leaded panes in the eastern windows. I heard my slippers clapping noisily, as it seemed, over the exquisite, if worn, parquetry floors. The sound and its echo were uncomfortably like pursuing feet. I had only the vaguest notion of my way down to the garden where, in all likelihood, the poor, starving cat would long since have lost all its nine lives in the indifferent hands of Cobb, the butler.

Making my way from the upper floors to the intervening stairs and then to the salt-rimed ground floor with its unpleasant seepage, was an experience I thought of and dreaded more in retrospect than at the time. My earliest memories in Ireland, after the death of my parents on their way to Dublin Fair, had been concerned with survival. And many an evening in my childhood, when I was employed at scrubbing the floors of the gentry, I found warmth and an odd sort of companionship with the cats of Ireland who were my fellow creatures of the night. At this moment in far away Venice, that lean, persistent cat on the urn in the garden was, in some strange way, myself, the Anne Wicklow of my childhood. In saving that cat, I would save myself.

I reached the garden door without meeting a soul. Somehow, Master Bartrum had reached his own apartments without running upon me. I was relieved. The young man might prove to be as coldhearted as his mother, and I felt that it would be difficult enough to do battle with the efficient Mr. Cobb.

And a curious battle it was! I stepped out into the garden just in time to see the precise and proper Mr. Cobb, assisted by a small, ferret-faced scullion, pursuing the gray cat over hedges, around the urns, beneath the stone slabs that served as benches. Though outnumbered, the lank cat streaked just out of reach of the two who managed now to get at either end of the garden, so that the cat could only escape to the palazzo or the canal at the western side of the garden. The cat leaped upon his favorite urn again, just as I came out into the dying garden. As the urns stood a trifle higher than our heads, the cat huddled there above us, spitting in terror, then hung his small, graceful head over the cold stone of the urn and looked down at me. I saw his eyes gleam as they caught the light from the heavens.

"Come, Puss," I whispered softly. "Come, Puss . . . pretty Puss." Still, the cat stared at me, wide-eyed in his terror, and I held out my hands for him to come down to me. He moved forward, his ribs gleaming in the light, his attenuated length making him seem larger than he was. He must have recognized a sympathy in my voice as I began again. Or perhaps it recalled to him the tones of his only friend, the vanished parlormaid.

Meanwhile, however, shadows crossed my face and I became chillingly aware of being enclosed, boxlike, by Cobb and the ferret-like little scullion. Cobb urged me in his unpleasantly familiar voice, "How charming you look in the moonlight, so oddly dressed, Miss Anne!" Thus putting me on the defense. "You do well with animals. When you have him safe, Angelo will slit his gullet. Do you have your knife at the ready, Boy?"

I was angered despite my knowledge that this was a commonplace solution to the problem of an unwanted feline, and determined upon the spot that they should not have the cat. The latter hesitated, his great, unreadable gaze shifting from me to Cobb and back again.

The scullion, creeping up on my left side with a frightful kitchen knife in hand, muttered, "The creature will not leave the great urn. Back it comes always to that urn. You see, Signore Cobb?"

"I see. Doubtless it is where Maria-Elisa's food was thrown to him," Cobb observed calmly. "She often tossed out bits of food from her window. It would probably land upon the hard-packed earth in the urn."

I held my arms out again and called softly to the cat who, with the unpredictability of his kind, drew himself up, all hackles alert, and his two executioners made futile grabs at him, supposing he would leap. I too moved, hoping to forestall them. Cobb and the scullion rushed toward the urn. Alarmed, I cried,

"Go, Puss!"

Obviously, he understood this and streaked off just as the urn swayed on its aged pedestal and crashed away from us upon the patch of ground between two cobbled walks. The dust and stone chips flying nearly blinded us, and the roar must have been heard by the half of Venice.

"Now, then," said the butler, with biting anger, "If the urn is broken, mark me, there'll be trouble for you, Boy!"

While the two examined the urn, I peered through the dusty air and made out the cat who had not run far but halted abruptly, just beyond the few handfuls of earth that spilled from the cracked urn.

The shrill voice of Mrs. Huddle cut through the confusion in the garden. "What in the devil's name is all this noise? Come inside, all of you."

We all made out her sharp face at an upper window of the palazzo and Cobb was the first to recover. He mentioned the pursuit of the cat, but Elvira Huddle ruled against this.

"Another time. Come within and let be."

I smiled to myself as the two, Cobb and Angelo, glanced in the cat's direction, the little scullion fingering his knife blade in a promising way, and then they both stepped over the debris that had poured out of the urn, and went to the door.

"Will you come, Miss Anne?" asked Cobb, expectantly.

"A moment." I noticed that most of the dirt was still tight-packed in the huge cracked urn, a matter of no importance except that as soon as the two would-be executioners went inside the palazzo, the starved little cat scuttled back and curled up once more on the earth at the mouth of the urn. As I moved slowly closer, wondering, he raised his head, his pointed ears alert. Then, satisfied that I would do him no harm, he relaxed slightly. I went to the garden door. As I opened it, I heard a strange, unexpected little sound behind me. For a few seconds I couldn't place it. Then I remembered. Two years ago, when I knew my husband would never return to his home at Moura, one of the ancient chateau's cats, a favorite of his, used to make the same, plaintive, mewing sound. A keening for the dead. In my heart I had joined the mourning cat.

Maria-Elisa's cat lay there long after I had gone inside, keening for the lost Elisa, curled up in his misery upon that huge, earth-filled urn.

IV

THOSE REMINDERS of death at this dark moment of the night, under an unknown sky, had made me shiver. I fumbled my way as rapidly as I could up the two flights of stairs and through echoing chambers to my own room with less difficulty than I had expected. Perhaps it was because my thoughts were so busy, I had not time to concern myself with twists and turns and passages through which I might lose myself on my way.

I looked out once before returning to bed. I was sure I saw the eyes of the little cat as he gazed up at me from his curious bed of earth, at the mouth of the urn.

Surprisingly, after so much exertion and so much to think on, I went to sleep. I dreamed of Edmond, my husband. Of our courtship and of his voice speaking to me. . . . I felt my cheeks wet with tears at the poignant, beautiful sound. . . . And then, the voice I loved and remembered so vividly changed in mood and tone to something frightening, the voice of my husband speaking in anger and bitterness, as he had spoken to others, but never to me.

At this point in my dreams it was not, of course, my husband's voice I heard but that of Julie Sanson's sinister French guardian. The dark silence of sleep eventually blurred all these sad memories that had been evoked earlier in the evening by the touch of similarity in the voice of the great, dark man I had seen in the garden, and then, by the strange conduct of the mourning cat.

I awoke at dawn, and missed the tray of strong Irish Tea that I was used to. But there was no use in repining over what could not be helped. I washed in cold water when no one came in answer to my summons. I dressed carefully in my lilac, full-skirted day gown after removing the ribbon at the bodice. Mrs. Huddle would never approve of furbelows. I only hoped she would make no objections to my hair which I usually wore secured by a ribbon in a loose bundle at the nape of my neck.

I looked out, saw the fallen urn, but the cat was gone. By daylight I could see how huge was the urn, with the cracks down its length, and I wondered why the earth within had not poured out.

"Very solidly packed, it is," I thought. "There'll be a bit of a dustup over the clearing of it."

Then the cat reappeared and curling up as usual, carefully cleaned his whiskers and fur. He had probably found a succulent rat somewhere around the canal waters that washed against the stone garden. Little as I personally shared his feline taste for rodents, I was glad he had eaten.

A heavy sound, like the slamming of a door, made

the toilet articles on the little lacquer table beat a quick tattoo. As for me, I nearly dropped my brush a minute or so later when it seemed to me that the entire palazzo was rocked by a woman's shriek. I rushed to the door, fumbled with the rusty bolt and by the time I got out into the salon I was in such a furious, not to say alarmed, state that I myself gasped when a black monolith crossed my path with great strides.

The monolith paused long enough to dismiss me and my gasp impatiently, "Stop screaming! First the servants, and now you! Are you all imbeciles in this house?"

Julie Sanson's great, dark guardian had aroused all my Irish temper, but possibly because his voice, if not his tone, held those haunting echoes of my husband, I said as quietly as may be, in his own language:

"I am the new housekeeper, Monsieur. May I help you?"

He was striding on when my voice, or the French of it, stopped him. He looked at me, the scowl on his leonine face softening to a puzzled frown and even that, to my surprise, was very human.

"So you are the Irish Aphrodite I saw at the window last night! I wondered then who . . ." He looked me up and down with such attention I felt as though I were seven again and facing my first employer. Although he was not a handsome man, and to some, his powerful physique and lion's head might even appear ugly, I found that his luminous dark eyes had a power which mesmerized their object.

I cleared my throat uneasily and tried again. "May I help you? I heard someone scream so I suppose you must have lost your way and startled one of the maids."

This time the harsh features before me were definitely softened by his amusement.

"Hardly. That virago was Elvira Huddle. She is bound to entice my ward into a marriage with this mincing little Casanova of a son, and I am equally determined that they will not marry."

Hoping to keep him in his lighter mood I smiled and said, "You sound very like the Capulets and the Montagues."

His black eyebrows went up. He asked me teasingly, "What? Both at once?"

Surprisingly, after all his haste and huge strides across the salon to some destination at the other end of the palazzo, he now seemed in no hurry to be on his way. I was about to suggest that I lead him to wherever he was going when I realized I knew less than he about the inhabitants of these rooms whose heavy closed doors hinted at either emptiness or some Bluebeard's Chamber. He noticed my puzzlement at the knowledge that I, and not he, was the real intruder. I was not often put out of countenance, but he had done so. He took one gloved hand and raised my chin—a great piece of impertinence!—with one finger.

"Now what have I done? Or said, to give you that scowl? If Young Bartrum makes no move to stop me, you yourself will hardly be held accountable for my actions." This remark and the way he looked behind me made me turn just in time to see that extraordinarily handsome young blade, Bartrum Huddle, looking a bit sheepish at Monsieur Sanson's pointed reminder. The young man had apparently come in upon the end of my remark to the Frenchman and said eagerly, "Julie will be most happy to see you, Sir. She only came to visit Mother this morning. A trifle early, I grant you. But I am persuaded you will not be cross with her merely upon that account."

"You are persuaded nothing of the sort," said the Frenchman as his hand drew away from my face with a gentleness that almost made his withdrawal seem reluctant. "Well, I suppose I had better be on my way to play the Outraged Father, though I was beginning to wish . . ." He looked down at me. I felt the power of those splendid eyes in the heavy, mature face and found, to my own astonishment, I was as reluctant to have him leave me as he seemed to be.

When he moved, he moved with speed and force. "No matter," he said briskly and went off toward a far corridor leading to the front of the building. "Come along if you like, My Brave Galahad!"

My own dismissal had been so abrupt it was almost offensive, but I was curious about him, and still too much under the spell he wove to take offense. As Young Bartrum passed me he gave me a wry grin and a nod in the direction of the Frenchman's back, as though he and I shared a joke at the Frenchman's expense. I resented this, probably because I could not so easily dismiss Monsieur Sanson's overwhelming personality.

"I am to report to your mother, Sir," I told Bartrum, dropping a respectful curtsey. "There'll be the question of removing the urn that was broken in the night. And other household matters. Would you be so good as to tell me how I may find your mother?"

"Cross as two sticks, I'll warrant, M'dear!" As I clearly did not show any appreciation of his humor, Bartrum pointed to the staircase somewhat concealed behind a delicately pillared alcove and said, "Suite at the front, on the First Floor. One story above the ground floor. The *Piano Prima* or *Nobile* or some such flummery they call it here. But must you rush off, Beautiful Anne?"

I noted this over-familiar use of my name, and having worked in such households before, knew that I would have to be politely on my guard against his easy familiarities, but it was one of the hazards of my trade, as my friend and mentor, Miss Nutting, often reminded me. I thanked my young employer and hurried after the Frenchman, his carefully polished boots flashing in the morning light. Master Bartrum must be about my own age, perhaps even past twenty-three; yet he seemed very young to me. Ten to one but he was spoiled, I thought, and indulged as an only child by his miserly mother. Still, my eyes told me, if my heart did not, that his looks, with their mischievous hazel eyes and mouth, his trim, graceful build, were sheer perfection, and I was not surprised that the Frenchman's ward had succumbed to those looks.

As for me, I told myself my own position in the household gave me no right to criticize either of my employers for miserliness or for a way with women. If Monsieur Sanson, or whatever he called himself, could not keep his ward from the arms of the handsome Bartrum, then it should hardly be my concern which was, strictly, the welfare of the Huddles and their household. I went quickly down the stairs, following Master Bartrum's instructions, and on the First Floor I hesitated long enough to get my bearings, as the seamen say. Despite a bright golden sunrise, the salons and corridors here were still dark and gloomy. The rococo decorated doors that opened upon balconies on the east side of the palazzo had not yet been folded back and it was not the pleasantest place to find myself at this hour, especially as I had not yet had my morning tea.

A soft voice spoke almost at my ear, exactly as had happened last night, so close and so soft I started and was angry at what I could only think of as that sneaking Mr. Cobb, the butler.

"How charming to find you faithful to the hour and your duties, Miss Anne! You were about to present yourself to our patroness; were you not?"

I had been right in my hastily formed opinion of him last night. He was a stealthy little man and as I looked at him—for he was not quite my own height—I was acutely aware of his sharp nose and lips. There was nothing for it, however, but to let him take my arm and escort me ahead to the great rococo doors of Mrs. Huddle's suite. His bony, pinching fingers pressed so tightly into the flesh of my forearm that I may as well not have worn sleeves at all.

"I heard Monsieur Sanson's highly distinctive voice a few moments since," he began as we reached the door of Mrs. Huddle's suite, and he freed me in order to knock in his usual cautious manner. "I daresay little Miss Julie has run away from home again. A sad business. She generally runs here, by the by."

The suggestion did not set well with me. I was developing prejudices about the household much too soon.

"You'll not be telling me her guardian mistreats her!"

His prim, careful words issued from his prim, careful lips in a way calculated to turn me against any opinion he might express. "That is not for me to say." There was cowardice in his unwillingness either to confirm or deny an accusation. Because the hint was there, all the same.

Mrs. Huddle's scratchy voice called out: "Come in. Come in. Don't dawdle. Always prowling about like a damnable cat. I tell you to your head, Cobb, if you didn't come so cheap, I'd have you gone from this house in a trice. If not before. I hate sneaking people."

I wondered at the little man, so elegantly and correctly dressed in what was essentially a livery, while suggesting a proper gentleman of 1820. Why, as a matter of fact, had he chosen to remain here and work "cheap" as even Mrs. Huddle recognized? But I was not being just to the butler. Very likely, I myself soon would be hard put to explain why I remained here. Quite suddenly, and for no reason, I thought of Julie Sanson's guardian in one of the rooms overhead, and wondered if he was even now exerting his overpowering personality upon the young lady. Poor man! What impressed a woman like me was not likely to have much positive effect upon a girl who thought Bartrum Huddle her dream come true. As for me, I had never been that young. Nor did I feel that in missing such charms I had missed anything vital. Still, I worried a bit about Mademoiselle Julie and her guardian. I felt sure that a word or two of common sense between them might have saved many of their painful scenes. The mysterious Frenchman vanished abruptly from my mind's eye as I felt myself jabbed in the ribs by a blunt but painful stick. It was a gentleman's walking stick wielded with accuracy by Mrs. Huddle.

"And you, Girl! You will have the palazzo cleaned, from attics to cellars, scrubbed and polished, for the betrothal ball. You are not, on any account, to leave a corner untended. That great thundercloud, Michael Sanson, shall have no excuses this time."

It was curious that Monsieur Sanson should raise barriers to his ward's marriage to a young gentleman as rich and eligible as Bartrum Huddle. Sanson himself struck me as a man of the people, no more the aristocrat than these tradesmen-Huddles. Could his prejudice stem from Elvira's miserliness, or Bartrum's obvious eye for females? I thought not. It was something else between Sanson and Mrs. Huddle. Something very deep, even violent, to judge by Sanson's attitude.

"And mind, now, the garden debris will be tended this evening, I trust, when the servants are free of household duties."

"Just so, Ma'am. As you wish," I said, but my ears, already attuned to every imagined sound overhead, had caught the distant tread of Michael Sanson on the staircase, even before the indignant, quarreling voices of the two lovers were heard.

"How is my son behaving?" Mrs. Huddle asked abruptly, glancing from Cobb to the still open door. "I am persuaded he went to the rescue of his beloved without entirely putting off Sanson."

Cobb gave a slight, behind-the-hand cough.

"I believe so, Ma'am. That is to say, the young gentleman accompanied Mr. Sanson to the parlor where Miss Julie was resting after her escape."

"Escape! Ha!" said Elvira Huddle. "The infant simply dotes on my son. She came here, not to escape her guardian but to put herself in the way of my son. Probably Young Miss is afraid Bartrum will change his mind. Shouldn't surprise me at all."

By this time Cobb and I had turned and were watching, on my part with some excitement, as a pretty, petulant blonde girl, about eighteen, came hurrying into the room, her slender figure quivering as if she were in mortal danger. This could hardly be so, as she was followed, in haste, by Bartrum who was trying incoherently, to calm her, and, at a reasonable distance, by Michael Sanson who looked cross but far from dangerous. In fact, his manner was so suggestive of an impatient, uncomprehending father that I wanted very much to smile in sympathy. I did not do so, however, and remained as unobtrusive as possible while young Julie wailed,

"I won't go home! He's not my father. He killed my father. Now he won't let me marry Bartrum. And I will. *I will!*"

"Of course you will, Child," Mrs. Huddle agreed. "Bartrum, do calm the child. Take her out of here until I can settle matters with this impossible man."

With obvious relief Bartrum put all his gallantry into play and reached for the girl. To everyone's surprise she spun around, hysterically accusing her lover: "You are as bad as Uncle Sanson. You let him take me out of that room. You are heartless as he is. You probably killed that poor Elisa just because she loved you."

"Make your mind clear, at least," Sanson said dryly. "Am I the murderer of your father, or is Young Huddle the murderer of the parlormaid? Or are we all murderers today?"

I kept a straight face through this, but found Michael Sanson's manner and his words salutary to say the least. Bartrum, however, appeared terribly shocked and stammered out that he was innocent of everything, but the girl had turned to me in her confusion and I could not help pitying the poor, silly little thing.

"Oh, Miss, men are all dreadful!"

This time, as I put an arm around her and tried what comfort I could give, I did find myself smiling faintly over her bowed head. Michael Sanson had caught my eye and I saw that he was torn between exasperation and concern.

"Aren't they?" the girl persisted.

"Yes, yes. Dreadful," I soothed her, and felt like a traitor to the child when her words and my response amused Sanson.

Seeing this, Mrs. Huddle cut in quickly. "Come, come, Michael. No more nonsense. You see now how dangerous is your resistance to the marriage. The child is now calling you a murderer. Miss Anne, take the girl away. Anywhere."

It seemed odd, indeed, that the woman should repeat Julie's absurd accusation; more incredible, that she should speak of such things while still contemplating a marriage between her own son and a member of Sanson's family. But I had my orders and as neither Julie nor her guardian made any objections, I led her out of the bare, cold room into the wide salon beyond. Monsieur Sanson looked at me as we passed. I tried very hard to let him know through my single, long gaze at him, that all would be well. I wanted him to know that he need not worry. I was annoyed that this thoughtless, selfish girl should cause so much worry and concern to a man like Michael Sanson who seemed, by the behavior I had witnessed, to have a guardian's normal and perfectly understandable worries about her.

As soon as I was beyond the physical influence of Sanson, I realized how preposterous had been my faith in him, this man of whom I knew nothing whatever beyond an accusation by his ward that he was a murderer, and the casual remark of Princess Ketta da Rimini that she liked him because she was fond of "sinister characters."

"Thank you, Miss Whoever You Are," the girl told me, sniffing back tears as I walked with her to the balcony across the salon. "If only you would go with us today, act as my duenna, Bartrum and I could at least be together to—to talk and hold hands at Florian's while we drink chocolate. At least, we would have that."

Avoiding this plea for the moment, I reminded her as gently as may be, "Miss Julie, it is a very bad thing to talk of murders, of matters like the parlormaid, unless you know for a certainty what happened to this Maria-Elisa."

"Oh, that!" She wrinkled her nose and gave me an impish grin which set oddly on her face; for the signs of easy tears remained. "Look. I'll show you where they think she died." She pushed open the balcony doors and we stood on the very narrow balcony, looking far down, between the ancient grillwork, at the murky green canal waters, afloat at this hour with cabbage leaves and long-dead meat, dead fish and debris of all sorts. The odor was somewhat pungent, too. "You see? She went over this rail, most likely."

I was more shocked at her light treatment of a possible tragedy than at the scene itself. "Miss Julie, you cannot believe your betrothed tossed a helpless girl over to her death!"

"Stupid! She committed suicide because Bartrum would not love her, of course."

I looked down at the water, imagining the whole scene, including the poor girl's white face, eyes staring up at me, from beneath those opaque green depths. I turned away quickly and I must have covered my lips with my fingers to hide my feelings, because Julie glanced at me, puzzled, and then admitted in a shame-faced way, "It must have been very sad. And then, she may not have died at all. Cobb says the current in this canal would never have carried her away. But—" I heard the sound of Mrs. Huddle's doors opening across the salon behind us, and her unctious remark,

"All settled, you see. I was sure you would agree, once you discovered the sensible way of it. And I am discreet, My Dear Sanson. In fact, you know me well on that article."

I listened vainly for Sanson's reply. Meanwhile, Julie was rambling on and I had to ask her to repeat.

"I said—if Elisa didn't jump into the canal, where did she go? No one's seen her now in nearly a fortnight. So you see? Where . . . ?"

"Where, indeed?" I echoed vaguely, not thinking of her offhand question.

"Well, Julie," said Michael Sanson, coming up behind us. "You are to see Young Huddle at Florian's for chocolate this afternoon." Childlike, she started to clap her hands as he added, much to my surprise, "Providing Miss Wicklow is permitted to play the duenna."

"Certainly, certainly," Mrs. Huddle cut in with her usual abruptness. "But you must see that I am reimbursed for the use of her time."

For one slow, infinitely pleasant moment, Michael Sanson glanced at me, before he added with just the suggestion of humor to lighten his moody face, "I've no objection. I feel sure her time will be worth it."

Then he and Julie left, with Bartrum trailing down the stairs after them, effusively thanking Sanson. Elvira watched the group, frowning.

"My son would do well to thank me. Not that creature." A curious way of speaking about a man so soon to be closely related to her. She recovered her brisk air. "Cobb tells me something in the way of a bookroom and den may be made of one of the servant wings that is presently unused. You will start there immediately. Organize the cleaning and see what can be contrived."

Cobb was standing beyond her in that part of the salon which cast a green, sickly hue over him, from the sun's reflection on the leaded window panes. He said gently, "Let me show you the way, Miss Anne. It is quite a charming little wing, actually. And occupied until a fortnight ago, so that it is not too fusty and unpleasant. She was a very clean young wench."

So it was Maria-Elisa's quarters I was to remake into a bookroom. Whatever the truth might be, it was obvious that neither Mrs. Huddle nor Cobb had any expectation of her return. Remembering suddenly Julie's question, so casually tossed to me: "Where *did* she go?" I was aware of a certain malaise, a sense that there had been more in Julie's question than I had supposed at the time.

V

THERE WAS about the missing parlormaid's room an immediacy, a sense of the girl's presence so vital that I was briefly shaken and retreated a step, almost treading on the butler, Cobb. His clawed fingers made the most of the opportunity provided and by grasping me under the arm, he nearly lifted me off the chill, uncarpeted floor. I freed myself as unobtrusively as possible.

He said, "I'm afraid you must have the wench's clothing and other possessions removed. She left hurriedly, as you may observe."

"How very . . . odd!" It was the least offensive word that occurred to me; for to confess the truth, the condition of the girl's property was extraordinary. There were neat piles of clothing on the narrow, monastically severe bed, and even on the footstool. A small and somehow pitiful collection of toilet articles had been placed upon a black, masquerade cloak as though their owner intended to tie them in the cloak and carry it away. The chemises, petticoats, gowns, none of them rich, but all delicately edged in ribbon or frills, were stacked as though they had been about to be packed.

What had delayed her? What act, or emotion had brought all this to a sudden stop? Would a girl who had progressed so far in her packing and her plans, leave this geometrically neat array in order to leap to her death? There was something exceedingly unnatural about it. I found it almost as difficult to follow Cobb's expressed theory that she simply dropped everything and ran away.

He moved about the pleasant, tiny room, throwing open the window which, like my own quarters one floor below, gave on the garden. I saw the gray stone benches and the high urns and the broken one still deep in morning shadow. Cheerless enough, so very lifeless in their old age, but at the further end of the garden, waving over a narrow, westerly canal, were a series of young trees, scrawny and half-dead from want of care, but they were a breath of life and spring amid all that stone.

"That cat seems hungry," I said, seeing the lank little gray beast leap up, gracefully to its place of refuge on the broken urn when an early morning garbage barge moved through the canal.

"What? The creature still there? I really must have its neck wrung." Cobb glanced out and then he dismissed trivialities for the important matter of clearing the room of its recent owner's property.

I felt an icy prickle of distaste at his persistent indifference to a living thing, even a starved cat, but I did not want to make an enemy of the powerful little butler on my first day in service here; so I said, "If you've no objection, I should prefer to keep the cat. He may be useful. I saw a—a rat last night in one of the corridors."

Cobb's pale eyes examined my face curiously. He flicked another careless glance at the garden below. He then became much too ingratiating for those cold eyes.

"If Mrs. Huddle wishes, Miss Anne. It's of no consequence. Maria-Elisa had a similar attachment to the cat. I doubt that the cat has been fed since the girl departed so . . . shall we say, precipitously?"

He would say it. Not I. My stubborn Irish tongue

45

could scarcely get around it. I began to gather up the missing girl's property while I tried to put all my imagination to the problem of making a dour bookroom out of a bedchamber whose every corner glowed with the signs of a pretty young female. Nevertheless, several times during that hour I found myself thinking of my friend, the cat who had been fed by the vanished Maria-Elisa, the cat who would not go away.

Once I had worked out several changes in the furnishings, substituting shelves and cabinets for the armoire and, of course, the bed, I asked Cobb politely but firmly to leave me. While my breakfast was served to me here, I gave myself time to think over the other needed changes in the room and its similar-sized neighbor beyond. I could see that Cobb preferred to supervise my every move and plan, but as my post was the equal of his in almost any English household, and would supercede it in some cases, he could do nothing but agree.

In many ways I felt much more secure alone, with only the missing girl's possessions for company. When Cobb had left me, leaving the door on the latch, I went over and closed the door. Afterward, I replaced chairs and the bedstand, and considered the new arrangement, but all the while, my thoughts kept wandering to the absent girl and her unclaimed belongings. As the moments passed, I found the room a trifle sinister, although it was cheerful enough in appearance. A sunny day with occasional rainclouds gave the room a healthy brightness, but always there was the presence of the unworn clothes, the unclaimed ribbons and laces. They took on a semblance of life in themselves.

So real it all was that when Barbarita brought my tray of breakfast, I was so startled, I half expected the missing Maria-Elisa to appear when the door was kicked open. She set down the tray and looked around at the piles of articles belonging to the vanished girl.

"It is very—what you call—proper. All in order. Elisa left her things . . . so. In the cloak. Now, you make all her things all . . . proper."

"I? But I've scarcely touched them. Only these, and the furniture." I had begun to drink the tea I expected, which was chocolate, of course. I looked over the dainty china cup and its steaming contents to stare at her, with the beginnings of that uneasiness I had felt before in this house. Yet, there was no reason. Absurd to question the fact that someone else had been in the room during the past two weeks to put Elisa's things in some kind of order. Yet I had been so sure. I had pictured the girl carefully placing these piles of clothing, here, the toilet articles in the cloak, there, the petticoats and the laces. And the rest elsewhere. Now, it seemed that Elisa may not have done these things at all. Who had? And why?

The matter was not, should not, be of any consequence to me. My post was that of housekeeper. If a Bow Street Runner was wanted to solve the girl's disappearance, let them send to London for him. I drank my chocolate, ate the rice in its odd porridge form, and enjoyed the warm, flaking biscuits, careful to be keeping my thoughts upon my personal responsibilities.

I felt also that the absent parlormaid would be pleased, wherever she was, when I dropped bits of my breakfast out of the window and had the warm pleasure of seeing the gray cat scramble to eat every bite. He looked almost frisky afterward before returning to his vigil, this time on a stone bench beneath his favorite urn.

By early afternoon the unused servants' quarters had been cleaned, dusted, and were readied for use in whatever capacity Elvira Huddle preferred. The notion of a bookroom did not suite my ideas about Mrs. Huddle; not at all. But it was not my affair. There remained only the removal and storage of Maria-Elisa's properties. The ferret-faced youth, Angelo, lent me considerable aid in fetching and carrying. Along with two upstairs maids, we managed very well. Cobb came several times to see how we did and upon being reassured, went his way.

In mid-afternoon, however, it became less easy to be rid of Bartrum Huddle who came and managed to put himself in our way almost constantly. I soon found myself less than respectful to him, his manners being so free and with so little formality. They became even more so when my maids assisting me had gone off to luncheon.

"But may I not assist? There must be something . . . Elisa had some pretty laces. See here?"

"Why do you speak of her in the past?" I asked, pretending to give the question little weight as I completed removal of the last few handkerchiefs and one of the bonnets from the armoire.

"Well, damme! She isn't here now. She was here. And now she is . . . What can I say? In my past. Somewhere else at this minute she is doubtless living a delightful present." He leaned over the chairs stacked between us and for a ridiculous few seconds he tried to seize me about the waist, while I, a little breathless from wanting to laugh, managed to squeeze out of his over-eager hands.

"Master Bartrum, I am not Maria-Elisa. I am very much afraid you have us confused."

"Lord, no! You are much the prettier. Silly little creature she was. Always sneaking about. Listening at keyholes, I daresay."

Relieved at the turn in his flippant thoughts, I reminded him coolly, "Then you do not subscribe to the theory generally held in this house."

He looked, I thought, just a bit stiff, on his guard. Rather surprising. He was not a young man to be concerned with subleties or worries about brokenhearts and possible suicides.

"I don't understand. What theory?"

"That Elisa destroyed herself out of love for you."

He flushed but denied everything. "What? All that for a mere flirtation? Scarcely more than a kiss. Believe me, Anne, I only permit Julie to believe it because she finds it romantic. I've no doubt we'll find Elisa is off somewhere spying for the Austrian Empire or the Spaniards or the Papal States. Something quite unconnected with me." Hoping to change the subject again, he asked me with a great pretense of interest, "What are you doing, looking for love letters? If so, they aren't from me, I assure you. Come, be kind, Angel Anne." He flashed me an engaging grin and reached out as if to catch me again, but I got Maria-Elisa's leghorn hat between us and accidentally pricked his hand with a hair bodkin stuck through the straw. "Devilish Anne!" he added, snatching his hand away and sucking the wound like a small boy.

As for me, I laughed at his foolishness and having dropped the hat in our scuffle, stooped to pick it up now. A very expensive hat for a parlormaid. Then I rebuked myself silently for this snobbish notion that Maria-Elisa had not the right to spend her paltry earnings in any way she chose.

As I reached for the leghorn hat, Bartrum obligingly did the same. This time, he found himself with the sky-blue ribbon tie running through his fingers while I had the broad-brimmed hat. At the same time a white bit of paper drifted to the floor. I picked it up, exceedingly curious; since it was obvious the paper had been concealed within the ribbon that trimmed the hat.

"Aha! You see? A love letter!" Bartrum cried dramatically, although he seemed to feel that it was all a joke, perpetrated by me for his amusement. Since he showed every sign of peering into my hand to read the note, I could do nothing but unfold it.

Whatever else it might be, the note was certainly not a love letter. It did appear to be a journal, in a very feminine hand with flourishes of pale ink. Other pages had gone before it, and the note was clearly a continuation of a report or observation on this inexpensive letter paper.

Bartrum prompted me in good humor and expectation: "What does it say?"

I read aloud: "—believe it is a secret worth a substantial life competence to me. It is best to put it to paper and make a certainty that no threats are made against me. Who would dare, knowing I heard the unbelievable truth? A double truth, surely. I will then be safe for so long as I choose. But to be paid for a lifetime! What joy! Yet, has anyone ever before lived with such a knowledge, such an amazing—" I looked up. "That is all, Sir."

"What a turn she has for being mysterious!" Bartrum made no urgent effort to take the paper, but his broad, unlined forehead wrinkled up with his puzzlement. "Sounds rather as though she'd stumbled into a bit of a doing."

His was not a powerful intellect. So much was evident. Almost too evident. I looked at the note again, wondering that he did not see what was clearer than ever, that the girl, Maria-Elisa, had been party to a secret so terrible that her mere knowledge of it would force someone to pay her what she called a "substantial competence for life." The corollary of this was the obvious danger in which it placed her. To me, it seemed horrifyingly apparent that someone had chosen not to pay her for the "life competence."

Bartrum asked cheerfully, "What will you do with it, Anne? Give it over to Cobb, I expect. He is rather a knowing one. He'll find her and her secret as well, undoubtedly."

"Undoubtedly." My voice was dry as my mouth was dry, with a creeping fear for what may have been done a fortnight ago to silence the too clever, too knowing parlormaid. I put the note into the bodice of my gown, not wanting to leave it where someone with a special interest might take it up. It occurred to me at the same time that if my suspicions were known, I might very possibly follow Maria-Elisa. For a moment I had a cowardly desire to take myself out of this murky atmosphere of hatreds and secrets and hints of murder.

Then Cobb was with us in his stealthy manner, remarking from the doorway, "How very serious we are! What is your thought, Master Bartrum? Shall this charming little chamber become a bookroom?"

"Not my sort of pleasure—books," said the young man lightheartedly. "Matter of fact, Anne and I are about to leave this dull place and go off to Florian's."

"Oh?" Cobb's pale eyebrows were elevated ever so slightly. "Then Miss Anne will be happy to know that the garden debris will not be removed until later in the day. Meanwhile, have you completed your examination of this chamber?" He looked around and I, in my present state of suspicion, wondered whether he suspected we had found something. "I thought perhaps

Miss Anne and I might begin the inspection of the other chambers on this floor."

Bartrum reached for my arm, smiling in triumph.

"My dear Cobb, forget the garden urns and other such trivialities. I have Mother's permission. Anne is mine until evening."

Knowing precisely my use to Bartrum and his betrothed, it amused me to observe Cobb's scarcely concealed anger, but there was no arguing with his employers. We went out of the room and past the butler, I with eyes correctly cast down, Bartrum as though he had won a major battle and not a minor skirmish.

"What a fellow! Always underfoot. Probably knows all about Elisa's flight."

"Flight? You still think she ran away?"

"Or was paid to take flight. Most natural thing in the world, after that note." Bartrum glanced over his shoulder. "You know, I do wonder what Cobb would say about it. I've always suspected he spread those stories about Elisa's suicide."

"But why?"

"Just his cursed nature. Undoubtedly imagined it would give him some power over me. He is mighty fond of ruling the household, and everyone in it. Except Mother, of course." He paused. I hoped he had forgotten his earlier remark, but unfortunately he blundered on. "Devil take it! I believe I'll tickle him a bit. Hint that I think it was he who sent Elisa away to keep her quiet."

Almost too quickly, I whispered, "But you would not tell him! He may be dangerous."

"What? That little toad? Rubbish. Let us tease him about it."

"No, please. It—" I didn't know what else to say and desperately snatched at a farfetched excuse that might stay his chattering. "Don't you see? It might involve Miss Julie somehow. And if so, your mother may set the betrothal at an end."

During the seconds he hesitated, I held my breath, not even sure myself why I was so anxious that Cobb remain in ignorance of our discovery. I had no real reason to suspect him of any crime, or even any knowledge of Maria-Elisa's disappearance, yet it seemed so logical to me that if the girl had been spying on someone in the houshold, Cobb must be involved.

VI

Bartrum laughed and patted me between the shoulderblades. "Well, well, as you say."

I was too relieved at his capitulation to resent his familiarity. We went very companionably down the stairs to the second story. He escorted me to my own room and promised to collect me in ten minutes: "Fifteen at the outside."

As I changed to a less dusty gown, one a trifle more suited to a fashionable cafe at sunset, I looked around my small chamber, reflecting how pleasant it had seemed only this morning. Now, I began to notice the very strong similarities to the chamber abovestairs, with which, I made no doubt, Maria-Elisa had also been pleased.

The note I had found in Elisa's room was now a problem to me. I trusted no one in the household, and ended by tucking it into my new morocco street slippers. In this way I would tread on it throughout the time we visited the Square of St. Mark's, and be continually mindful of it. Perhaps, I thought, there would be someone in civil or military authority to whom I could entrust the matter. As a duenna for the two lovers, I would very likely have considerable time to myself.

When Master Bartrum and I stepped into the gondola at the quai beyond the garden, passing the overturned urn and seeing no sign of Elisa's gray cat, I began to believe that the cat might have found a safe haven, that the ensuing hour for me in St. Mark's might be pleasant, and in the end I would find Venice charming in despite of the horrid suspicions I was entertaining. We were taken through the Grand Canal toward the distant lagoon and the Piazetta with a bright, gaudy sunset at our backs. Already, the carnival masquers were out in force, making the occupants of each passing gondola look very like the other, all in black, all cloaked, most of them slightly under the influence of spirits, if one judged by the laughter and singing, which were more noise than melody. Some of the masqueraders were obviously female, but without their giggles and gay screams I would not have guessed either their sex or identity. Still, I confessed, in the midst of my disapproval, they seemed so carefree, with no thought of possible murders, disappearances, deadly secrets...

"It's great sport, this month of Carnival," Bartrum commented gaily, saluting and blowing a kiss to three black shrouded figures in a passing gondola. I laughed too, because his light spirits were contagious.

"But Sir, how can you know those ladies? They are all masked and exactly alike."

"No matter. I know them all."

I believed it. I could see how an impressionable girl like young Miss Julie had fallen under that spell.

When we came among the mooring poles at the Piazetta and tied up there, Master Bartrum helped me out of the rocking gondola with exaggerated gallantry, and escorted me past the ancient Palace of the Doges which shown like pale pink flesh in the afterglow of sunset. The great tower which my companion called "Campanile" cut a harsh, lean shadow like a sword blade against the Cathedral which I scarcely saw before Bartrum hurried me over the stones of the Square to the out-of-doors tables of Florian's cafe. I had seen few cafes of this sort in my life and I found it fascinating. The custom drawn by such a place was in itself captivating, and mysterious, too. Half the coffee drinkers and the chocolate-drinkers were masked, their bodies concealed or disguised by the all-enveloping cloaks. It was an eerie sensation to feel those eyes behind the masks watching us, surveying us, some hailing to Bartrum, those with women's voices. And one or two with jeweled male fingers reached out and tried to seize my skirts as I passed.

But Julie Sanson's light, high voice summoned us to a table just beyond the busiest area. She was alone, which surprised me. I had half-expected, or more honestly, I had hoped, that her guardian would have accompanied Miss Julie to the cafe. The girl called to me as well, before I could look about at the scene of St. Mark's Square so often extolled by poets, travelers and even my husband's commander-in-chief, the Emperor Napoleon.

"I knew you would bring Bartrum to me, Anne. I may call you Anne?" Miss Julie chattered on as her betrothed drew out a chair for me and seated himself beside her. He leaned over her and adoringly kissed her hand while I tried to appear not only blind but deaf to the murmured endearments between them. Once I had turned slightly in my chair and gotten a full view of the Square climaxed by the Byzantine splendors of the Cathedral, I could scarcely remember my companions.

I must have stared for several minutes, enthralled by the progress of the late sun down the face of the Cathedral until, with a stunning suddenness, this busy end of the Square was plunged in deep shadow. Dimly, I fancied I heard my name called, and supposing it was Master Bartrum, I glanced back in confusion only to find the lovers engrossed in each other. My name was called again, from somewhere in the shadows, and this time I could not mistake the resonant voice of Michael Sanson. I looked around, peering into Carnival faces with their extraordinary anonymity, saw many teeth grinning in the dim light below abbreviated masks. Beyond these faces Sanson was standing, quite a different figure from these laughing, half-drunken carnival crowds. He was not masked, although he was otherwise correctly dressed. His black hair that was beginning to whiten in three or four streaks off his face, and his figure that seemed larger than the life I was used to, were marks of the man I remembered so well from a few moments' acquaintance.

I was surprised at Michael Sanson's familiarity; for he had called me "Anne!" but ironically enough, though I considered this a distinct liberty on Master Bartrum's tongue, Sanson made my name sound wondrously endearing. I arose and Sanson made his way between tables, taking my hand.

"Come. I want to talk to you."

I went as though obedient to my own husband's instructions, hardly aware of hands again tugging at my skirts or the laughing invitations from the masked gentlemen along the way.

"They envy me," said Michael Sanson with a little smile that relieved his normally grim look.

I colored at the hint in his voice as much as his comment, but hoped he shared the gentlemen's interest. I was beginning to feel quite warm and satisfied with my luck during these precious moments, until we came to his table and I saw, staring up at me, the sparkling eyes and witty face of the Princess Ketta da Rimini.

"How very good of you to join us, My Dear! I told Michael you would be a delightful addition."

What a setdown this was! Not only did I find myself the awkward third at a table for two, but it had been her suggestion and not his that I join them! Tentatively, I accepted the odd little chair provided by Sanson but was determined to leave at the first opportunity.

"And how did you find that delightful old harridan Elvira?" asked the Princess. She stirred dark, thick coffee in a tiny cup. The drink looked very strong and I hesitated when Sanson ordered a cup for me. I knew how dangerous these beverages from the Levant could be. Too much strong coffee could play havoc with the nerves, and drive a man mad, I had been told. The saints knew what it would do to a female! Especially Saint Mark, I thought with amusement, glancing at the strange oriental facade of his church. But I took the coffee and sipped it, keenly aware of Monsieur Sanson's brilliant dark eyes upon me. I did not mind that. Not in the least! But there was the Princess watching too, and democratic as she might be, it was clear to me that she would not be human if she did not resent my presence, more especially because of Sanson's inexplicable interest.

I tried to finish my coffee hurriedly, at the same time replying that I had very little to do with Mistress Elvira, as Cobb, the butler and I had managed the problems of the household between us.

"Starves you, I daresay," Sanson remarked.

"Not quite, Sir. Only the parlormaid's cat. Poor thing."

The Princess gave a startled laugh. "A starving cat! How perfectly typical of Elvira! I had some sort of notion she disliked felines."

I explained. "She does. But it seems the parlormaid used to feed a lank gray cat out in the garden and I really believe the poor creature will not move away until Maria-Elisa returns."

Princess Ketta ordered more coffee for herself. Then as she watched Bartrum and Julie who kissed at that moment, she asked, "Is the parlormaid away? It isn't like Elvira to permit free visits and desertion of her."

Sanson surprised me by cutting in abruptly to the Princess, "Julie insists the girl is a suicide."

"Devil take me! Why?"

"Over the dubious charms of young Huddle, of course."

The Princess and I laughed together but I could see that Michael Sanson was not in the least amused. He had gone into an abstracted mood and when the Princess, still laughing, tapped my fingers to call attention to the two lovers, I felt I must take my departure quickly. Sanson would have escorted me back to the young pair but I explained, "Elisa's cat caused us a deal of trouble last night, and I am afraid I must go back and help the servants remove the debris. One of those great stone urns was broken."

Sanson had given his hand to me but paused with a quick gesture that made me keenly aware of his interest.

"Good God! Did Elvira personally wring the cat's neck?"

The Princess laughed and charmingly pinched his coat sleeve between two fingers.

"Come, now, Michele. You know Elvira. She is most likely preparing the cat for dinner."

I made my departure as quietly and unobtrusively as I could, despite Sanson's restraining hand. I was fully aware, however, as I evaded him, smiling, and went my way, that his thoughts were not entirely upon me. Nor yet upon the Princess. I wondered what I could have said that troubled him.

Julie Sanson made a little move of displeasure at

my arrival, but Bartrum whispered something in her ear. She brightened at once, nodded, and as her guardian came to take Bartrum's place with her, Bartrum and I left together. I heard Julie teasing in her voice that had just a hint of a whine, "But I must go to the mercer's shop. It's just in the Merceria. And the most heavenly lengths of gauze for a ball gown!"

Sanson looked worn, his face set in its harsh lines as I glanced back, but he apparently agreed to her wish; for she clapped her hands, called him a "dear," an unusual pleasantry in my experience of their relationship. I remarked to Bartrum on the dislike between the Sansons.

"Quite natural," Bartrum agreed as though such unhealthy bitterness were a commonplace. "Julie's father was Sanson's friend, as I am told, and Sanson was a smuggler, not very respectable. When Julie's father died some years since, Julie became Sanson's ward. There is no blood tie between them and my little girl believes Sanson was responsible for her father's death. Whether this is true or not . . . and frankly, I doubt it . . . Julie is quite sincere in her feelings. Come! Let us walk the way back. You may find it intriguing. Everyone in masquerade; the little bridges all shadowed like a series of mad sketches. Julie adores them."

I ventured with care, "I should think she would frighten easily."

"Of course. Then the charming little creature clings to me for protection. And—" he added significantly, "may I hope that my previous luck will repeat itself?"

I laughed, assured him that his betrothed's tender arms should be quite enough to satisfy him, and he had the grace to join me in my amusement. We left the marvelous Square of St. Mark's by a little passage I had not suspected to exist, on the western side of the Square. Beyond, as he had predicted, we found ourselves in deep shadow, a paved little street, hardly wider than a London alley, where small shops were rapidly closing, and the crowds had thinned to an occasional masked and cloaked passerby.

Again, we went rapidly through an even narrower passage, beyond which I could make out the silhouette of a small bridge with a humped back. A gondola slithered under it and along the canal beneath, its single lantern taking the light away from us as it vanished in the distant night.

"Ah, you are frightened! Confess it, Miss Anne," Bartrum teased me gaily.

I reacted, probably as he had intended, by making a vigorous, if shaken, denial. He looked back several times and I wondered curiously if he himself was frightened, or if he had something else on his mind. It proved to be "something else." We had gone across the bridge, taken another narrow, heavily shadowed alley, and were rapidly approaching another bridge when Bartrum said abruptly, "Did you mean that, Anne? You are not afraid?"

To protect my pride I said, "Certainly, I am not!"

"Excellent, Angel Anne! You see, I made a small rendezvous with Julie at the mercer's shop, and I shall be late. If only—"

I looked around. I saw nothing but the early night sky, dark as midnight, the high walls of windowless buildings enclosing us, and some slight distance ahead, another humped bridge, in equally heavy shadow. Bartrum took my arms and clutched me painfully.

"If I point out the rooftops of Mother's house—the palazzo—can you possibly reach it alone?" Before I could answer, he was turning me to face the bridge. "You see? Against the horizon. There. Beyond those rooftops you will see the half-story which raises the palazzo above the others. A ten minute walk. No more."

"Yes. But—"

"Remember to take the bridge to the left each time. Four bridges. You cannot miss the way. You will come out upon the back of the garden from the last bridge, Dear Anne." He began to wheedle me, "Will you do this for two lovers who invariably have such short minutes together?"

I did not like it by half, but there seemed nothing for it except to agree, and let my gallant escort go his way. I made very certain that I saw the correct rooftops he had indicated, as well as the fact that we had seen no one in the past few minutes and I hoped I would continue to see no one on my hurried return to Mrs. Huddle's palazzo.

"You are quite certain you aren't angry?" Bartrum pleased, wanting to have his way and at the same time to keep my good opinion.

"I am not angry," I said. I was many other things: disgusted, impatient, slightly afraid and rather nervous, but anger was a wasted emotion when one dealt with a grown child like Bartrum Huddle. I turned quickly away, freed myself from his still pleading hands, and hurried along the alley, keeping the Huddle rooftops in sight as best I could. I looked back just before I reached a sharp turn in the alley where another bridge looomed up ahead and the black, murky waters of another canal washed over the stones of a deserted quai.

I could no longer see Bartrum. He must have run to his rendezvous. It was surprising to perceive the depth of his feeling for Miss Julie, although, in my cynicism, I suspected Julie was very probably the heiress to a fortune. This fortune might beckon Bartrum on the run.

Meanwhile, I myself speeded my steps. I did not like the look of that deserted quai on either side of the bridge ahead. The wash of canal water had left a wide swathe of slime which glistened in the light from the first stars overhead. And as I reached it, a light suddenly blinded me from a silent gondola stationed under the bridge. The fact that the light had been heretofore concealed or hooded, was not a pleasant thought, nor was my sudden awareness of a silent carnival creature in the waist of the gondola, out of whose masked face the eyes glowed, vivid and very much alive as they stared at me.

VII

Upon my first sight of that perfectly motionless masked and cloaked creature, I felt a shameful cowardice, not like myself. How alive the eyes were, glowing at me from the lifeless black surrounding them! I supposed that all eyes must look so, in such context, but I could not mistake the evil directed toward me in that gaze.

I stopped sharp. This was stupidly done of me and only told the creature by my behavior that I had been intimidated. I resisted glancing behind me. Indeed, I knew what I should see there, which is to say—nothing but the darkness, the gray expanse of walls imprisoning the walker who ventured through that Venetian alley.

My panic was absurd, I told myself. Any sinister qualities this masked man possessed were, thus far, confined to his costume, his lack of personal identification. He might have been the Devil, beneath that costume, and no one could guess. Or, and much more likely, the man was another guest of Venice, waiting in the gondola for—whom? There were no doors, no entrances hereabouts?

No matter! It occurred to me upon a brief survey of the path ahead that I might reach the bridge before this masquerader could leap up to the quai and to the bridge itself, in the unlikely event that he chose to stop me. I moved swiftly, though without running. I stepped onto the bridge and had walked halfway across when I heard the single scrape of the gondola against the stone quai as the masquerader stepped out and swung onto the bridge behind me. It was difficult to guess, even now, whether those footsteps were male or female. The creature wore soft, padded slippers, suited to the costume which I saw clearly as I looked over my shoulder. The gondola light flared brightly upward over the unprotected bridge, illuminated what I saw now was the habit of a monk, an excellent disguise, if one was needed. My momentary pause brought the creature horrifyingly close. Out of the dark folds that hid my pursuer, a gloved hand snatched at me.

At least, I was satisfied now that I was the silent masquerader's object, though for what reason beyond the obvious one of my sex, I could not guess. I began to run, thanking my Irish childhood for the strength and speed that must have surprised my mysterious pursuer; I soon put myself far enough ahead to choose a left turn in the darkness beyond the bridge.

This brought me between two ancient and seemingly deserted palaces, within an alley so narrow my outstretched arms could have touched both walls, but my swift choice, following Bartrum's instruction, gave me a few minutes' respite. My pursuer had obviously taken the other way.

I hurried on, having glimpsed again the high roof of Mrs. Huddle's palazzo, hearteningly close, but separated from me by space which suggested at least two canals and an area of buildings in an unsavory, slum area of the city. The stench of rotting vegetation reached me almost immediately, but I was not a lady born and bred. I had seen a deal of refuse and rubbish in my twenty-three years. I only hoped my pursuer would be hindered by the stench. If his interest in me was a sensual thing, these filthy canal waters would surely have an adverse effect upon his desire.

I stopped at the next canal to catch my breath, and to slip my foot back into the shoe I had walked out of, and more important, to try and make out my way in the darkness across the canal, for the alley through which I had been running ended abruptly at the canal. A black and white cat, as starved as the parlormaid's gray tom, sped out of a slimy corner and across my path. It was a lucky chance, I thought, for the streak of white was easy to see and I followed it over a bridge somewhat down the canal. The bridge was so low, hardly above the garbage-strewn water, that I knew there would be no gondolas here. I was beginning to long for the sight of a gondola, alive with laughter and lights.

I had not seen nor heard my mysterious pursuer for several minutes, and decided, optimistically, that he had given up the horrid chase. But it was a curious thing entirely, the "monk's" persistence, far more sinister than romantic. Yet what purpose could he serve? What enemies had I made within but twenty hours of my arrival at Carnival Venice?

It was a maddening, not to say unnerving, moment when I discovered my instinct in following the cat had been misplaced. I was now on the right and not the left side of another of those infernal canals and there seemed very little chance of reaching the palazzo without retracing my steps. I whirled around in a brief panic, then my anger at my impotence got the better of my good judgment and I went on, hearing my footsteps louder, resounding upon the roughened stones underfoot and against the walls of the ancient buildings that all but imprisoned me.

Quite suddenly, from a short distance in front of me, I was blinded, made terribly vulnerable by many lights at the end of the passage. I was still angered by my helplessness, so that I did not stop at once and found myself almost swallowed by waving lanterns. I stumbled, reached out and found only the cold stone that entrapped me.

Behind the lights, a merry, drunken voice called out in Italian, "She will do very well for Julio. What do you say, Julio?"

There was a scramble, lanterns swinging, confusion, other voices. Faces hideously masked, but blessedly vocal. I did not know whether to be relieved or shocked at this new but more recognizable danger, but girded myself to do battle in my own way.

"No, Signori," I called to them. "You will anger my husband." My voice was stern in what I thought of as my "house-keeper manner." "He is to meet me yonder, over the bridge."

Two more slightly staggering figures moved in front of the lanterns. Surprisingly, one of them was a female, small, giggling and, like the men, smotheringly disguised by the usual carnival costume.

"Her husband . . ." There was a barrage of comments, sputtering laughter.

I raised my chin, pulled my cloak about me uncompromisingly and walked toward the merrymakers. "Yes, Signori . . . Signora . . . My husband who is Butcher-in-Chief at the Cafe Fenice."

I very nearly committed the stupidity of laughing at their confusion. It was quite clear as I passed among the lanterns and black-clad figures, that no one cared to challenge the butcher and the butcher's wife. And now, as the drunken merrymakers stumbled back into their gondola while I walked firmly over their heads, across still another of the city's endless footbridges, I saw just to my left, as Bartrum had promised, the great stone urns of a garden, marking the untended property of Elvira Huddle.

Greatly relieved, and suddenly aware of every tired bone and muscle, I reached the sharp, broken hedge, leaned against the base of the nearest urn and once more stepped out of my slipper, massaging my reddened heel. Home, at last, and small thanks to the gallant Bartrum!

I was startled out of my revery by the rush of something soft and light as air across my ankle.

"Puss?" I whispered and the creature stopped in midflight, crept back to me and curled up on my foot. I stooped and petted the cat, feeling the ribs hard against my stroking fingers. Then the cat stiffened. The ears went up. The cat scented danger. Another presence, and an alien one.

I looked around the garden, suddenly tense again, as aware as the cat that we were not alone here. The thing that I thought I had thrown off my trail was here, watching me and the cat. Masked and silent it was, just as before and, I was sure, with the hideous glove ready to claw out at me. Leaving my shoe on the cobblestone where I had stepped out of it, I turned to hurry into the house, hoping against all hopes that Cobb or even the ferret, Angelo, would be at hand. Then, with a weapon, we might face down the masked and silent Thing, standing there, shrouded in the dark behind one of the westerly urns.

Although the starlight was faint, I knew what obstacles lay between me and the garden door—merely the overturned urn and the surprisingly small amount of earth which had trickled out after last night's scramble for the gray cat. I made the first step successfully, avoiding the higher piled earth close to the mouth of the urn, but then I miscalculated with my other foot and stepped into the crumbling dirt. Had I been wearing a shoe on that foot, it is possible I should have felt nothing beneath my foot except the grains of earth and a few small pebbles. But now, so unexpected was the cylindrical object under the yielding earth that I nearly lost my balance before scrambling on to the doorstep.

I slapped the door hard, unable to find the brass

lion's head knocker. Behind me I heard the crunch of a shoe upon the dirt-strewn walk. I called out, so loud it was scarcely less than a shout. To my enormous relief, the door began to yield under my pounding. Barbarita's pert, never-more-welcome face appeared in the doorway.

"Sh! The Old Witch hates our making a disturbance when we come in. There is a servants' entrance on the canal, but it leads into the cellars, and it's often too wet to use. Seepage. You understand."

"Let me in. We will discuss the seepage later."

The girl wrinkled her nose at my abruptness, and in confusion, barred my way.

"What is it, Signorina? You look so very white!"

"Out there! Someone is out there." I waved behind me as I stepped into the passage. At the sametime I heard Elisa's gray cat mewing, that curious, mourning sound which had disturbed me before. It was because of the cat that I looked back and caught a glimpse of the strange figure in the monk's habit and the mask. He—if, indeed, it was a man—seemed almost to float upon the periphery of my vision and to vanish into the night beyond the garden hedge as I watched. I motioned to Barbarita, but by the time she focused her eyes upon the darkness after the candlelight indoors, I abandoned any hope of her seeing my pursuer. She reacted very much as though she had seen nothing whatever and thought me mad, beside all else.

She was not blind to my bad temper, and said hastily, hoping, I daresay, to soothe me, "That cat, with his moaning!"

And so it was I finally looked down, and in the flickering candlelight, made out the curious object I had stumbled over a few minutes before, in the earth from the broken urn. Starlight seemed to glance off the bony object, giving it a color like darkened flesh. Staring at it, I must have murmured something, exclaimed, for Barbarita asked nervously, "What is it, Signorina? What is the thing that cat uncovered?"

I was beyond fearing the monk-like creature who had vanished. I limped back out, retracing my steps. The cylindrical thing was evident even as I stared; yet it was so monstrous, so shocking, I did not wish to believe what I saw.

A bit of flesh, once human, once young. With my stockinged foot I uncovered more, seeing what was plainly the forearm, then the elbow, the lower arm and hand of a young female.

"What . . . is it?" whispered Barbarita, standing on tiptoe to see over my shoulder.

"I'm very much afraid it may be Maria-Elisa."

Barbarita shrieked. I scarcely blamed her. I knew my voice had been shaking as I spoke, and I tried to take hold of myself, since the girl was still beyond control. "Come, now. Listen to me. Is Mrs. Huddle at home? You must take me to her at once!"

The girl began to scream again. I cupped my hand over her mouth and almost dragged her inside the passage. Poor soul! I knew exactly her panic, her sick revulsion.

"Then she was not a s-suicide?" the girl stammered, still cold and shaken.

"That is evident." I looked around the passage. Barbarita had left her candle on a step leading up to the first story of the palazzo and I took the candlestick, searching the shadowy corners around us. I had begun to suspect every member of the household. "Is Cobb within the palazzo? Or the scullion Angelo?"

She did not know. She kept glancing at the garden door which was still ajar. I said, "Now, possibly, you may believe in that thing I saw masquerading in a monk's habit a moment since."

"Si, Signorina. Si. You say you saw the thing? Very good. I saw we saw. You think it is by this person that Maria-Elisa is murdered?"

Whatever the girl's confusion, mine was as great. There was Mrs. Huddle yet to see. I sent Barbarita scuttling up the worn and sloping steps.

"Ask her to come at once and bring all the servants."

"Si, Signorina. But she does not like to employ—" She saw my look and added hastily, "I ask." Barbarita then obeyed in exemplary fashion.

Meanwhile, I went to the door, found my fingers shaking uncontrollably as I set the door at an angle so that it would not shut unassisted. I took the candlestick from the steps and went out into the garden, holding the light high. It flared briefly while I held my breath, but then I was able to see the garden, to observe that my nemesis was gone and that the unfortunate dead girl's arm had been exposed, partly during the instant I had stumbled over it and partly too, by the cat who loved his benefactress and had done his small, feline best to call our attention to the crime. Knowing cats as I did, I felt I should have guessed the truth when I saw the persistence with which the Puss remained about that urn where his benefactress had been so brutally concealed.

After a careful glance around the garden and being assured I was alone, I knelt by the broken urn and, with a dreadful, gnawing sickness at my stomach, I began to brush away the earth, uncovering, inch by inch, the poor remains of a young woman who was all too obviously the missing Maria-Elisa. Even her parlormaid's uniform was still visible, though dirt-stained and with several bad rents in the cheap worsted material. It was impossible to guess how she had died. The discolored flesh told me very little except that, during the brief second or two I stared at the still visible lineaments of the young face I knew she had not been strangled. She must have been very pretty, once. I thanked God her eyes were closed.

The gray cat, mewing more faintly now, crawled to me where I knelt beside the high-piled earth.

"Yes, Puss," I whispered, taking him up and rising to my feet. "I know. I know." I could not bear any more. With the cat huddled in the hollow of my left arm, held there securely by my hand, I hurried back to the house after a last glance at the now deserted garden.

I met Elvira Huddle coming down the steps from the first story, with Barbarita clattering along behind her. My employer showed what, to me, was a surprising presence of mind, both in her questioning of me and her brief, almost indifferent examination of the body.

"Ay. That'll be the girl. Maria-Elisa she was called." She took my candle, and asked me to cover the body with a robe of some kind until the authorities could be called in to investigate. She looked at the gray cat in my left arm, seemed about to mention it, then added instead, "And a sorry business they will make of it, I warrant," and she rustled back into the palazzo, looking like her own scullery maid in worn, food-stained clothing.

I went rapidly behind her to fetch a blanket or sheet in which to shroud the unfortunate girl; since the sheet in which she had been wrapped was badly rotted by the damp earth. All the time I was wondering if Mrs. Huddle realized the significance of this appalling crime. When joined to the evidence of the paper I had in my shoe, the evidence that Maria-Elisa possessed dangerous information—

And then I remembered how I had stepped out of that shoe and, with remarkable lack of good sense, had left it in the dirt beside the dead girl.

"A moment, if you please, Ma'am," I said to Mrs. Huddle and turned to retrace my steps, with the gray cat cautiously sticking his head out and looking around, wide-eyed at my flurry of skirts and noisy, limping descent to the garden door. I burst out into the garden, imagining I should find it exactly as we left it, deserted and silent except for the faint breeze which stirred the canals at their junction on the southwest corner beyond the garden.

I was shocked to discover my monkish pursuer waiting for me, as it seemed by the broken urn, but before I could make more than a gasping sound of protest, the man stepped into the light from the doorway. He was not my weird pursuer, at all, though he seemed somewhat taller and might be in some ways, equally frightening.

"One shoe off and one shoe on," observed Monsieur Sanson, gesturing with my missing shoe. "Was this what you came for?"

I was breathless at my haste, my fright, and the unexpectedness of seeing this man who had filled my thoughts until the terrors of my pursuit through the back alleys of Venice, so I barely managed to say, "It was. Thank you. Did you see—that?"

I took the shoe that he made no attempt to retain,

and pointed at the terrible thing which lay half revealed in the dirt, illuminated now in all its ghastliness by the light through the open door. I cannot say why I watched him so carefully for his reaction. I was certain the crime had been committed by a member of the household. It could have nothing to do with Michael Sanson, and yet, I found myself sensing an oddness about him as he studied what we had uncovered of the poor girl's body. It was more than surprise and shock. Nor was it legitimate horror at such a crime.

. . . "He studies it," I remember thinking, "as though he were more curious than surprised. He analyzes what has occurred, or else, what will be discovered."

Either way, I was chilled by this sudden knowledge that the decaying body of a once vital and pretty young girl could not surprise him.

"A vile business," he said brusquely, his voice hard. "Come inside. This is no place for you." Before I could protest or put on my shoe, whose folded bit of paper I had been trying surreptitiously to get out, he took my arm which still sheltered the cat. "Puss" was made indignant by this pushing, pinching and crushing to which he was subjected and as we walked into the palazzo, he leaped out of my arm with a squawk and a protest, and went shooting off into the nether regions on the ground floor passage where water seepage gave the place a sickly stench. The stench of decay, I thought with a shudder, remembering that body outside.

I was still limping, and felt the damp cold of the stone steps on my stockinged foot, even beneath the threadbare carpeting. We reached a salon at the head of the stairs, ill-lighted as all of the palazzo, and I stopped and was about to step into my shoe when we both heard someone coming toward us from what I remembered as Mrs. Huddle's own apartments on the front of the palazzo.

"Good evening, Mister Sanson," said Cobb in his milky voice. "And is it our bright-eyed Miss Anne with you? This is a charming surprise. We had wondered what kept her so long, what with the garden debris and the cellars to oversee." I was persuaded he knew all about Maria-Elisa's body. He had just come from Mrs. Huddle's rooms. Still, he continued his little cat-and-mouse game. "But with you, of course, Mister Sanson . . . ah, well, you Frenchmen!" He shrugged. Worlds of meaning, all of it soiled and detestable, went into that shrug.

"I met Mademoiselle at the garden door," Sanson said with a sharp, cutting decisiveness that would have crushed anyone else, but Cobb was far from disconcerted.

"Did you really?" he remarked with his careful, unamused smile. His eyes flicked over me in my disheveled condition and, with a gleam of success, rested upon my shoe which I had dropped when I heard Cobb's footsteps.

"But you have turned your ankle, Miss Anne!" he cried, all solicitude as he and Sanson reached down at the same time to take up my shoe for me. This conflict gave Sanson the shoe but as he lifted it, to my consternation, the folded note from Maria-Elisa's journel fluttered out. Cobb's fingers, having missed the shoe, closed over the square of paper.

"Whatever can this be? Small wonder you were limping, Miss Anne, with this wedged into your shoe."

Furious at his effrontery and at my own carelessness in letting him see it, I tried to snatch the paper out of his fingers, explaining somewhat incoherently, "It is to make the shoe sole even. You understand. Give it to me, if you please."

Cobb had very cleverly opened the paper between two of his lean, bony fingers and as Michael Sanson reached for it, scowling at the man's attitude, Cobb was able to read much of the contents in the brief seconds before he offered it to Michael for me.

"How very curious!" Cobb murmured softly, watching my slightest expression. He was still smiling. I think he sometimes forgot he had put on his utilitarian smile.

I did not ask him what he found so curious. At this crucial time, the young ferret-faced Angelo came into the salon to make himself useful to his mentor, Cobb.

"The girl Barbarita, she says you wish me for some work Signore."

It was clear, from Angelo's pallor, and his darting glances at each of us, that Barbarita had told him the nature of his work. But though I tried to discover whether there was any understanding look between him and Cobb, Michael gave me the bit of Elisa's journal just then, without having attempted to look at it himself. He must, surely, have noticed Cobb's quick perusal; yet he deliberately avoided glancing at the paper. It was almost as if Michael had no need to read that bit of terrible forewarning in what I had steadily assumed was Maria-Elisa's hand.

Was it conceivable that Michael knew what was on the paper?

VIII

"WHO IS out there?" Elvira Huddle's voice called suddenly from her apartments. "Is it the police or whoever the devil deals in such matters here?"

"Quite as unpleasant, I'm afraid. I wish to talk to you, Madame," Michael replied in the way he had of being heard though he had not raised his voice. He took my hands between his, crushing them painfully, and gave me that smile I was learning to wait for. My suspicions had been absurd. Whatever Michael knew, it could not be evil. He said to me as he released my hands, "It promises to be a vicious business, but you are not involved. You must not be afraid."

A little stiffly, I contradicted him, "I am not afraid."

"Then you must not shake so. *Bon soir*, my dear Anne." For an instant, as he looked at me, I had a pulse-pounding thought that he might kiss me. He did not, of course. But his face had been so close, and his eyes so very tender in their expression that I felt we had known each other forever. "Remain, Anne. Let me see you after this unpleasant thing is finished."

I nodded.

I watched his broad, powerful back as he strode to Mrs. Huddle's apartments. Cobb, following my gaze, remarked softly:

"What a sinister creature he is! One could scarcely understand what the Princess da Rimini sees in him to love."

"And does Her Highness love him?" I asked ironically, to conceal the quick pinch of jealousy.

He shrugged. "There is even talk of a marriage one day. Naturally, his fortune plays a significant part. No woman of any refinement, any taste and discrimination would find the fellow in the least attractive."

I would have argued this, but something more important needed explaining. Before I realized the youth, Angelo, was listening, I said, "But if the Princess may marry Monsieur Sanson, why does she refer to him as a *sinister character?*"

Angelo put in flippantly, "Perhaps the Princess has a liking for the Bad Ones. You know?"

I did not feel it necessary to defend the Princess, and Angelo, as a scullion, was in my department of authority, whatever his relations with Cobb. So I sent him for the local police, and after getting a bed sheet from the nearest cupboard, I went down and covered the dead girl. It was a painful thing to do and I was badly shaken by the time I returned to the house. I would like to have discussed the identity of my masked pursuer with someone I could trust, and Michael Sanson was the logical confidant.

As I stared at Mrs. Huddle's apartments with their closed doors, and wondered what business Michael and the woman could possibly share, I knew I was afraid to tell him about the "monk" who had seemed so menacing on my homeward walk. I was afraid because I could not be absolutely certain the monk had not been Michael himself!

During the following half-hour Michael remained closeted with Elvira Huddle, while the servants talked among themselves about dreaded investigations by the *sbirri*. This was their ancient name for the local police and suggested terrors invoked in the name of the all-powerful Serenissima, as the Venetian Republic had been addressed so respectfully by the world for over a thousand years. But I knew that modernity, in the form of General Bonaparte and the armies of the French Revolution, had swept away almost all of the archaic forms which made the Serenissima nothing but a glorious, decaying anacronism. Rather like the palazzo of Mrs. Huddle itself, I thought.

And I was less surprised than the rest of the household, perhaps less worried, too, when a well-mannered tawny haired young gentleman in a tight-buttoned black surcoat called upon us late that evening. He spoke to Cobb and then to me, while Sanson and Mrs. Huddle, in their curious unity, remained above the turmoil.

The Inspector looked so very French, dressed much as a country Prefect of Police might dress, that I felt Capitano Dandolo was not in the least frightening. In point of fact, during our first moments together, I thought I liked him.

"One understands, Signorina, that you are newly come to this household. But it would appear that you knew at once the identity of the unfortunate girl."

I explained that the household had acquainted me with Maria-Elisa's disappearance, her possible suicide—

"Which we must obviously discard," he cut in, though very pleasantly. He questioned me about the household's general theory that she was dead, before, presumably, there was any demonstrable proof.

I said, "Very true," and he looked surprised; so I gave him the note I had taken from my slipper, explained where I found it originally, and waited with some expectations of an explosive reaction from him.

To my astonishment he said merely, "You believe this has some significance?"

"Certainly. It tells us why she was murdered; does it not?"

He read the note again, then handed it to me in silence. I read the lines, scarcely crediting my own eyes. The hand was undoubtedly that of the girl who scrawled those lines boasting of a secret which would bring her a life competence, a secret or "double secret" as I seemed to recall, which was earthshaking. But now, on paper similar to that used in the warning lines, I read:

"—but when has she not worked us to the last ducat, the last *lire* and *scudi*? What a miser the creature is! I should never remain but for the possibilities. How attractive—"

I took a breath and hoped I appeared calm.

"This is not the paper, Signore."

"Ah?" His ingenuous blue eyes began to look a trifle less innocent. "And yet, you tell me you yourself removed it from your slipper. Perhaps the writing differs from that on the bit of paper you say you found?"

I confessed it seemed the same, as nearly as I could remember. But I ended stubbornly, because I knew I was right, "Another writing in the same hand has been substituted."

"When?" The question as sharp as a whip's end.

I had, of course, begun to ask myself this single, all-important question, and the answers were frightening. As I did not reply at once, he pursued my first brief comment.

"Signorina, did the young Huddle substitute this bit of nonsense for what you say it contained?"

"Master Bartrum!" I asked, surprised. My thoughts and suspicions had been concerned with a few quite different moments, during which almost anyone might have found my morocco slipper in the garden beside Maria-Elisa's body and substituted the innocuous message I now returned to the Captain. "In any case, this is not what I read to Master Bartrum this morning and he could not possibly have substituted it then. It never left my hands." I hesitated, not sure just how anyone could have guessed that my slipper would be there in the garden, or that the note would have been in the slipper. And if all this had been foreseen through some miracle, how would the thief come to be in possession of a substitute portion of the journal?

"Are you sure the Young Huddle did not see you place it in your slipper?"

I felt a certain treachery toward Bartrum when I confessed, "Yes. He saw, but he was not present later when I removed my slipper." Then I remembered. "No! He did not see me put it in my slipper. In the girl's room I put the note into my—" I felt the embarrassment of speaking it aloud, and yet, there sat Captain Dandolo urging me, totally without humor. I said, "—in my b-bodice. You see," I added in haste, as he glanced at that particular part of my person, "I put it in my slipper sometime later, when I dressed to act as duenna for Master Bartrum and Mademoiselle Sanson."

"I see. Then he had no occasion to discover the truth?"

I laughed, though I was far from feeling amused. "Not unless it was he who pursued me from the Piazza of San Marco." I described the sinister monk, but I could see that the creature meant nothing to Captain Dandolo. His pale, expressionless blue eyes were beginning to terrify me.

"It is conceivable, Signorina, that your monkish friend had quite another design in following you." Apropos of absolutely nothing, he went on abruptly, "You are very young to be holding your present post."

I thought, with a rudeness I managed to conceal, *And so are you, Captain!* But I only gave him a smile that had a lack of mirth which would have done credit to Humphrey Cobb himself.

He started to rise and though he did not look around, I guessed that he heard, as I did, the swift, light footsteps of Bartrum Huddle on the steps from the garden door. His approach sounded so very happy it seemed a pity that he must be reminded of a sordid reality in his recent flirtation with Maria-Elisa. I was sure he had totally forgotten the poor girl. Captain Dandolo continued glancing at the innocuous bit from the dead girl's journal. "In spite of your youth, Signorina, I am prepared to accept your word upon this matter. But I would be remiss if I did not warn you that your knowledge places you in grave danger."

"From a member of the household?"

"Undoubtedly."

"But what is to be done about the missing page from the girl's journal? There must be the rest of the journal somewhere. And there will be portions in which she talks of this information she possessed."

"That, forgive me, will no longer be your concern. You have been most helpful, Signorina. But for the rest, there is in actuality, only your word for the contents of that paper which ... disappeared."

As Bartrum Huddle came bounding gaily into the salon, kissing his fingers to me across the wide room,

Captain Dandolo tilted his head slightly in that direction and reminded me, "If you are frightened at any time, you must not trust these Huddles. That one, for example! He marries my poor Julie for her guardian's fortune. Only that. Good night."

He dismissed me so quickly and with so little ceremony I had scarcely time to agree that I would do as he asked before he was calling to Master Bartrum. As the Captain seemed intimately involved with Julie Sanson, I could well imagine why he seemed determined upon the guilt of Bartrum Huddle. He had said nothing whatever about the possibility of Cobb's having stolen the journal page and made the substitution.

Or Michael.

As I passed the surprised Bartrum and started up tiredly to my own room on the floor above, I wondered with a terrible, gnawing doubt, whether it had been Michael Sanson all the time. How strange it had been to find him out there in the garden with my slipper in his hand! And for a few seconds I had even thought him my pursuer. On the stairs I stopped now, looked back at Mrs. Huddle's apartments on the far end of the salon below me. I was remembering the mysterious link between Elvira Huddle and Sanson. A secret they shared? Something with which she had forced a strong, harsh man like Michael Sanson to obey her.

"I won't think that!" I decided. "It can't be true. If he were guilty, if he followed me from the Square tonight, he could have killed me when I met him in the garden."

What idiocy I had been thinking! I tried to hurry my steps to get to my room and take a very long breath for the first time since that far away hour when I left St. Mark's Square with my inconstant escort, Bartrum Huddle. But I got no further than the top of the stairs when I heard furious voices, one, Mrs. Huddle, and the other, a male voice, far deeper than any in the household, that voice which brought me such poignant memories. I looked back, feeling my own weakness where this mysterious and unknown man was concerned. He was speaking in French as the door of Mrs. Huddle's apartment was flung open and he came storming out into the salon.

I remembered his promise that he would see me when his interview with the woman was ended, so I waited there at the top of the stairs, no longer tired, my fatigue and worries momentarily washed away by my hope of speaking with him. Then it came to me, the meaning of that parting French phrase with which he had regaled the angry Elvira:

"Then I will put an end to it, you evil harpy!"

"Harpy" was the only translation I could make of the last word and it was enough to thrill me with fear for him; since Captain Dandolo came hurrying across the parquetry floor to intercept him. I started back down the stairs with some vague notion of defending the Frenchman. Or perhaps only of putting myself in the way of meeting him as he left the palazzo.

"Signore Sanson," the young man greeted him in a friendly, almost placating tone, which was far from the attitude I expected of the policeman.

"If you please, I have not seen Julie—the Signorina —these past few days. May I go and call upon her soon?"

The Captain did not even intend to question Sanson! I hoped the Frenchman appreciated his good luck. But I winced as he clearly did not.

"You may go to the devil!" and Sanson himself went impatiently down the steps to the garden door.

The fact that he had completely forgotten me was a wound of sorts, but far more important was the fact that he risked antagonizing Captain Dandolo who, I suspected, would make a dangerous enemy.

Very slowly, and tired in every bone, I climbed back up the stairs and made my way to my room.

All that night there was a great amount of confusion, of digging, and breaking off of stone chips from the cracked urn two stories below my window. Since these appeared to be Captain Dandolo's men and they finally cleared away all the debris a little before dawn, I felt no guilt in letting them work while I tried to sleep. Once or twice I thought of Maria-Elisa's loyal friend, the gray cat, who had done his feline best to lead us to her body. I hoped he was finding something to eat and a cozy corner in the cellars in which to sleep. I would have to go through those miserable, wet cellars later in the day and see what could be done about them, and about Puss.

When the noise below ceased, I got a couple of hours of invigorating, dreamless sleep which had more than once aided me in a time of crisis. Arising in new spirits, I summoned my morning tea and was less angry than amused when Angelo, the scullion, delivered it to me, it had joggled and spilled over in the pot, and soaked the soft, worn and mended napkin.

He seemed determined to watch me drink, and I was about to send him away when I became curious over the thoughts, if any, behind his little black button eyes.

"Have the Captain's men gone from the house, Angelo?"

"They are gone in the night, Signorina. But the Signore Cobb tells me something most interesting." He leaned forward, across the tray, and I caught a whiff of garlic-laden breath. It struck me as exceedingly odd, this custom of garlic for breakfast, but I suspected I would have to become accustomed to it.

"Well, well, what is this interesting thing?" I prompted him after a pause sufficient to give an appearance of indifference.

With what glee he confided his little secret! "I am to make search when I am not needed in the kitchen or the stillroom. Always, I am to search. And if you are agreed to, you are to do so, you and Cobb."

Bewildered, I repeated, "Search? For what?"

"But for the other bodies, certainly."

"Other bodies!"

"The Captain believes the Signore Bartrum strikes on the back of the skull—so!—all the servant girls when he has done with them. It is only that he waits for a matter of proof."

"Good God! It is not possible." I set my cup down so hard I feared the French china would break. To ignore completely all references to the original paper I had found, to ignore as well, the obvious undercurrents of deadly secrets in the household, it was the outside of enough! There could only be one reason for Captain Dandolo's insistence on this interpretation of the crime. The rivalry between him and Bartrum Huddle over Sanson's ward was his real spur.

With deep irony I asked, "And how many other pretty parlormaids have disappeared recently?"

The boy pursed his thick, red lips, and squinted, in thought.

"There was the little Frenchy named Isabeau. She was here a short time before Vespers. That is Twelfth Night."

I began to feel the slight prickle of uneasiness.

"You'll not be telling me she disappeared!"

He grinned. "In the family way, she called it. We all know it is the young Signore who—"

"I understand," I cut in hastily. "And you have not seen her since?"

"But of course I have seen her. She is in the hospital of the Blessed Virgin. The child was born three days ago. It is a mere female. Had it been a male, it is possible that the Old One, the Signora, would have given some assistance."

I was angry at how gullible I had been with this young rogue, believing he knew of another heinous crime like the murder of Maria-Elisa.

"I suppose there must be other girls who vanished from here in the same way, and upon the same cause."

"Oh, many. There was the little Siciliana. And several females last year. Or so Capitano Dandolo insists."

I pushed aside the tray, told him he could take it away. As he was reluctantly leaving, I said cheerfully, "I am certain that if you search hard enough, you and Captain Dandolo will find all those young women are still very much above ground."

"So was Elisa," Angelo reminded me as he closed the door between us. It was rather an effective exit, I thought.

IX

DESPITE MY refusal to believe the scullion's preposterous story, or more importantly, the suspicions of Captain Dandolo, I found my work throughout the aged palace even less comfortable that day than it had threatened to be on the night of my arrival. For one thing, the feeling within the household was unhealthy, to say the least. For this reason among others, we soon completed the cleaning up of the garden debris. I was as anxious as the other servants to be done with that place of death and desolation.

It was Cobb who reminded me that nothing had been done about the kitchen and stillroom, that Cook was threatening to be quit of the place if her salary was not improved, and that since the indiscreet talk of Captain Dandolo, none of the servants were willing to go into the cellars.

By the time we had gotten a few of the problems on the upper floors settled, I approached the proud, stiff Frenchwoman, D'Entragues, who presided over the kitchen. Cobb had assured me that D'Entragues responded only to commands, and to manners more freezing than her own.

"I take leave to doubt it," I told him dryly, but I was puzzled as to just how much of the little man's advice I could trust.

"May one ask why you doubt?"

"Because I know the French," I said. "They are very like the Irish when it is a matter of reaction to arrogance."

His thin, high eyebrows arched. "That is as may be. You would naturally know better, Miss Anne. I am told your late husband was a spy in the service of the Usurper."

Restraining myself with difficulty, I corrected him. "You need not judge my husband by his peasant wife. He was an aristocrat, and the Emperor's friend. In an attempt to restore the Emperor, he was killed."

"Executed, I believe."

This was a gratuitous cruelty and I pretended to ignore it, but in the end, his remark proved to be of far greater help than he intended. We had spoken as we crossed a pantry into the kitchen whose narrow windows overlooked the canal bridge at the back of the garden. I glanced out the window at that bridge which looked so bright and so unshadowed this afternoon. It was charming, this delicate anacronism in the modern world of 1820. I could hardly believe that it and those bridges and corners like it which I had seen in my headlong flight last night could look so innocent in the sunlight. Nothing less dangerous or deadly could be imagined at this hour.

D'Entragues, the cook, was overseeing the dinner for the two Huddles when we entered. There was a frightened little scullery maid stirring a savory pot of stew that swung on a hook. Angelo was busy rebuilding the fire beneath the stew pot and other smoke-blackened utensils. As he saw Cobb, he finished his work quickly and hustled out the door, squeezing behind us to do so.

"I leave you . . . ladies," said Cobb with a silent suggestion that D'Entragues and I were exactly what I called myself, "peasants," as opposed to his own higher status. "I would merely be intrusive. The kitchens are not my province."

"Out!" cried the cook, hefting a meat-ax from the worn deal table near her hand. Her threat was unmistakably meant for the butler who retreated backward, his suave surface a bit ruffled, I was happy to note. The cook turned around just in time to catch me smiling, but her stiff, dark-complexioned face yielded nothing to encourage me. "And you! You are here to talk to me about money; isn't it so?" Her Italian was bad, and I thought we might go on better in her own language.

In that tongue I explained as pleasantly as possible that money was only one of the matters of interest, and that I hoped we need not speak of them over the blade of a meat-ax. The stern facade cracked a bit. I thought it possible she might even smile one day, given sufficient stimulus. Meanwhile, she laid down the ax.

"Well, then! I thought none but myself in this household could speak the beautiful tongue. Myself," she added, to be fair, "and Monsieur Sanson. A true Son of the Revolution, that man. None of the cursed Aristo about him."

"No, indeed!" Her politics were so evident I thought they might eventually be of use to me in getting her cooperation. While I was wondering how to best broach the subject of my husband's politics, she issued one of her dogmatic orders to the little scullery maid in her bad Italian:

"The water is on the boil. Where is the macaroni, for the domestics?"

The little maid's teeth began to chatter. "Th-there is no more in the stillroom, Signora. We had the last at noon."

"Then fetch some from the storage cellar."

The maid clutched her skirts and shook all over.

"Oh, pray, Signora, not the cellar. It is so dark down there!"

"Well, take a candle, Little Imbecile! You will not find the macaroni in the cold storage, but the dry storage room."

The girl's face creased into childish, blubbering protests. She was little more than twelve, and while I could scarcely admire her courage, her terror was sincere.

"But it is cold and wet. Things creep over my feet."

As she had no stockings and probably never possessed any in her life, her thin-soled, flat sandals could offer very little protection against the rats and slimy creatures that inhabited the lower regions of this city on water. Before the child could get further into the bad graces of D'Entragues, the cook, I put in quickly, "Perhaps the girl can show me the storage cellars. I have been intending to see them. Then I'll bring up your macaroni."

The woman looked hard at me, as if suspecting me of an undue sympathy with an underling, but as I merely turned to the girl and asked where we might find the steps to the dry cellar, D'Entragues went about her work with a brisk efficiency I could not but admire. The girl beckoned to me after furtive side-glances at the cook, and I followed her out into the passage which was so gray and gloomy it blinded me momentarily after the bright afternoon sunlight of the kitchen.

"Take care, Mademoiselle Wicklow," the cook called to me surprisingly. "You will not find a sure footing in the cellars beyond the storage room. You had best take the candle yourself. Rosa has an uncertain hand."

I called a brief "Thank you" in her own language, but when I reached for the scullery maid's candlestick, I could see that it represented a measure of protection to her, and I had just resigned myself to taking the cook's advice in good earnest when Humphrey Cobb came around an ell in the passage. It was evident he had heard D'Entragues' advice to me, and he looked a surprise and sympathy I'm sure he was far from feeling.

"Dear me, Miss Anne! I am persuaded you need not commit yourself to the errands of a scullery wench." The pompousness of this did not fool me. There was nothing pompous about the real man beneath Cobb's careful facade. In fact, far more alarming was the man I vaguely perceived beneath the facade.

"You yourself suggested I find out what can be done about the cellars," I explained. "When better than at this moment?"

"So that's it! Admirable. And I thought you had some absurd concern for this weeping ninny." Before I could prevent him, he took the candle-end from the girl who cowered as if she expected to be struck, and then ducked away, leaving us, Cobb to laugh softly and I with a quickening temper I strove to keep even.

"I'll be thanking you not to interfere in what you called my province. Rosa! Come back here." But the girl had pattered on to the kitchen. It would probably take an unpleasant and noisy scene to get her started to the cellars again. "Very well," I agreed, determined that, somehow, I must get the upper hand of this odious little man. "It is getting on toward the staff's dinner time, and we need that macaroni. If you will oblige?"

He did not like the notion of being used to fetch for the servants, but had gone so far he could not retreat.

"Macaroni! Do you know that these benighted creatures eat macaroni twice and often three times a day? Well, come along."

I did not remind him that he and I drank tea three and very often four times a day, but it amused me to feel that I had given him a setdown. I was less amused when he led me around the ell in the passage and waved the candlestick over what seemed a sheer drop of uncarpeted steps plunging down into a black pit.

"Have a care with those long skirts, Miss Anne. Do watch your step,"

He looked as though he might stand back and politely urge me to go before him, but I motioned him to the steps. "You are quite right, Mr. Cobb. If you'll be so good. Hold the candle higher. I will follow." By this means, I was able to make out each step as we descended; and also, by holding the candle so high, he was himself forced to proceed with great care.

"And no more than you deserve," I thought as I followed his advice to the letter.

It was a curious place entirely, and as we descended, a vile sick-sweet odor filled the moldy atmosphere.

"Rather like decaying flesh," murmured Cobb as he turned to see how I reacted to the stench. His remark was in monumental bad taste, so bad that I fought nausea to remind him coolly, "Do not stop so suddenly next time. I nearly trod upon you."

Even in the flare of the candlelight, I saw him change color, the muscles of his face tighten. "Here before me, on the left, is the dry cellar. The rice and the pasta are stored here."

It was scarcely more than a cupboard and was built into the stone foundation, intersected twice by wood pilings of the type I assumed were used under the rest of the buildings of Venice. The stone floor of the cupboard was at a level with my waist, which must make it difficult for the shorter local women who were generally employed by Mrs. Huddle. The wooden door, rotting and splintered, was swinging open on discolored brass hinges, a clear sign of the panic displayed by the last servant who visited this cupboard.

"Careless, silly girls!" murmured Cobb as he held the

door with his free hand while I reached in and took out a huge bag filled with the macaroni that seemed to be the daily portion of the household. The bag itself was coarse-woven, and when I felt the bottom of it I realized that a form of flour was also stored in the bag. Oddly enough, none of the contents seemed damp or moldy. The cupboard must be tightly built. I thought the pasta might be a pleasant change to me, after the polenta so common in Northern Italy.

Meanwhile, what light there was began to fade. I swung around so quickly I only just missed lashing Cobb across the back of the head with the sack.

"Were you leaving, Mr. Cobb?" This time even the impervious butler could not miss my sarcasm. He had been moving further down into the depths of the cellar, but he stopped, held the candle toward me, making a beautiful pretense of innocence. His direct motives in all this were transparent. He wanted to alarm me, frighten me away from Elvira Huddle's service. Beyond that, I could not be sure. My suspicions were so horrible I hardly dared to acknowledge them, even to myself; yet I had no real proof of anything except his petty and malicious tricks against me, and these were the tricks often practiced between those two rival claimants to the running of a household: the housekeeper, and the steward or butler.

"Dear Miss Anne, did I fail to light you? I was assuming you would wish to see the remaining cellars, while we are about it."

Without thinking of how the heavy gesture would look to the effete little man, I hoisted the big sack on one shoulder as I had done with heavy loads in my Irish childhood, and said, "Very well. Can we come up out of the cellars at the far end? They are, after all, expecting this in the kitchen."

"Only the domestics. They will wait."

"Hurry, then. You are wasting time." This crossing through the cellars was sheer bravado. I did it now, at this hour when I should be doing a dozen other things, merely because I could not bear to be set down by the odious Cobb.

I soon discovered why the servants avoided the place.

With a choice, I would do so myself. We descended another dozen steps, now far below the dry storage cupboard. The steps seemed to be badly sunken in the center, possibly from long immersion in the tidal floods of the winter season, but once we stepped onto the floor of the cellar I saw that these stones too were sinking, often into the ooze and slime that bubbled up around them along what appeared to be the center aisle of the cellar. Indeed, so far as I could see, there was very little more of the cellars than this cave, enclosed by walls green with slime, the slime sometimes gently moving, as if the walls themselves breathed in a somnolent way.

"Beyond that wall is the second cellar," said Cobb. "There are some rather good wines in storage there. Not of the first order. But tolerable. At one time, during the great days of the Republic, servants and guardsmen of the palazzo were quartered down here, where the cellar widens under the canal windows."

After moving into this area which caught a filtered light from the high, barred windows, I remarked that it was unlikely the servants who lived down here in this tomb had called those "the great days" of the Serenissima.

Cobb agreed. "I rather think not. From time to time there were drownings when that canal overflowed its bank. One can imagine their agony, trapped here." Cobb turned and looked at me. I had a remarkable sensation that the candle flame was reflected endlessly in his eyes, back and back. Each little flame further within and behind that unreadable face.

"Why where they trapped, these servants down here?"

He was bland as he raised the candle toward the nearest window which looked for all the world like the barred aperture of a prison.

"But Miss Anne, you must know it was a commonplace at night to lock the staff in their quarters down here—for fear they might rob the palace, or their masters abovestairs."

I felt the shocking truth of this, but was concerned to keep from stepping in the stagnant water beneath the windows. It was not easy. There was apparently constant seepage, and the cellar itself was so thick with mud that I felt the horrid stuff oozing into my shoe as I walked.

"Where is the canal entrance?" I asked. "Barbarita mentioned it last night." I was devoutly hoping we should arrive at it very soon and at least take a few steps upward, out of this accursed place.

"Very soon. Beyond these pilings. One crossed from there to an inside staircase into a corridor on the ground floor."

I had no notion that the barrier beyond the windows, which I imagined to be a stone partition, was in actuality one of the thousands of pilings that prevented the huge palazzo overhead from collapsing into the lagoon. The knowledge gave me an even greater feeling of insecurity. I would remember this place at night when I slept in my comfortable little room three stories overhead, and I would wonder when it would all collapse. From the look of the low ceiling above us, we had not long to wait. The beams were sagging. Splits and splinters were all too evident, even where stone had reinforced it, and we could see it clearly in spite of the dim light from the windows.

Cobb was moving on to the canal entrance and I heard the crunch of his shoes upon what I assumed must be the steps leading up to the canalside. Much as I disliked these cellars, I knew that I had best get a brief idea of what to do with this wasted space. Then, during my hours with other and more physical concerns elsewhere, my mind might be occupied with the problem of this useless and unhealthy place. But, in the meantime, I must be quite sure Cobb did not play any of his little tricks on me. I had no desire to be locked in these cellars like the servants of long ago, whether or not there was flooding.

I hurried around to the canal steps, saw Cobb's small, neat back, his rigid stance in the open doorway above. Something about that rigidity, despite the steadiness of the candle in his hand, suggested an emotion that I could only guess at, though it must be powerful.

"Mr. Cobb," I called up to him. "Are you quite well?"

The candlestick dangled a few seconds in his fingers. Then it fell and shivered to bits. The noise startled Cobb out of his strange mesmerized state. His shoulders seemed to shiver, to lose their stiff, correct balance. Clearly, his knees too were shaking as he knelt to pick up the bits of crockery that remained of the candlestick. He was so confused, he crawled across the stones reaching for scattered pieces. I laid down the sack I was carrying and went up the steps, partly to help the man, but partly, I confess, to satisfy my curiosity as to the cause of his mysterious change. At close range he looked very pale. He was unquestionably disturbed. Just before kneeling to help him, I glanced around, wondering if I could glimpse the occasion for this extraordinary change in him.

A gondola was just passing out of sight on the southerly canal and I had a second's pleasant panic when I saw Michael Sanson and his gondolier, obviously headed for the garden entrance of the palazzo. Surely, it was not the sight of Sanson that had caused the strange behavior of Cobb! And yet, it seemed more possible than anything else I saw on the canals. I began to hope we could get out of these tiresome cellars in time for me to see him.

Another gondola passed this time down the canal in front of us, but unlike most of the Venetian Carnival celebrants, the gondola's occupants were only a respectable-looking, elderly pair of gentlemen, unmasked. I wondered if anyone else had passed Cobb before I reached the gondola mooring pole here. There was no quai, only the narrow stone wall which presumably held in the dull green waters of the canal. It would take an athlete to walk along the stony path that marked the canal's border, and I assumed those who entered the palazzo from gondolas here would have no choice but to step out of their boats and onto the block of stone where we stood now, before the cellar steps. In any case, neither the afternoon sun nor the deep shadows revealed anything the least alarming.

Cobb spoke suddenly. He still seemed unlike himself. That is to say, he was much too pleasant and either nervous or in a hurry.

"I am quite—well now. Thank you. I had a slight seizure. My heart. I believe I must avoid these many flights of steps."

It was a lie, I was sure, but the reason for his behavior baffled me. And he had certainly been terrified. I offered to take his arm, though he ignored my offer, as we went back down the steps and tried to avoid the muddy seepage that covered the cellar's uneven floor. I took up the now damp bag of macaroni, thinking ruefully of all those hungry mouths waiting in the staff dining room. I was too puzzled over Cobb's behavior to give much more attention to the cellars, but Cobb had not forgotten my original interest. When I started to take his arm again, he unobtrusively moved away and made a good deal out of the gesture of pointing at the wine cellar that lined the western walls of the palazzo, parallel to the forlorn garden, but this cellar looked so cave-like, and so dark, I decided to postpone any work there, at least until I was armed with a substantial lamp.

There was no question about Cobb's condition, however. His hand still shook as he pointed out the various vintages, speaking rapidly about bottles, a cask, the straw, et cetera, which he could not possibly see with only the light from the open doors across the cellars.

Just as I was feeling smug about my own lack of nerves, Cobb started so violently, I felt the contagion of his fear and asked in a hoarse, low voice, "What is it?"

"A light. A pinpoint of light there among the straw. Very small . . . it—Good Lord! It moved!"

Before I could recover from this borrowed panic, something flung itself at us out of the cave of the wine cellar, and I felt sharp needles pierce my limbs through my skirts.

X

I CRIED OUT. Cobb simply stared. But the moment I felt those needle claws I knew the dead girl's friend, Puss, had come to me, and from his fawning, clinging attitude now, painful as that clinging was, I knew he accepted me for his protector as he had once accepted Maria-Elisa. I only hoped I would have a little more luck than Elisa found, in protecting Puss, *and myself!*

"That insufferable little beast!" Cobb exclaimed, and dabbed a handkerchief at his sweating brow. "We really must be on our way, Miss Anne."

I took up Puss after painfully releasing each of his extended claws, and followed Cobb up into a corridor on the ground floor, near the front of the palace. We both heard Michael Sanson's distinctive voice somewhere on the steps above the garden door, speaking to one of the servants. He sounded surprisingly agreeable, by comparison with his manner the last time he had come to see Elvira Huddle, when Captain Dandolo was present. Cobb flashed me a swift glance. I looked elaborately unconscious, and for the first time since his odd behavior a while ago, he smiled. I felt sure he guessed my liking for the Frenchman. I broke off this silent interrogation abruptly.

"You were an excellent guide, Mr. Cobb. Now, I must get this to the stillroom."

"Of course. And I must—but then, my little tasks can hardly be of interest to you with your household reorganization problems." He bowed elegantly and as I went toward the back of the house, I looked over my shoulder and saw him hurrying to some mysterious region in the front of the house. He had been very wrong when he said his "little tasks" could hardly interest me. The man, and his tasks, interested me enormously. I found him more suspicious every hour. The difficulty was that there had been no overt criminal action by the man. Captain Dandolo would think me mad if I set Maria-Elisa's death at Humphrey Cobb's door. At the same time, I was not so bold nor so foolish that I wished to challenge Cobb to his face, merely to end as Maria-Elisa, a poor cadaver in a dying garden. And then too, his strange actions in the cellars today were not those of a murderous creature, but of a frightened one. Perhaps my dislike of him had blinded me into exaggerating every suspicious action of his.

I delivered the pasta to the stillroom and was told

severely by D'Entragues that I had brought to ruin a good quarter of the bag's contents when I set the bag down on the cellar floor. This also dampened any hopes I had for special food to satisfy Puss; so I kept hold on him. He seemed content and sleepy in the hollow of my arm.

"The old miser will be cross as a witch if she discovers so much as a grain of polenta is lost," complained the cook.

"Need she know?" I asked conspiratorially.

The Frenchwoman winked. "The less she knows of my kitchens, the better. That one! I think we get on well, you and I . . . I heard what the little toad, Monsieur Cobb, says of your late husband. He died for the Empire. Not for these fat Bourbons today. It is they who are the usurpers, after all. I would not put it beyond them to have killed the little prince, Louis Seventeenth, in prison, years ago."

This was going it a bit far, as I had heard vaguely that the heir to the throne of France died in the Temple prison in Paris during the Revolution, but I was careful not to disagree with her; since I could not have cared less about politics.

As an Irishwoman who grew to womanhood in England, I had seen nothing but war with Revolutionary, and later, Imperial France. But my conversion through an overwhelming love was likely to prove fortunate in my present post. The woman was as passionately Bonapartist as my beloved husband. One might wonder at these aberrations, but one respected the passion.

I made a careful little remark in agreement with the cook, and after discussing her "demands," I felt that she had softened them considerably since they were transmitted to me by Mr. Cobb. D'Entragues did not so much demand a rise in payment. Rather, she stood firm for better conditions in her own domain belowstairs. She was particularly firm about Mr. Cobb. I felt, in the circumstances, that the butler's interference in areas which did not concern him had brought on what I thought of as the Kitchen Crisis. The logical person to address was Mrs. Huddle, and I felt that if I could point out a saving in expenses by solving this Kitchen

Crisis, even the miserly Elvira would give her consent.

Meanwhile, to judge by the usual interviews between my employer and Michael Sanson, I would not be able to see her until tomorrow. I said finally to D'Entragues, "Madame, will you have a supper tray sent up to me in my room? And a little something for Puss? I will have your problem arranged by tomorrow evening . . . I devoutly hope."

"Very well, young Madame . . . Wicklow? Wicklow. That is not a French name." Then her narrow eyes widened slightly. "Ah! But it is dangerous to use the good French name of your husband?"

"Precisely. Here I am Mademoiselle. Good night, Madame D'Entragues."

I started up to my room at once and briskly, with the cat who raised his gray head and looked around, then curled up again. I was wondering all the while if Michael Sanson would be closeted long with Elvira Huddle and asking myself once again the nagging question: "What business did these two irreconcilable opposites share?" When I heard steps hurrying up the last flight of stairs behind me, I had the sudden, preposterous hope that this was Michael Sanson, but I realized almost immediately that it was a female, and her feet clattered far too lightly to be the Frenchman. Barbarita called to me.

"Signorina! She will not take dinner. What shall I do? She has always eaten a very hearty dinner, but not a bite will she take tonight!"

I looked down, wondering, then turned and went back down several steps.

"The Signora Huddle will not eat her dinner? Is she ill?"

Barbarita shrugged. "I left the tray upon the tabaret in the salon outside her doors. She was insulting. You know how she can be. The Signore Sanson was with her, and they quarrel always. She called to me, and then Signore Sanson said, 'Let be. She will eat when she is hungry.' So . . . I let be. But it is most odd."

"I know. Is he with her now?"

She rolled her big eyes. "He went into her sitting

room. What Cobb calls the Little Salon. They quarrel maybe, and she has no appetite. You think so?"

I was sure of it, but I knew neither my employer nor Sanson would forgive me for interferring. I suggested Barbarita go and find Master Bartrum. He might have some effect upon his obstinate mother.

"If I could," Barbarita explained, "there is nothing I would wish more, Mademoiselle. It is only that the Young Signore has gone to the theater of La Fenice. He makes little flirtations with the females there."

"Great Heaven!" I cried, washing my hands of Master Bartrum. "Send up a supper tray to me, and if the Mistress has not eaten by late evening, let me know and I will see if she is ill, or merely in a temper."

I hurried to my room and dropped into the chair and closed my eyes. I had a roaring headache. I expected Puss to jump out of my hands and leave me, but he merely stretched out in his lean, graceful way, claws and the forepaws and then his entire body, and afterward, he curled up again companionably on my lap. He was a comfort to me in an odd sort of way, as though he might join in my defense in this strange, unhealthy house. However, I had second thoughts on that, recalling that his defense of Maria-Elisa had not been quite powerful enough to prevent that awful business in the garden urn.

I did not expect to give much thought to Elvira Huddle's eating habits that night. There seemed nothing ominous in the fact that she chose to delay her evening meal until her visitor had gone. Still, as I got up presently and started to close my window, I found myself wondering about Mrs. Huddle's small departure from what the servants apparently considered long habit.

The garden far below my window was as still as death. Even the muggy night breeze had not swept in yet to ruffle the dry, prickling hedges and the water-starved trees which looked gaunt, and in the twilight formed weird, gnarled shapes, like a dozen robed and cowled monks with fingers groping toward each other, and occasionally toward me. That was a disconcerting thought.

I was still at the window, staring out at the deepening night, wondering where Maria-Elisa had been murdered, "struck on the back of the head," Captain Dandolo said, and who had placed her body in the tall urn, when I began to fancy again that my monkish pursuer of the previous day was standing at the far side of the garden staring up at me.

"So much for vivid imaginings!" I told myself angrily. There was nothing human in the garden at this hour. No servants, no visitors. No prowlers. Nothing but the gray, inanimate trees, sparsely leafed, and with meager buds, yet there it stood, that curious thing at the far end of the garden, backing upon the westerly canal, almost as I had fancied it the previous night. An illusion due solely to the hour, which was beyond dusk but not quite dark. Tall and gray it was, and unidentifiable as to shape, but with a bit of flesh-color just where the hands ought to be. By studying it very hard, I thought I made out the black holes in the mask, where the eyes would be, staring fixedly at me. Then, an instant later, the changing light would make it all appear a fancy, and I would be certain that nothing stood there at all, blending into the thin, gnarled tree trunk as if a part of it.

Because I had been so intent upon this thing out there, I was shaken by the quick, nervous stiffening of Puss at my feet. He had sensed something outside my door before I heard a betraying sound on the floor in the salon, followed by a decisive knock at my door. Puss had arched his back so fiercely he looked twice his normal scrawny size, and when I went to the door he made a dash, in the most cowardly way, to a refuge under the great armoire whose little carved legs were so short I winced for Puss in that narrow space. He remained there, with feline discretion, until I had welcomed my visitor and Puss felt that this big strange, dark-haired man was a friend, not a foe; for, to my surprise and pleasure, Michael Sanson stood in the doorway, carrying my supper tray.

Whatever Michael's troubles with my employer, it was clear there had been no arguing tonight. He was in excellent spirits and looking especially attractive to me.

"Good heavens!" I exclaimed in a bit of a flurry. "The Huddle family apartments are on the floor below."

"Very amusing, but even an Irish goddess must eat," said Michael Sanson, quite as sober as though he were giving orders to his ward, Julie. I caught the glint of humor in his eyes, and tried to appear as nonchalant, as easily charming. It was an effort; I am serious by nature, and find it excessively difficult to behave lightly at moments which I feel, in my heart, are crucial to my life. My moments with Michael Sanson, I felt, in those far-off Venetian nights, were just such crucial times.

"Thank you, Sir. If you will put the tray upon that —this— That is to say . . ." There was no table. It was absurdly unlikely, but I had no place to eat except upon my lap.

"Sit down," Michael ordered, and all obedient, I dropped down into the one chair the room afforded. He came into the room, kicked the door closed with his booted foot, and set the tray upon my knees with a slight rattle of china and a definite spilling of tea. He was as bad a servant as the boy, Angelo, but I did not say so.

I grimaced as the tea dripped, lukewarm, over the edge of the tray, through my dress to my thigh. I did not like to mention this because of the location of the spots, but Michael leaned over me in the chair, said "Sorry," and briskly applied the napkin from the tray to my soaked skirts. I jumped, ready to take instant offense, but he made it seem so very much in the line of a businesslike gesture that I dared not object. I was afraid his prickly temper might take him away from me entirely.

I said a bit faintly, "I suppose Mrs. Huddle is well. I understand she was too busy to touch her supper tray."

"Or to touch me, for the matter of that," said Michael. "The stew looks very inviting. Must be a French cook."

I laughed, but still a little flustered. "The cook is French, and the stew smells wonderful. I thought it was to be macaroni. In any case, there are two spoons. One for the wine-cake. You may have it . . . if the stew looks inviting." I had added this last, about the extra spoon, in a tentative way, to let him know I was not discouraging his friendly overtures, while yet I hoped he would not attempt some ungentlemanly advantage.

He accepted this offer in a spirit I had hardly dared hope for, pulling forward the little bedside step-stool, which placed him beside me. He took up the dessert spoon and began to share the savory stew with me. Although we smiled at each other, and ate like children, seeming unconscious of each other's nearness, I, for one, felt none of my childhood innocence under his dark-eyed brilliant gaze. He said suddenly,

"You are a very remarkable child."

"Child?" I echoed and then, realizing by his tantalizing grin, the implication I had left, I scrambled back mentally. "Nor will you be finding me remarkable; though, I own, it is very handsome of you to go about saying such things."

"Not handsome of me at all. I mean it, in many ways."

I began to smile under his warmth and his surprising gaiety that, for the moment, had not been clouded by his naturally sombre moods.

"Glory be!" I teased him. "You should have been a Donegal Man, by the tongue of you." I had gone about my eating as though genuinely hungry which, indeed, I was, and he, who had made his delightful pretense of racing me to the finish of my meal, watched me now. I was sure that part of his amused interest was aroused because my appetite showed me to be no lady. Miss Julie Sanson would never eat off every bite of a dish of stew. But then, it was unlikely that Miss Julie had ever known hunger. I said something of this aloud, beginning, "I daresay you'll have noticed I'm no lady. But food is food, and not meant to be wasted."

"Quite right."

Still his eyes watched me in that warm way which turned my bones to water.

"And—and—your ward has lovely manners. They do you credit, Sir."

He frowned. I was suddenly sorry I had brought forward the girl's name.

"Julie is an—obligation. An obligation for whose safety and happiness I would pay in my blood." It was a strange and melodramatic statement. I took leave to doubt it, setting its vehemence to the man's naturally dramatic temper. He went on, "But she is no more. I haven't the talent, nor the feeling to play the kindly, doting father."

"I cannot believe that, Sir. All people love children, at heart. Pardon me, but perhaps you do not recognize the depths of your own parental feelings toward her."

His heavy lips, which might have been sensuous in a less tragic, less dramatic face, curled slightly with scorn at my reading of his character.

"My dear child, who could possibly find anything filial or enchanting in a little ninny like that girl, who is afraid of her own shadow, who goes about screaming imperiously to get her own way, who falls into an infatuation with a womanizing, wenching rascal like young Huddle, and who will, if permitted, give over to him every sou I have built up through the years for—" He paused just a second. "—an expiation."

It was a curious word. I wondered if, perhaps, he had killed Julie's father as she once accused him, and now his care of her was what he called "an expiation." It was possible. It did not change my feelings for him which were rooted in emotion, not logic or sense. I felt him perfectly capable of murdering a man in a fit of rage, but not, of course, in cold blood, with calculation.

"What are you thinking?" he asked me suddenly. "You have a lovely brow. Did you know that?"

Although the compliment and the first question caught me unawares, and I knew I had flushed, I said straightway, "I was thinking that you might kill a man in anger, but never with calculation, in cold blood."

He stared at me, then gave a sudden, startling bark of laughter, as though I had uttered the most amusing joke in nature. It was only as I watched him, that I realized his laughter was not amusement, but something else. Ridicule, perhaps. I could not understand why, and I retained my firm conviction that Michael Sanson was incapable, by his very nature, of taking a life with premeditation and cunning. To recover from what had clearly been a mistaken frankness on my part, I said in a light tone, "I find the creatures who follow one about Venice are far more frightening than you, Sir."

His good humor returned, I was happy to observe. "So you've been followed already by these blades! I am not surprised. I hope they cause you no concern, rogues like Bartrum Huddle."

"Oh—poor fellow!" I waved away the whole idea of my employer's handsome son. "His arsenal of charm is formidable, but a trifle outmoded."

"How he would hate to hear you say that! The masked dandies will be after you, Anne. But you will find them what they are, harmless egoists."

"In general." I glanced at the window, remembering. "All but my religious friend, perhaps. He does give me a bit of a malaise."

"Oh?" Michael followed my glance. "And does he serenade you beneath your window?"

"No. Just watches me from the darkness. After I said good night to you in the Square last evening, I saw this monk a few minutes later. I had quite a run to out distance him. Tonight, I thought I saw him out there again. Only a trifling time before you knocked."

Michael said nothing, but got up and went to the window. I waited, suddenly aware that my fingers were chilled and I was nervous for some unaccountable reason. Surely, no one could be more protective than Sanson. He said finally, "I see nothing. Are you sure it was not one of those trees out there? The night breeze has blown in and they look like a starveling army."

Offended at his easy dismissal of my supposed danger, I said in a clipped voice, "I daresay I have fancied the whole of it, including the amazingly horrid discovery of the parlormaid last night."

He looked once more out the window, but briefly, then brought the window closed and came slowly across the room toward me, his dark clothing and his big shadow giving my little bedchamber a strangely close and crowded look. I felt as though I were suffocating and could not instill strength into my weakening limbs. I had felt this overwhelming physical attraction to but one other person in my life. My husband. The power of this man, his masculine command, the virile flesh of his hands and his face, even his throat above the very correct froth of his white cravat, all drew me. I remained perfectly still, while the exquisite sensation I had thought never to experience again, washed over me.

"Lovely, lovely Anne." He stopped before me and with his knuckle bent, raised my chin so that I looked up into the great darkness of his eyes, wondering all the while that there was such an overpowering light in that darkness. I felt my tongue flick over my lips, that telltale sign of my own aroused senses. In another moment we should be in each other's arms.

But Puss, who had settled down on the high bed, raised his head, his ears pointed like a hunter's bitch, and then he looked at the window. I knew from my previous experience with the cat that he heard things before I did and that, this time, he had heard something in the salon, or even in the garden below the window.

Our mood was broken, Michael's and mine, and he straightened to his impressive height, with that look of business and stubborn, dictatorial perversity that threatened to make his dealings with Elvira Huddle all the more difficult. He took my hands which I yielded as though they were his property, and he touched the palm of each to his lips.

"For once," he said then, "I am grateful to Elvira for one of her peremptory messages, since it enabled me to see you."

When he opened the door and went out, I stood a few steps out in the dark salon and called, "Good night, Sir."

He waved to me without turning, and went rapidly down the stairs at the side of the salon. Because I was still under the spell of his overpowering personality, I moved to the head of the stairs and looked down. The little ferret-faced scullion, Angelo, was at the foot of the stairs, looking up at Michael.

"Signore, I come to take away the Signora's supper tray, but she does not eat anything. Not even the tea. Do you still wish to see the Signora?"

"Certainly. I'll go and speak to her . . ." His voice faded slightly as they walked to Mrs. Huddle's apartments. "You say she will not eat. Have you spoken with her?"

"Yes, Signore. Just before your arrival. But now, she will not answer me."

"No matter," said Michael in that calm voice of conviction I associated with him. "She will speak to me. Come along."

I heard no more about it then, having retreated to my own room where Barbarita presently came to fetch my tray, explaining with a sly smile that the Signore Sanson had insisted on taking my tray from her earlier, and serving me himself. I said nothing to this which disappointed her, but she was bent upon gossip and said finally, "If the Signore wishes to see you when he has finished his business with the old one, shall I tell him you are awake and will receive him?"

"Certainly not! That will be all, Barbarita."

Her mouth turned down and I think she might have made some impudent remark but did not quite dare. I was glad when she was gone. If Michael did not behave more discreetly, and I continued to set my heart on my sleeve, like a schoolgirl, we should find ourselves in a pretty scandal! I determined to behave more circumspectly in future.

After making the rounds of the silent palace, locking up and going over the morrow's menu with D'Entragues whom I found most biddable, I changed to my bedgown and was brushing my hair when someone rapped on the door. My first thought was of Barbarita's remark about Michael Sanson and I was of a mind not to answer, but the sound was lighter, more tentative, not at all like the Frenchman.

"Who is it?"

"Bartrum Huddle, Ma'am. We need you. Urgently!"

The young man's name was hardly one to make me rush out in my bedgown at midnight, but that obviously troubled plea "we need you" was enough to send all my conceited suspicions glimmering.

"Yes. A moment. I'll be with you."

What on earth could be wrong in the household? Not, I hoped, another quarrel between Michael Sanson and Bartrum's mother!

XI

I BUTTONED myself closely into my good day coat, stepped into my day slippers and hurried out to the salon which I had left in darkness. Behind me, as I glanced back, I saw Puss sensibly stretch, then return to the comfortable place I had been about to take in the big bed. There were now several lights burning, including a candelabrum on a sideboard at the far end of the big room. Master Bartrum, looking romatically disheveled, was so excited he made no effort to play off his charms upon me.

"Anne! She is—ill. I never saw her like this. You must help us. Her personal maid left her a month ago, and one of the girls from the kitchen is usually called upon to serve her. Very difficult, you may imagine. They are exceedingly incompetent. Mother has no gift with them, as I have told her repeatedly."

"Yes, yes. But what is it? How is she ill? You are talking of your mother?"

"Naturally."

He hurried me to the stairs, though I made out two, perhaps three servants scattered through that salon we had just left. They said nothing, merely stared at me with scared expressions until we were gone from their sight.

"What happened to your mother, Sir?" I asked as we crossed the large and imposing Renaissance salon to Mrs. Huddle's apartments on the floor below. Silent as were those rooms of the palazzo at midnight, the air outside, on the canals, was full of Carnival sounds. Snatches of singing, off-key and happily drunk, came to us now and then, even through closed windows, as gondolas passed carrying celebrants to sleep off their festive time.

"It is ghastly. Simply incredible!" Bartrum murmured. "I don't pretend to understand. We've sent for a surgeon to come directly."

"Is she so ill then?"

We reached the pleasant little sitting room which adjoined Mrs. Huddle's bedchamber, and I saw the maid, Rosa, standing in the open doorway, still in uniform, shivering violently and clutching her bare arms. Mr. Cobb was behind her, very grave and correct. He set her aside with a swift, businesslike gesture and came to meet us.

"My dear Miss Anne! A shocking thing, to be sure. But your good offices will set all to rights."

"How is she now?" Bartrum asked in a strained voice.

"Bad, Sir. Very bad. I believe she is resting quietly at the moment, but—" He shrugged, as if the whole matter were somehow beyond words.

I hurried into the bedroom, having guessed, of course, that this excitement involved the health of my employer. The puzzling, the frightening thing was the cause of the woman's illness. Elvira Huddle lay sunk deep in the blankets of her huge four-poster bed, looked shriveled and very tiny. By the light of the one low-burning candle beside her bed, her flesh looked dark, an ugly, unhealthy gray. At the bedside I carefully touched her forehead with the back of my hand. She was sweating heavily and felt clammy to my touch. But at least she was alive. My first glance had made me wonder if she might be dead.

"How is she?" Bartrum asked nervously.

I could see that everyone was watching me expectantly. I had a notion it was one of those times when no one wished to shoulder any responsibilities. The poor woman could die while these people stared. "Has she eaten or drunk anything recently? I know she refused her supper tray." When there were vague, indecisive replies to this, I asked the girl, Rosa, to go to the far side of the bed and help me move Mrs. Huddle, to examine her. This was a wholly wasted effort. Rosa trembled and scuttled behind Bartrum whom I signaled to help me.

"She is dying; isn't she?" he asked in suitably doleful tones.

Disgusted with the insincerity in their commotion, I said, "She will be, if we do not discover what ails her. And someone fetch in more lights."

While they scuttled around, attempting to be helpful and falling into each other's way, I took the one candle the room afforded and while her son moved Elvira Huddle gently, I raised the candle and looked at her with care. She appeared to be in a stupor and when, with my free hand, I felt her heartbeat which was heavy and torpid, despite the heavy sweating which may have been due to the tightness of the room, she showed signs of a laudanum poisoning such as I once witnessed at a Young Ladies' Academy where the unfortunate girl had found herself in the family way.

"I pinched the poor old girl's arms and her legs," Bartrum volunteered. As I looked at him in amazement, he explained weakly, "She moved. She cannot be paralyzed."

Put this way, it made a trifling of sense, and I ruled out the possibility of paralysis, but decided after looking over the woman, that my early theory had been a very likely one. On the other occasion, we had walked the schoolgirl up and down the corridors all night until the effects of the drug had worn away. I suggested the possibility to Bartrum who was willing to believe me but hadn't the faintest idea of how to proceed. I explained the necessity of getting her on her feet, and of the danger if it should prove to be other than a laudanum poisoning. If, instead, she should be suffering from a form of lung sickness which did not demonstrate itself by her coughing and sneezing, we might even kill her by this method.

I was not too reassured by Bartrum's quick, nervous glance at Cobb, and his agreement, "Let's chance it."

I followed his glance, suggesting, "A surgeon has been sent for, I understand."

Cobb said, "It was done at once upon Rosa's discovery, Miss Anne."

Mrs. Huddle was sinking more deeply into this torpor so near to death, and I began to see new similarities to the poisoning I had suspected. We had to do something rapidly. Bartrum understood my latest unspoken question, nodded, and we raised the woman to a sitting position, though her thin neck was like a flower stem, the head lolling heavily. Her long, limp, graying hair dragged across my hands like infinite spider legs and presently we got her to sit on the side of the bed, her lower limbs dangling, her surprisingly frilled bedgown all wrinkled and damp with sweat. I pointed to her night robe. Cobb handed it to me, his face a cold, white mask. I wrapped the woman in it as best I could.

It was exceedingly difficult to get her on her feet. The poor woman kept collapsing under us. But finally, Bartrum had his arm around her waist, and I guided her, more or less with my hand tight around her thin forearm.

"They will kill her!" murmured the newly arrived unhelpful Barbarita to Cobb. I flashed an angry glance their way, in time to catch Cobb's nod of agreement. What a revolting creature he was! To be silently critical of others, the while he offered no help himself. If Elvira Huddle had been left to Cobb, she might have died without so much as a sympathetic sigh from him.

Contrary to Barbarita's opinion, our patient began to rouse from her stupor. Her legs worked better, one foot moving before the other, not dragging helplessly, as before.

"What do you think?" Bartrum whispered over his mother's bent head.

I tried to read his real emotions but they were concealed behind the tense expression which revealed the physical effort of our work, I said, "Better, I think. I do wish that tiresome surgeon would arrive."

"The canals are crowded at this hour, Miss Anne," Cobb said in a slightly defensive voice. "So many celebrants returning home."

Mrs. Huddle groaned. We all looked at her. Her eyelids fluttered. She opened her eyes, stared vaguely ahead at the shadowed far end of her room.

"How the devil did it happen, Mother?" Bartrum asked sharply. "What did you take?"

She groaned again, licked her lips and almost fell over her bedstool which I kicked out of the way impatiently. Now that the deadliest effects of the drug—if, indeed, it had been a drug—were wearing off, I suggested, "A trifle later. We do not want to risk giving her a chill. That might take her off straightway."

As if in answer to this, Mrs. Huddle yawned and sneezed.

"Quick! Get her into bed," I whispered.

Bartrum lifted his mother into his arms and put her back on the great bed.

"Do you think she will live?"

I said "undoubtedly!" in such a crisp voice I startled myself, but it really gave me an immovable disgust to have so many faces watching and, I daresay, hoping, for a woman's death. Including, I made no doubt, her own son and heir!

When we had gotten the woman back under the covers and I was rubbing her gaunt, chilled feet to restore the circulation, I glanced up at the faces of the group crowded into the room.

"You had best go back to your quarters, most of you, if someone will stay up long enough to show in the surgeon when he arrives."

"Of course. Let me," Bartrum volunteered quickly.

"And I will sit by with the mistress," Cobb put in almost as soon. "The poor lady will need care for the next few hours."

I thought: Very likely! When it was you who may have poisoned the woman! I said aloud, "Nonsense! I will stay with her. The rest of you, I advise you to go to bed. All except Mrs. Huddle's maid. I may need you."

There was considerable grumbling among those gathered in the chamber and spilling out into Mrs. Huddle's sitting room, but they eventually scattered, leaving young Rosa to tremble, in a very disconcerting way, merely because I stared at her. I had forgotten the absurd choice of Rose to serve in this room tonight. It was so like Elvira Huddle, with her choice of cheap, inadequate service. I wondered if I, too, had been considered cheap.

"Me, Signorina?" the girl Rosa asked shakily "Must I stay in this room? What if she dies?"

What a little silly!

"No, no. You may lie upon the chaise in the sitting room. I will call you if I need you."

Cobb turned back and put in impatiently, for the first time, "Really, Miss Anne! You would find me far more useful than this . . . child."

"A man of your utility in the household needs his sleep," I reminded him. He departed without another word, but I felt certain he was either hurt or angry at my bad manners, my failure to respond to his offer. I hoped that his emotion was based solely upon pique at being eliminated from service in these unnerving moments, and not regret at an opportunity missed.

I sat by the bed in the silent bedchamber, surrounded by long-fingered shadows from the fireplace across the room, and examined my conduct in the matter of Humphrey Cobb. I had been high-handed, to the the very least. There was nothing, not really a bit of evidence to make me suspect the precise and proper little man of any wrongdoing. As a matter of fact, why should there be any suspicious thoughts concerned with Elvira Huddle's poisoning, until we were at least certain she had been poisoned? And in any event, was it not possible she had taken the laudanum merely for purposes of a night's sleep? A common enough practice, though a foolish one, from my observation.

The surgeon was taking an unconscionable time, in spite of all the talk about crowded canals. I got up from my chair and looked down at the sick woman. Though the light from the low-burning fire was very faint, and I had removed all the candles to the sitting room to give the woman more rest, I saw that Mrs. Huddle was breathing more naturally now, without the previous stertorious sound. I felt that she would recover after a few hours of normal sleep. Though I could not really like her, I was greatly relieved at her improvement. One does not like to think that even one precious life can be snuffed unnaturally, and in such a fashion.

I sat back in my chair and eased my tired back. I did not close my eyes. I had sat in this fashion less than ten minutes by Mrs. Huddle's shelf clock with its well-worn Roman numerals, when I heard an unearthly screech, followed by a clatter. I jerked upright, got up and glanced at my patient. She stirred fretfully, groaned and went on sleeping.

I went to the open doorway, saw that the door across the sitting room was ajar into the big salon. The sitting room itself was totally dark. For some reason, Rosa had taken the entire branch of candles with her and gone out into the salon where I could see crazy, moving shadows, exaggerated, looking like tortured figures in some panorama of hell. I went rapidly through the sitting room, feeling the cold breath of night around my limbs, beneath my thin robe. A door had been opened somewhere, letting in the miasma off the canals.

The surgeon must have come. I followed the source of light and found it on the steps leading down to the garden door. The candlestick lay overturned but all the candles still intact, and Rosa, too, lay across the bottom step, in a heap of petticoats, moaning over a twisted ankle.

"What is it, Rosa? What happened?"

She pointed upward without looking at me.

"I t-tripped."

I went down the steps rapidly, seeing the hole in the threadbare carpeting which must have caught her shoe. But when I got to her, and after examining her ankle which was reddened and swelling rapidly, I saw her sandal. The flat sole could never have caught in the small rip of the carpet.

"At the door, Signorina . . . the surgeon."

I left her and opened the door. A little, white-haired man in a black taffeta coat and breeches of the past century was standing there with Angelo who had fetched him out of bed, he explained.

"I am afraid you will find two patients," I said as I led the little man and Angelo to the steps, and indicated the tumbled, moaning Rosa. Examination here was brief and ended in an order to Angelo to carry Rosa to her quarters and bind her ankle. To all of which, Angelo agreed so promptly I very nearly smiled. Young Rosa made no objection either and I left them to their own devices.

I led the surgeon, Signore Grassini, across the salon, holding high the branch of candles I had taken up from the foot of the steps. It was here, a trifle tardy, that we met Master Bartrum, making his way in gingerly fashion between the furniture obstacles of the salon. He was still putting one arm into a beautifully cut jacket, and his cravat was awry. His entire wardrobe differed from the one he had worn earlier in the evening. Clearly, he had been aroused from his bed. There had been no thought of sitting up for the surgeon, or to assist in the event his mother relapsed.

"Good Lord! Frightfully sorry. I seem to have heard nothing. Good to see you, Grassini. Pity you had to be called out at this ungodly hour. But Mother's had a bit of a difficulty. Takes that wretched laudanum to help her sleep. Tonight she was too generous by half." He was still rattling on pleasantly as he took my place beside the little surgeon, and I went ahead to light the way.

"How does Mother go on, Anne?"

"Very well a few minutes since. She had begun to sleep naturally. Rosa's scream disturbed her a bit."

Bartrum wanted to know at once what had caused Rosa to scream and I left this explanation to Grassini. As we entered Mrs. Huddle's sitting room and the discussion behind me grew louder, I asked the gentlemen to oblige by lowering their voices. The silence that followed was so eerily full of whispers, I regretted my own request. Mrs. Huddle's bedchamber was very much as I had left it several minutes before, but she must have drifted off into a dreamless sleep. She was quiet now.

The two men tiptoed in after me, Bartrum's carefully polished boots squeaking a bit. I held the light at the bedside the while Grassini removed his gloves and stood on the bedstool to examine our patient.

"Closer, Signorina, with the light."

He had appeared a fluttery and unimpressive little

man, but once he was occupied with his patient, he was confident and thoroughly adequate.

I raised higher the candles, observing now that they were burning dangerously low. Trying to keep my hand steady, I turned and signaled to the first person in the sitting room doorway. It was Cobb. Unlike Master Bartrum, he had not undressed. He was always prepared.

"Fresh candles," I murmured and held out my free hand.

He obliged with commendable promptness and remained standing near my elbow. As two of the candle wicks burned down, I was able to change the candlesticks and bring up the light Grassini needed. The little surgeon's face looked stiff, expressionless as he bent over the sleeping woman.

"It is an affair of the powders for sleeping. Of that we may be fairly certain. A basin, if you please. It is possible, even yet, that if she were to yield up these powders... does someone have a feather?"

Bartrum became thoroughly upset. "What is it? Why a feather?"

I put my finger to my tongue in pantomime. He swallowed hard and understood that it would be necessary to force his mother to regurgitate the poison. Cobb had left my side and gone to find a feather. No easy task, surely. But I did not know Cobb.

The surgeon had not yet looked up at me again, and I ventured the low-voiced question, "She is better now; is she not? She was breathing with great difficulty an hour ago. But after we had walked her, she recovered somewhat."

Grassini looked at me.

"Forgive my frankness, Signorina. But I fear your observation is at fault."

I was so alarmed I looked the question I dared not speak. He said abruptly, "The feather!"

"Here, Signore Grassini." Over my shoulder Cobb handed a slightly frayed feather to the surgeon. I had an uncomfortable suspicion that the feather came from an ill-used duster.

In any case, it was not used. I watched Grassini,

expecting him to apply the feather to Mrs. Huddle's throat to induce vomiting, but he studied the sick woman closely, placed his hand over her forehead and then fingered the inside of her thin wrist.

"Oblige me by massaging the throat and bosom, Signorina."

I gave over the candles to Cobb and did as I was instructed to do, working upon the woman gently but with all the firmness at my command. Her flesh felt hot to my touch, which reassured me at least that it was not the cold of death. But then, the room was very warm and unventilated, as well.

"I can feel no response," I murmured finally, hoping I was wrong.

Grassini had been about to apply the feather inside the woman's mouth, but he paused now, crumpled the feather and threw it down upon the bed.

"The feather, it will not be of use now," he said in normal tones, startling after our careful whispers.

I looked down at Elvira Huddle, as Cobb moved the light closer for my view. There could be very little doubt. The disturbed sleep in which I had left my employer had turned to death.

XII

TWO DAYS LATER, Elvira Huddle was removed in the black funeral gondola to her burial place on San Michele, the Isle of the Dead, in the Lagoon. Although I was persuaded that her death was not a normal one, nor due to her own overdose of a sleeping draught, the only person whose word might be accepted on such a matter was the surgeon, Grassini. He, unfortunately, took the view that Mrs. Huddle had been dying of the poison during the entire night, that I had not "walked" her long enough, or else too long, and my leaving her alone briefly in answer to Rosa's scream had merely hastened the lady's death. Undoubtedly, during those minutes she had a recurrence of her illness, and no one was present to bring her out of her coma. In short, if anyone was responsible for Elvira Huddle's death, it was I.

I felt ghastly. Everyone was excessively kind to me, Master Bartrum in particular. He continued to insist, even when the matter was no longer under discussion, that it was "absurd to suppose our Anne was in any way culpable. The dear girl is merely human. She took fright in the most natural and feminine way, upon hearing the chambermaid scream."

I winced at being supposed such a tiresome little helpless creature, but there was much to be done in the house during those two days and I had little time for repining over the words of Master Bartrum. I only hoped Michael Sanson would not share the general gossip that I had been either careless or frightened, as Bartrum, Grassini and Cobb made me out to be.

"The dark gondola is waiting at the canal door," Barbarita told me as I answered her knock the afternoon of the funeral. It was awkward to have no black gowns, but I had followed carefully my husband's wishes: "Never wear black. It saddens me. I have seen too much of black, and it is not how I think of you." So, when I came to the door, I startled Barbarita, who looked fetching in black, including a lace shawl over her head and shoulders.

"You are ready?" the girl asked uncertainly, looking me up and down.

The darkest gown in my wardrobe of four was my only elegant one, a green shot silk. Fortunately, it was not low in the bosom. I wore it that day. It was this gown with its high collar and long, tight sleeves which startled Barbarita, though I cushioned the shock to her correct Catholic eyes by buttoning my long coat over the dress, and the coat, luckily, was of a brown nearly as dark as a peat bog.

"We are to ride in the second gondola, Signorina Behind the body of the old . . . of her. There will be two staff gondolas. What luck to be in the first one, behind the funeral boat!"

We were on our way down to the canal entrance out of the cellar. There Cobb and I had earlier seen to the placing of blocks for the coffin which would rest there briefly before its removal to the sombre funeral gondola.

"It is unfortunate Maria-Elisa could not have received so elegant a funeral," I remarked, still angry over the failure of anyone in or out of the palazzo to make connection between the young girl's murder and the peculiar death of Elvira Huddle an hour after she had begun to recover from a highly suspicious poisoning.

Barbarita's eyes sparkled. "Captain Dandolo say it is a lucky thing the old miser doesn't know how much the funeral is costing."

Captain Dandolo! I thought. And a fine policing we'd had from that silly fellow! He had come to the palazzo the morning after Mrs. Huddle's death, listened to Dr. Grassini's analysis with its sly hint that I had failed in my attentions to the sick woman, and had asked innumerable questions about the location of Bartrum during the entire evening. In the end, the Captain announced that it was quite evident the lady had died of a careless dose of laudanum, administered by her own hand, and complicated by inattention on the part of the domestic staff.

"Signorina! You do not listen to me. You think of very deep seriousness."

Startled, I said absently as we descended the cellar stairs at the front of the palazzo, "I believe we have been completely taken in by . . . someone. Only conceive how very odd it is that Mrs. Huddle was recovering when I left her, and she was dead or dying when I returned scarcely ten minutes later!"

Barbarita gave me a side-glance that told me she shared the general opinion of my guilt.

"Excuse me, but you use words so hard to understand."

"My Italian is inadequate, I've no doubt."

"No, Signorina, though the accent is strange. It is not that. But you say we are *taken in*. That means?"

We had to hold our skirts carefully as we crossed the slime-covered blocks of stone to join other members of the household. The cellar was now usually light, what with the open canal door above the steps, and the four tapers at the corners of the highly ornamental coffin. Four men, strangers to the household, removed the tapers as we watched, and covered the silver-trimmed coffin with a black cloth, embroidered in silver, and of a costliness so evident that many of us would not have been surprised to see the dead woman rise to protest.

Bartrum Huddle stood in a shadowed corner half concealed by the piling barrier beside the steps. He was not alone and as the servants, with Madame D'Entragues, Cobb and myself, stood at the opposite end of the coffin, I wondered how many of Mrs. Huddle's friends were with him. I did not look in that direction until Barbarita pulled on my coat sleeve and whispered,

"What a scandal! That Frenchman is here, and everyone knows he hated her."

This time I raised my eyes and then, slightly shaken, I looked away quickly. Down the length of the black draped coffin, I had seen Michael Sanson's gaze fixed upon me as though he read me to my very bones. It was far from a forbidding gaze. Obviously, he did not share the degrading belief that I was responsible for Mrs. Huddle's death. So great was the effect of his gaze upon me that I felt the color rise in my face and hoped no one would notice my emotion, against which I struggled sternly and uselessly.

When I looked his way again, at the moment Mrs. Huddle's coffin was borne up the steps to the dark gondola at the canal's edge, it was a considerable shock to see the Princess da Rimini, richly gowned in black from proud head to dainty toe, walking beside him and talking lightly. It was for some strange reason, even more humiliating that the Princess spoke to me before Sanson did, taking my arm and saying companionably, "Anne! How good to see you here! We must have tea and a pleasant gossip one day. One can scarcely be astonished at this affair today. Poor Elvira! That miserly brain of hers persisted in functioning night and day. Hence the drugs, I imagine."

I said nothing to that, though I managed to smile at what I assumed was her humor, and since her remark plucked upon the very harpstring of my indignation, I attempted to change the subject.

"I did not have the opportunity of knowing Mrs. Huddle very well," I said.

As the daylight at the top of the steps struck upon her eyes, and they were very beautiful, I wondered that Sanson had not revealed more love for her, if the gossip was true that she loved him. She was so very light, gay and cheerful. I envied her that eternally light mood.

"No, Cherie," she laughed. "Of course not. And then, with the talk that goes on since her death . . . utter nonsense. But you must find it annoying." This was cutting rather too close to my nerves. "That is to say," she went on, doubtless at the stiffening of my features. "Dismiss all gossip. That is my advice, absolutely, in all circumstances. I follow it all my life. And I should know, for they dearly love to gossip about me."

Hardly knowing how to answer this veiled insinuation about my guilt, I said quickly, "I believe the priest is looking at us."

The priest, as a matter of fact, had joined the group around the coffin, consisting of Bartrum, Julie Sanson and Michael. The latter looked over at Princess Ketta and me. The Princess smiled delightfully at him. The priest, apparently assuming Her Highness' smile was for him, beamed with respect and reverence toward her, bowing over the coffin which he halted by his act of obeisance just as it was about to be lifted onto the funeral boat.

"Dear Capriccio!" the Princess murmured, plainly referring to the priest. "We shared the same governess at one time. Had I not fancied myself in love with my insufferable Tito da Rimini—and a sad mistake that was!—I should certainly have married Capriccio."

Feeling like a gossip myself I ventured, because my thoughts were upon him, "I was astonished to see Your Highness in the company of Monsieur Sanson in San Marco the other day."

"Oh?" the lady asked, arching her delicate, tawny eyebrows. "How so?" And then she laughed, but pleasantly, cheerfully. "You refer to my friend, the *sinister character*. Yes, I did call him that. He is a mysterious dog, and I've charged him with mystery. But he and I have been friends this past year. One hardly knows how it began. At Elvira's, if I do not mistake. I had come to lease this palazzo for the summer, and discovered that she herself merely lived in it by sufferance."

I stared at her. "Ma'am! You cannot mean that Mrs. Huddle did not own this house!" Was it possible the dead woman had reason for her miserliness? Perhaps she had not been rich at all, in which case all our conceptions of her must change.

"But, my dear, you know Michael. Generous. Secretive . . . He simply permitted Elvira and that young dandy of hers to reside in a house he owned. Now, one wonders what will become of the entire situation. If Bart and Julie marry, I daresay all will be resolved very handily. Together, they will inherit this broken-down palazzo."

My suspicions about recent events at the palazzo were beginning to coalesce and I found their direction more terrifying than ever. Only a few hours before Mrs. Huddle died, Michael and I had lightly discussed his possible murderous tendencies. I made the statement then that he could never commit a calculated murder. But Elvira Huddle with whom he constantly quarreled, was dead, so short a time after his latest visit to the palazzo! No one had mentioned this coincidence, and despite my own secret fears about him, I too, had failed to mention the coincidence of the visit.

"Are you quite well?" the Princess asked me abruptly, peering into my face.

"Perfectly, Your Highness." But when I heard my own voice I was shocked at its stiff, unnatural quality.

The Princess, I felt sure, was aware of the effect upon me of her gossiping remark. She was silent as we separated after the coffin had been laid in the leading black gondola, with its silver-ornamented covering carefully readjusted over the box. Bartrum stepped into the gondola, following the priest, and then put out his hand to young Julie who looked young and rather scared, with her frail blondeness enhanced by the black lace head covering and her mourning garments. I stepped back for the Princess to go before me into the first gondola and I moved away to join part of the domestic staff in the second boat.

I had just made the first awkward step down into the rocking gondola when a masculine hand reached out behind me to steady my descent. I did not look back until I was seated beside D'Entragues who surprised everybody but me by softening her severe expression to beam at someone over my head. I knew quite well, from her reaction, that, as I suspected, it was Michael Sanson behind me. I looked up at him, aware of the interested gaze of the others in the gondola.

In his own way and without any of Bartrum's aristocratic elegance, he looked exceedingly impressive as he stepped down into the gondola beside me. I was uneasily aware that we were the object of much attention from those around us, but he looked as if he attended every day the funerals of those people with whom he had notoriously quarreled.

D'Entragues nudged me in the side with her sharp elbow and winked. She followed this with a whispered comment, "Be charming to him, M'amselle. He has an eye for you."

I was relieved that Sanson himself made it unnecessary for me to reply. He motioned to Humphrey Cobb on the stone block by the gondola mooring pole. Cobb, nearly as resplendant as Bartrum all in black and white, bowed to Michael and took Michael's place in the funeral boat ahead of us, careful to sit a respectable distance away from the Princess and Julie. The black-clad gondolier moved off, causing the canal breeze to ruffle the cloth over the coffin. The sun glinted brightly on one silver handle of the box. I found myself wondering if even the expensive coffin was paid for by Michael Sanson. And above all . . . why?

Then I recalled what I had wanted to ask him for two days. It was possible he could bear out my suspicions about Mrs. Huddle's poisoning. I turned slightly toward him and asked in an undervoice, "May I speak with you in private when this is over, Sir?"

"Certainly. Nothing would please me more." His

voice had its normal ring and everyone in the boat must have heard it. The fact that he sounded pleased was painful too, because my subject would not be the light conversation he probably expected. I said no more.

Michael had not crowded D'Entragues and me when he joined us, but I was very much aware of his body beside mine. When one of the palazzo servants released our mooring rope and Michael caught it, our gondolier shoved off. A faint, sibilant hiss of whispering started up between Barbarita, Rosa and Angelo behind us. I was thinking about Michael, aware that he had glanced at me once or twice, and rather belatedly realized that someone in the funeral gondola ahead had turned to stare at us.

"Acknowledge Her Majesty," Michael prompted me pleasantly when we were moving along the busy Grand Canal. "She is waving to you." It was as though I were his obedient ward and he had every right to instruct me on my behavior. I wanted to laugh, but this was hardly the place for levity. He was partially right in Princess Ketta, however. The Princess had turned awkwardly in her place to watch me and raised her black-gloved hand. But I was certain that the gesture was meant for Michael and I tried to satisfy both possibilities by smiling at her and making a slight motion to Michael beside me.

During the next half hour of the journey to the Isle of the Dead, I thought sympathetically, "The Princess must be wondering what in the name of all the Saints her *sinister Sanson* is doing in the wrong gondola!"

This was not the case with Julie Sanson. She did not look back once, nor did she indicate that her guardian existed. I was not surprised, therefore, to witness a shocking little scene between the girl and Michael shortly after the burial service on gloomy San Michele. Bartrum had been prompted in a quiet few words from Michael Sanson and came over to D'Entragues and me.

"You will oblige me, Ladies, by remaining in my service, at least until I can make my future plans. God knows what they will be." With his big, engaging grin and a shrug as to his prospects, he played on our sympathy and won. D'Entragues was flattered, though she kept her chilly French demeanor, and I was definitely pleased by his clear need of us.

Poor devil! He would need neither of us if his future father-in-law controlled the purse-strings. Sanson had always opposed the marriage, as I had seen, and with Elvira Huddle dead, whatever power she wielded to bring about the betrothal should, presumably, be gone. In fact, the disquieting thought had been with me all along: There was convincing evidence that no one would profit by her death so much as Michael Sanson.

The Frenchwoman and I indicated agreement to Bartrum by curtsying respectfully and at the same time, Michael, a short distance away, said something to Julie. She was looking sulky and mutinous like a stubborn child, and at his words, she cried shrilly, "No! At once! I will not wait. You must help him. You owe it to him."

Everyone turned and stared at them, from the priest and Princess Ketta who were reminiscing, to Barbarita and Rosa who were complimenting each other on their funeral raiment.

"Ah!" said D'Entragues in my ear. "There is trouble in that department. Mark me!"

Bartrum murmured quickly, "My poor Julie! This has all been too sad, too much for her delicate sensibilities. She should never be put through such an ordeal." And away he went to attend on his "delicate lass." It should have been touching and romantic, but for some perverse reason her conduct only succeeded in annoying the cook and me.

"What fools men are!" D'Entragues said, dismissing the whole sex with this sweeping condemnation.

We were about to leave the island when Julie's voice was raised to Bartrum as he joined the Sansons.

"He says we must wait. But we won't will we, Bart?"

Bartrum tried to silence her, smoothing her ruffled yellow hair, replacing the lace head piece that dangled from one of her curls. He and Sanson exchanged a few words which looked perfectly harmless, even pleasant to those of us who witnessed the scene, but Julie stamped her foot and insisted,

"If you don't, I'll tell the whole world what you did. First—my father. Now, Bart's mother . . . *Where is my father,* Monsieur? Where is he buried?"

"Julie! My pet!" Bartrum murmured, frantically trying to silence her. "Really, Sir, the child is beside herself. She means none of this."

Michael shrugged and moved away from the two lovers with the cold remark, "It's of no consequence whether she means it or not. The little fool will say anything to gain her ends."

"I say, Sir! Not a little fool. Really, Sir, that's going it a bit strong!"

D'Entragues and I could not but smile at this staunch defense by a stammering and embarrassed Bartrum. But Michael had already started past the tall, funeral cypress trees that stood sentinel over the dead, and headed toward the cook and me as we were about to step into the waiting gondola.

"Well, Anne? Shall we have our little talk?"

D'Entragues bobbed him a brief curtsey and was helped into the gondola by Cobb who watched us curiously as Michael and I walked away from the quai and out of their hearing.

"I beg pardon, Sir," I began, wondering at my own temerity, for it was not my business how Mrs. Huddle had died, since it had been ruled an involuntary suicide.

He looked down at me expectantly, the thread of a frown beginning to make its way between his brows. By this time he must guess that my business with him was not social, as he had supposed.

"Do you recall three nights ago when you were waiting to see my employer?"

"Perfectly. I am not like to forget it. I waited with you." This time there were the beginnings of a little smile, though the frown remained. I hastily moved away from the memory of those moments in my room which he was obviously thinking of now.

"When you left my room that evening, Sir, you said Mrs. Huddle would speak with you. What did she say to you? Was she ill when you saw her?"

His eyes narrowed. I began to be just a little afraid, but I stood my ground. I had to know, for my peace of mind and, I confess, to satisfy myself that I had not been guilty of a gross negligence to my patient.

"Quite simply, I did not see her. I went into that little salon in which she reigned over all her victims—"

The word "victim" was there as it had been since I first came into the palazzo. Michael Sanson had been Elvira's victim in some way.

"—the sitting room," I cut in. "But you must have seen her. The bedchamber is just beyond."

"Do you doubt my word?" he asked lightly, but I felt the hardness, or a twist of pain behind the simple question.

"No, no, Sir. It is only that Master Bartrum and I worked to throw off the stupor in which she had sunk, and I cannot believe her relapse could take her off without more—"

"Poison? No Anne. I went directly home after leaving the palazzo that evening. I must have been home before—" He paused almost imperceptibly. "—before ten. So if you are imagining that I concealed myself somewhere in those accursed cellars and crept up to poison the old harridan once more, while you were picking up that clumsy servant girl, you will be sadly disappointed."

"I did not mean quite that," I explained, biting my lip and trying to set things right between us. "I only wish to understand how . . . Sir?"

"Yes?"

"How did you happen to know that I was picking up Rosa while Mrs. Huddle was having her relapse?"

He took my arm and led me, not too gently, back toward the waiting staff in the gondola.

"Good God, Anne! Everyone in Venice knows about that night by this time. Grassini is a notorious gossip."

To save face, I said, "I still don't understand how that girl tripped and fell. She's gone up and down those steps a score of times a day and never tripped before. She wears sandals. The rip in the carpet was much too small to catch in . . ."

"What in God's name are you talking about?"

"Nothing," I said hastily. "I was only thinking aloud."

"An unhealthy practice. I advise you to give it up." And with that he helped me down into the gondola, bowed ever so slightly, and went off to join the mourning party in the first gondola. The Princess da Rimini seemed especially glad to see him.

In his place D'Entragues and I had the company of Humphrey Cobb. There was considerable talk among the servants about the ceremony and about how handsome the Chief Mourner, Bartrum Huddle was, what a beautiful pair he and the pretty Julie made and the usual remarks that go on about perfectly paired lovers. D'Entragues and I said very little. We were occupied with our own thoughts. But presently, when we had turned our backs upon the gloomy cypresses of San Michele, Cobb bestirred himself to remark, "It went off tolerably well, I thought. A surprising number of elegant mourners."

I said with a prick of curiosity, "I had not known the Princess da Rimini was such a close friend to Mrs. Huddle."

"Close, indeed! Mrs. Huddle was once housekeeper to the Princess, as she was to Mr. Sanson. Very democratic is Her Highness."

D'Entragues gave me a significant look before asking slyly, "What truth is there to the rumors that link the Princess with Monsieur Sanson? She seems very struck by him; whereas, he—well, my dear Cobb, one would scarcely call him attentive."

Cobb seemed to feel this was a personal affront.

"To the contrary, my dear Madam. Sanson is forever at the Palazzo Rimini. I happened to overhear the Princess speaking of their visits. Three nights ago she was at his home with him until all hours."

"Nonsense!" the cook argued cuttingly. "Three nights ago he visited Mrs. Huddle on business. Rosa told me so."

Cobb's little mouth creased into what he doubtless called a smile. "Quite true. And yet, he went immediately home from the palazzo. The Princess mentioned that he was there shortly after midnight and they had a glass of wine together."

No one but myself seemed to find this statement in the least odd. But then, only I had heard Michael Sanson say he went directly home from Mrs. Huddle and arrived before ten. How carefully and deliberately Michael had lied to me only minutes ago! Two hours were missing. The frightening reverse of the coin was that for a brief few minutes during those lost two hours, Mrs. Huddle may have been given that second and fatal dosage which I alone believed was the cause of her death.

XIII

But after all is said, nothing was either done or suspected immediately by anyone except me, and I preferred to bury my own suspicions after that encounter on the island; to bury them, at least, until Sanson could offer an explanation. I devoutly hoped that he would. I was susceptible to almost any excuse from him. Besides, I was too busy those next, rapidly passing days.

The week was scarcely out before the entire household was over turned and I was given instructions to prepare for the addition of two new members to the household, that is to say, of Michael Sanson and his ward. The day before the Carnival ended, Julie and Bartrum were to be married. The lovers had won Michael over. By what methods I preferred not to ask myself.

I was too concerned with cleaning and refurbishing the palazzo's main apartments to think much about this strange, sudden move of Sanson's, or his anxiety to get into this house. Still, if there was any special charm about the house, any secret attraction in it, he would hardly have permitted Elvira Huddle to live here so long. Or was it something Elvira herself had left here that Sanson was seeking? I had not forgotten Maria-Elisa's torn journal which had vanished.

I began to hate, even to fear this line of thought which involved Michael. At night I dreamed of it, of Michael searching, Michael standing over Elvira's bed, looking down at the sleeping woman ...

I always awakened before I could be sure that he had or had not taken that deadly step of feeding the woman a final dose of the powders.

By day I knew it was absurd, and a treacherous requittal of his kindness to me. Curiously enough, even with my suspicions, my feelings for him increased in spite of myself. He was direct and imperious and not at all warm to me for a few days after that near quarrel we had at San Michele. But I could not turn my feelings to indifference merely because he appeared indifferent to me. I had given him grounds for his manner by my own mistrust of him.

I asked Master Bartrum one day where the family would live, after the wedding, as some of the staff and I were busy putting sheets and coverlets on a newly cleaned and charming little apartment for Julie. Bartrum strolled around the room, complained of the smell of garbage from the canal below the narrow balcony and took up one of Julie's delicate perfume flasks, sprinkling the expensive stuff around lavishly.

"But, of course, we shall all live here, Anne. What could be cozier?"

This bland question I took to be ironic, but I did not say so. "Very well, Sir. But since the wedding is only a matter of weeks away, will Miss Julie be remaining in this apartment?"

"Good Gad, no! We shall have Mother's apartments. My esteemed father-in-law will move into smaller quarters. As Cobb says, one wonders why the fellow moved into Mother's room for such a brief time. Merely to inconvenience me, I make no doubt. Cobb tells me I should assert myself with the fellow. However, I am by nature a peaceable man, and I think the three of us, Julie, Sanson and I, may deal very well together."

. . . Besides, I thought . . . it must be awkward for you to assert yourself with the man who furnishes your food, lodging and the princely life you continue to lead . . . As Cobb had told those of us on the staff, Elvira Huddle left Bartrum almost no income of any kind. It appeared that there was nothing to leave. Poor Elvira! To be condemned as a miser when she was one out of necessity! The astonishing thing to me was

Bartrum's insouciance about the whole business. I seriously doubted if he held any "secret" over Michael's head; so it was clear that having been provided for until this moment, he assumed he would continue to lead his improvident, spendthrift life, out of his father-in-law's pocket.

Such people as Bartrum both annoyed and amused me. I often felt it must be a special gift of the Almighty, this confidence in a cloudless future uncomplicated by any thought of one's own contribution.

That was the day in which Julie offered to help Bartrum pack away his mother's property, and I began to revise my opinion of the girl's worth. She worked harder than her betrothed, neatly smoothing and folding each worn stocking, each corset and rusty, threadbare gown. I said as much to Michael Sanson when he came to the palazzo that morning to tell us not to expect him for the early dinner we had planned. He had business that took him to Pavia.

"They make an attractive picture, do they not, Sir?" I asked as he looked in on the lovers. They were kneeling on the floor of the bedchamber where Elvira had died, their handsome heads bent together over an old brassbound trunk whose contents were piled neatly beside Julie as she removed them.

Sanson shrugged, but I could see that he appreciated at least their calm, companionable occupation as we stepped back into the sitting room.

"Doubtless, they are hoping to discover Elvira's treasure. I wish them luck."

"And did she have a treasure?" I asked before I remembered that it was no concern of mine.

This time his glance at me had some of the old tender amusement that I had found so attractive at our earlier meetings.

"She may have had. But I take leave to doubt it. She was an extraordinarily ordinary woman. That is to say, she knew how to provide the elegances for the boy of hers, without providing him with a backbone on which to hang those elegances. I saw young Huddle at the Teatro Fenice only last night, dallying with one of the actresses there. He was so ignorant of the proprieties that he had even removed his mask. He with that girl, and Julie home moping for him."

I could not resist saying, "*You* saw him at the Teatro Fenice?"

He laughed. "But then, I do not have a girl home moping for me." I looked away hastily and he reached out and caught my shoulders, turning me slowly, almost playfully, to face him. "Or do I?"

I pleaded ignorance. "That is not for me to say, Sir."

His dark eyes searched my face. "Oh, yes it is! Very much so." His touch was unnerving to me. I wondered if he knew how unnerving it was, but Julie and Bartrum got into a loud squabble at that minute in the next room, and he left me go, and stepped into the bedchamber.

"Be quiet, youngsters! No quarreling until you are married."

Julie complained, "Bart says we must throw away this empty jewel case and I say I will keep it and he will one day fill it with jewels for me."

"But it is threadbare," said Bartrum. "Look at the red velvet. Julie must have new things. Besides, Cobb wants all the useless things, like this, for the Santa Maria Charity in Lent."

Michael left them to their quarrel and remarked to me as we went out into the big salon, "Imagine having no more than that to quarrel about! I wonder if either of them has any notion of the world's ills."

"They are young," I excused the two. I sometimes found myself wishing I might once have been so naive about life.

"My dearest creature! He is older than you by several years."

My ears found music in that "dearest creature" and I said softly, "But he is a male with the world before him, he believes. Do you remember when you were his age?"

"When I was his age," said Michael in an edged and frightening voice, "I had been twelve years at my profession."

I did not know why his words hung upon the air between us, bringing an emotion I did not even perceive for a few minutes. Then, when it was over and I had seen him out the garden door and he had taken my hand and kissed it, I stood there watching him stride away between the stone urns to the waiting gondola. I touched my cheek with my hand where he had kissed it, and found myself shivering. I blamed this upon a breeze, sweeping across the gaunt greenery, and went in and closed the door.

As I walked up the stairs, I felt again in memory that brief time in the salon when his voice, or the emotion behind it had such extraordinary effect, even upon the climate of the air around us. It had been misery that hovered there, so powerfully moving that I felt the prick of tears in my eyes as I remembered. And more than misery was there: the ghastly shape of horror.

All afternoon I could not get it out of my mind. I went on with my work, stimulated by the driving desire to keep so occupied I would not think of those few minutes again. But they were present at the back of all my thoughts, and they combined with the growing infatuation I felt for Michael Sanson, so that to my infatuation was added a deep and almost passionate pity for him in whatever suffering he had endured.

Though the refurbishing, cleaning and scrubbing of the palazzo might be expected to shed the atmosphere of death and decay everywhere, it did not do so. I was constantly aware of a haunting uneasiness when I walked through its salons and down its many flights of steps. Perhaps it was the sickening memory of Maria-Elisa's body, rotting away all those endless days and nights under the very windows of the palazzo, no one seeming to care. Were they simply used to such horrors in a historic pile like this?

I had not been beyond the palazzo since the funeral, and there was a considerable brightening of the day when the Princess da Rimini arrived, all in golden yellow, swinging a black mask from her long fingertips. She had come to take Julie and her guardian to eat the ices at Florian's.

"Oh, bother!" said Julie, wrinkling her nose. "Who wants Sanson along? He is a skeleton at the feast."

"A rather substantial skeleton," the Princess reminded

her lightly. "Bartrum, will you be a dear boy and fetch Michael to us?"

Bart had been teasing Julie by ruffling her hair and trying to take some of his mother's worn-out articles away from his betrothed, and he now looked around, confused.

"Anne, where is Sanson? I saw him with you a half hour since."

"I am afraid he is gone to Pavia again, on business, he said. I was told not to have dinner prepared for him."

The Princess concealed her disappointment charmingly. "Well then, we need not forego our own pleasure, need we, little Julie?

Julie looked eager, then hesitant, as she glanced from her fiance to the Princess. Bartrum had taken this opportunity to remove his mother's threadbare items from her arms, and seeing this, she held on with a death grip while attempting to strike a bargain.

"Oh, Bart! Come with us in Sanson's place. Do!"

The Princess smiled at me significantly. "Love!" said her tongue and her well-shaped lips with a cynical curve. It seemed a strange expression to me when one considered her presumed interest in Michael Sanson, though I confess I smiled in some sympathy with her mood. It was quite apparent that Bartrum had no interest in accompanying the Princess and his bride-to-be, just as it was plain that he had an unusual interest in an armful of objects, worn and old, that belonged to his mother. Nor could I believe it was sentiment for Elvira Huddle that prompted this extraordinary concentration on her property.

"No, my pet! I've things to do. Sorry." He brushed a flippant, light kiss upon Julie's nose, and while she beamed in a rather touching way, he removed the litter from her hands. It was a sleek, smooth gesture, almost an unobtrusive one, but the Princess noted it, as I did, though I wondered if she found anything odd about this interest of his.

Julie looked longingly out across the balcony to the walls of an ancient palace across the canal. It was a beautiful day and the murky waters of the canal sparkled in reflection upon the high, barred windows of the opposite palace.

"It's heavenly out. I would adore going with you, Ketta."

"Excellent, child. Where is your maid? Run along and dress. Something... suitable."

Looking a trifle abashed at the implied criticism in this remark, Julie started to hurry past me to her own apartment but stopped abruptly and tugged at my hand.

"M'amselle, come and help me. That tiresome old Babette is forever dressing me as though I was ancient and fusty."

This sounded very like the complaint I was forever hearing in Miss Nutting's Academy For Young Females; so I excused myself to Her Highness and allowed the girl to drag me off to her rooms. Just as I had suspected, the tiny, stout Frenchwoman of about sixty who was Julie's maid had chosen a ruffled, high-necked India muslin round gown of a style two or three years past. Unlike the Paris fashion which still revealed a considerable amount of flesh, the young Demoiselles of Venice were more carefully hidden from view than any but the ladies of the Turkish Empire. I understood poor Julie's complaint just as I understood Michael Sanson's masculine anxiety that she should behave like a properly reared young female. But I could see that the dress was shockingly unattractive on her and would make her look quite bundle under the bosom. Nor did its pallid pink color flatter Julie's bright blonde curls.

Julie's maid had a broad smile upon her plump face beneath its white-haired frame, but her eyes were fixed upon me in a manner that clearly showed her mistrust. Julie watched the two of us, and I knew she was mentally wagering upon the outcome of my impending duel with Babette. I knew I must disappoint that hope, just as I must manage to win Babette's trust. These staff matters often depended upon compromise, the third way out of the difficulty. I began by nodding to Babette, agreeing that the gown was charming, and then I remarked as I held up Julie's curls, "A pity her hair is a trifle bright for that color. One does not wish her to be noticed."

"Her father desires that she will be masked, as is proper, if she is out after sunset," said Babette stiffly, but she was examining the pink dress with a frown, seeing what I had suggested, that it might make Julie too much noticed.

Julie stamped her foot, cried, "Babette! He is not my father! You know that." But by this time I had found a pretty blue gown of delicate-looking but sturdy *gros de Naples*. It looked soft and deceptively sensuous, but the bosom was well covered, the silk sash very near the normal waistline, and there were puffed sleeves, correct for a maiden of seventeen. Babette glanced at me and then at the dress and started to say something. Very faintly, I shook my head.

"I wish I might wear such a color. But we are not all fortunate. A pity."

"It is a blonde color. Only for blondes," said Babette, playing the little game with verve.

In very short order Julie was dressed and looking charming. What was even more important, Julie was in excellent humor. As I tied the ribbons of her blue bonnet under her ear, she said to me gaily, "For once in my life Sanson is right, Anne. He thinks of you often. If you were a lady, he might marry you."

"Indeed!" I said, somewhat dashed by this frankness.

"But Anne, you would not wish to marry a murderer."

I gave a hard tug to the ribbon, pulled the bow out in my nervous haste and the girl calmly set it to rights.

"I wish you will not say those preposterous things, Miss Julie. You know Monsieur Sanson would not deliberately murder anyone, and you must not make jokes in this way."

Julie's limpid blue eyes gazed at me, looking so Germanic, so like a young Austrian student I once knew, that it was hard for me to think of her as French. I wondered why this curious idea had occurred to me now. How could it matter to me that this girl with her imperious little nose and her haughteur, might not be French? I did not know her mother who may well have been Alsatian. As a matter of fact, I did not even know what sort of man her father had been, except that she seemed to have loved him very much. Fully aware that it was no concern of mine, I tried to remember my place. It was no more proper of me to criticize my employer's ward than if her maid, Babette, had done so. Perhaps I had even less right than Babette.

Julie grinned pertly and surprised me by winking. "How clever you are! This gown is so much nicer than the odious pink. You must really encourage my . . . Sanson. Perhaps he will marry you, after all. Or make you his mistress. And then you and I can be friends and I need not look like a tiresome dowd, or be kept within doors, as though I were in a harem in Barbary."

I was both pleased and humiliated at this suggestion, but hurried her along to the waiting Princess Ketta. I hoped the girl would not go about making such indiscreet remarks in the hearing of Her Highness. I had a notion the lady would be displeased, and in the most cutting terms. Before we got to the great salon, Julie fussed busily with her lace gloves, admiring the delicate hands that the gloves revealed.

"Mother had dreadful, red hands. So big, too. Isn't it luck I inherit Papa's hands? They were nice. And graceful."

"Did you know your parents well?" It was a harmless, natural question in the circumstances, but I felt that I was prying, because I was so interested in the answer.

"Not really. Not either of them. You must promise not to tell." She startled me by leaning close and whispering, "Mama was a barmaid, and worse. She'd been a laundress. That is why her hands were so horrid."

As I had laundered many an object in my day, I could only feel the barb in this, and a strong sympathy for the vanished barmaid.

"Nonetheless, as she was your mother, you owe her your life, Miss Julie."

"Oh, fustian! It is an hourly humiliation—every time I think of her. Papa, now, he was clever, and so very handsome. And his temper was like mine. Like the fireworks display I saw before Twelfth Night. I inherit my dreadful nose from him, I think, with a hump in it."

"Whose nose is dreadful?" the Princess asked in her tinkling voice. She was coming to us, holding her hands out to Julie. "Dear little one! Your nose has not a hump. Who has been telling you this?" With just a flicker of her eyelids, the Princess indicated me, making it appear an accident, I was sure.

"Ketta! Nobody said it. No one but me would possibly be so beastly." Julie laughed and put her hand into Her Highness' arm confidingly as they walked away, leaving me prey to some vaguely troubling thoughts as I finished my morning's work.

I was a good deal surprised to discover that Bartrum Huddle shared Julie's horrid suspicions, and a few of his own. He came gallantly to my rescue a little after noon when Angelo hurried off because "The Signore Cobb asked me to take the earth from the urns in the garden." I had nothing to say against the project, being in favor of it myself, but I had been about to hang new curtains from the tester of Bartrum's bed, and was now standing on tiptoe on the bedstool, trying to reach the high tester when I felt myself seized under the arms. I stifled a scream, knowing perfectly well this must be the gallantry of the bed's prospective occupant. He was the sort of man one did well not to encourage.

"Ah! You recognize my touch, my adorable Anne."

I looked over my shoulder into the dazzling white teeth of Bartrum and unable to resist that enormous innocence of his, I smiled too.

"I am not your adorable Anne, Sir. And I am certainly not your adorable Julie."

"Touché, Ma'am." He released me much too slowly, adding the calculated response, "But you look so very tantalizing there, stretching tall, with those rounded arms, and those pretty ankles . . ."

The compliment might have been charming, if rather too exciting, on lips less practiced in compliments, but I could hear the faint echo of all the times he had said such things in the past, and I only laughed.

"I think, Sir, you rehearse at every opportunity."

"What ever do you mean?"

"Aside from that," I said, changing the subject rapidly, "you may be of great service to me at this moment."

"How? Tell me how."

"By fastening these curtains to that tester above my head."

Since he was more or less hoist by his own petard, Bartrum did a notable job of it, and ended by demanding a like service of me, that I accompany him that afternoon to an island in the Lagoon to purchase a set of crystal goblets for his bride. Since he had saved me more than an hour's work, I could hardly refuse him, though the island he named, Ile Isola, was a gloomy place, bearing signs of ancient habitation which had gradually deteriorated until even the ghostly past no longer seemed to trouble Venetians. They only went there by daylight, to the little glass factory which had a commendable name.

In hurriedly dressing to go, I was torn between the natural desire to look my best, and the consciousness that I must at no time be mistaken for a lady of his own class. Those who chanced to see us and recognize me, must know that I was serving him in my capacity as housekeeper, and no other. After a brief struggle with my vanity I decided to wear my lilac day gown and no frills or furbelows of any sort. To complete the picture of the respectable housekeeper, I swept my hair back and bundled it on the nape of my neck with hair bodkins. I wore my black, workaday shawl and joined Master Bartrum. He was his usual flattering self, but compliments from that quarter were coming so easily of late that I felt they had very little worth in the marketplace.

Our gondola journey did not begin propitiously. Bartrum was asked by the public gondolier for his pay at the moment of hiring as he did not like to carry passengers to the Ile Isola. It was a minor sum and I made no doubt that I would be reimbursed by Cobb who was, at the moment, my paymaster. Bartrum, of course, had no hesitation in asking me for the loan. I did wonder how he expected to purchase the goblets, but I did not mention the fact, out of fear that he might take the question for an offer.

It was dusk when we passed the Piazzetta leading to the great Cathedral of St. Mark's and the Capanile, and the time of day, as well as the location was a reminder of my previous excursion with Bartrum. Beside all else, we might be arriving at the glass factory after the shutters had gone up for the night. Bartrum was so confident, however, that I made the unpardonable mistake of trusting him.

"And do not trouble yourself, Anne, that I will let you wander the canals of Venice alone today. It was frightfully ungallant of me. I was given a distinct setdown by my esteemed future father. I would not dare to abandon you again."

"Thank you. I shall count upon your gallantry."

"I suspect you are being ironic, but I am sincere, Anne. I share several things with Sanson. One is the suspicion that Mother's interest in Sanson was financial. Some secret of his. I was sure there would be some evidence among Mother's things. But I found nothing." I looked at him quickly. He smiled and added significantly, "I share another thing with Sanson. My admiration for your beauty."

"How fortunate you are, Sir! To have such praise forever at the tip of your tongue."

He reached for me and for a second or two I thought we were going to have a ridiculous tussle in daylight out in the Lagoon, but as I drew away, so did his hands. He was staring over my head at something in the choppy waters beyond us.

"One of the ladies of the Teatro Fenice?" I asked lightly. But I saw that he was genuinely puzzled. "Good Lord! I was not mistaken the last time I saw him. What the devil does Sanson find so fascinating on Ile Isola?"

I glanced around. Even in the dark and by the faint gondola light, I recognized Michael Sanson's face. He was looking down, or staring into space, worn and troubled. I ached to comfort him. I was still thinking of this, of his deep problems, whatever they might be, when Bartrum settled back in our gondola, to the relief of the gondolier, and saying triumphantly, "That fellow has a secret!"

"Why do you say that?"

"Many reasons, my dear girl. This isn't the first time he had lied about going to Ile Isola. Always, he says he is off to the opposite direction. Today it was Pavia again; was it not?"

"Yes, but perhaps he returned early and went to this Isola place."

"Always?"

I stared at him. "Now, what'll you mean by that?"

He clapped his hands. "Three times, M'dear. Twice, he told Julie he was going to Pavia. Once to Mestri. I saw him returning from Isola each time. The opposite direction, mind. And still he lies."

I said so quickly he looked at me suspiciously, "Absurd. There is no reason why he could not change his mind and—and not go to Pavia. Or perhaps go to both places."

"The same day? Really, Anne! Quite an impossible feat, even for him! He has a very expensive secret, and I mean to possess it." He added with what I regarded as revolting and dangerous greed, "I've a serious need for a competence to support me for as long as—" He shrugged. "For life."

I had a sudden, horrible memory of another person who had hoped for a life competence. Maria-Elisa was already forgotten, by all but me. And by her killer, no doubt.

XIV

A NIGHT FOG was rising off the waters, so that Sanson's gondola soon dissolved into that thick, gray dusk and was gone. I was still thinking of him when Bartrum cut in with admirable coolness.

"Do you know, Anne, it was providential that we were bound for Ile Isola today."

"Tonight, from the look of it," I said tartly. "I'll wager we are too late for your precious glassware."

Bartrum took up my words at once. "A kiss to a ducat says you're wrong. But even if they should be closed, we have a superb chance to discover what secrets Sanson is hiding on the island."

"You're being ridiculous, if I may say so. Do you expect to find a mad wife, or a graveyard full of victims? Something of that sort? We are not dealing with some of Mrs. Radcliffe's odious characters now. I suspect you've been listening to the mischievous imaginings of a very young girl."

Bartrum looked at me, not in the least moved except to amusement. "That very young girl is scarcely four years younger than you, Anne."

"Six years," I corrected him. "And she has been reared as a lady. Sheltered. Ignorant of the world. And a little spoiled, I expect."

Embarrassingly, he did not deny this but persisted, like a terrier worrying a twisted rag, "At all events, we've nearly got to the quai. And it isn't dark yet. We've a deal of time for making the Grand Tour of the island."

The gondolier grunted and muttered something in Italian so rapid I didn't understand it, though I understood his mood. He did not at all like the place. Then, too, if it was not yet dark, as Bartrum claimed, it was certainly foggy, and I felt no passionate desire to grope blindly over an unsavory, deserted island full of ancient dead, and knowing no more of it than of the Plains of Cathay.

"Master Bartrum, how well do you know this island?"

As I had suspected, he seemed to have less common sense than a venturesome two-year-old.

"I've been to the little glass shop. When you've seen one island in this part of the world, you've seen all. It's very like Torcello . . . I think."

The gondolier looked down at us, his weathered face carved by deep lines.

"It is like Torcello. Like San Michele, too. It is a dark place. The ancient Roman gods are here yet. It is a dark of the heart, one hears."

The sound of that was nothing if not unpromising, and I glanced at Bartrum to see if it dampened his enthusiasm as it certainly chilled me. It did not. He looked up, made a leap for the warped and twisted mooring pole, and managed to hold us secure with that painful and dangerous gesture, while the gondolier brought us in parallel to the quai.

"You'll await us?" Bartrum asked the gondolier who agreed by holding out his hand, palm up.

Bartrum looked at me with a pleading, teasing grin. I ignored him as I held the proper *scudi* over the gondolier's palm and looked him in the eye:

"You will await *me*? I am returning almost at once."

"Now, Anne . . . ?"

"At once. How far is the glass shop?"

He pointed to a dark, low huddle of buildings at the end of what looked to be a straight, poplar-lined canal. There were lights in that shadowy hump against the Eastern skyline, for which I was grateful. Five minutes to reach the shop, a few minutes for Master Bartrum to make his choice, and five minutes back. No more! I was determined on that, though the trees were full and lush overhead, the canal looked clean in its foggy shroud, and I began to hope that Ile Isola had an unearned reputation.

The gondolier stood in his gently rocking boat, one hand on his hip, the other propping his great sweep against the mooring pole. He made no response to my request that he wait, but he had unquestionably taken my money. I could only hope for the best while taking a firm attitude with Bartrum. The latter took my arm as though we were politely strolling the Piazza of San Marco.

We were walking rapidly along the little dirt path that bordered the canal, and could still make out the difference between the thick, damp air and the water with its color, or lack of it, borrowed from the low-lying fog, but I should not have cared to wander here much deeper into the night. Bartrum must have had similar misgivings, because he said suddenly,

"You are being excessively good about this, Anne."

"I will not be paying for your glassware, and you may be sure of that, Sir."

"No, no. I am known here. They will set it to my account. They know I am marrying money, as the saying goes."

"I hope that is not—" I bit off the end of this prosy reminder. The marriage of Bartrum and Julie was not really my concern, though I did have an almost uncontrollable desire to tell him how base I considered his whole attitude toward the marriage. It was not, of course. It was a most natural and popular attitude for a man of his position, and in a cynical city like Venice; so I changed my remark, went on in as light a tone as I could muster, "I have an evening's work that needs doing. I shall be returning to the gondola just as I promised."

Bartrum peered around into the gathering puffs of fog, and made a pretense of shuddering. Or was it only a pretense? Beyond the column of trees the landscape was crowded with grassy clumps of vegetation that had crawled over old monuments, ancient foundations and fallen stone walls to soften the signs of a long dead civilization. Gradually, as we reached the low stone wall before the little glass shop and its outbuildings, we could both see that the island landscape in every direction was dissolving before our eyes, into indefinable shapes. The small world of this island would soon be obliterated by the fog.

"Please hurry," I said, rather surprising myself by the timid sound of my own voice. I half expected him to show some amusement.

It did not ease my own doubts when he answered my plea with a quick, slightly breathless: "Naturally. I think I had rather be caught in a tomb than this place. Damme! I've never seen it by night." Then he laughed at his own cowardice as his nervous rap on the warped wooden door produced a perfectly normal, if huge, bald man in a peculiar red garment like a tunic over his old-fashioned breeches. Although the man put me strongly in mind of a friendly butcher, his way of ushering us into the dark little shop was dignified and graceful.

I blinked at the alternate darkness and light in the room. Our way was illuminated by lamps through what appeared to be the sales area, though the floor was of alternate dirt and blocks of broken stone. The place may once have been more significant, in the dim past of the island. But beyond the lighted area with its customer's board, no better than a kitchen deal table, along with an insecure cerule chair taken out of its ancient context, I could see the work area, a huge fireplace burning bright orange flames, and beside it, all manner of glass tubing, a common stool, and a splendid collection of glassware of varied shapes and magic colors.

"These are freshly blown," boasted the big man whose face looked the color of his red tunic.

Even in the dark work area of the shop, I could see burned holes in the man's clothing, as well as the long, puckered brown scar of a burn on his massive forearm. The man had a number of exquisite glass sets from which Bartrum had a little difficulty choosing. As for me, I felt the silence, the desertion of this place, and when Bartrum turned to me for my choice among the glasses, I made a hasty choice of wine goblets which reflected the fire like frozen flame, and then asked quickly,

"Are you alone in the shop, Signore?"

The giant clapped me on the back and laughed to reveal the gaping holes where his teeth once had been.

"Is the Signorina wishing to be alone with me? You hear that, Signore Huddle?"

Bartrum, to my surprise, made no attempt to play on this notion. He indicated the desired glassware, put aside an elegant green epergne and looked into the shadowed corners of the shop.

"You live somewhere in the Merceria; do you not?"

"And leaving almost immediately, Signore. I've no objection to the island here, but my wife—ah, you know the nerves of a female when she is unwell. We did live here once, several years gone. But no more." Having made his sale to Bartrum who signed in a ledger but paid nothing, the glassmaker began to remove his tunic before us, revealing a huge, scarred chest that shone in the firelight.

"Your wife did not like the island?" I asked, seeing that Bartrum was looking at me expectantly.

"Not in the least," said the giant with great cheerfulness. He was covering the hairy flesh with a homespun shirt.

Bartrum took a breath, blurted out, "You mean there is a reason— Is there a reason? That is, do you find the island dangerous in some way?"

"*Por Dio!* Dangerous is the very word. My wife has

a lung sickness, and these miserable fogs! The climate! You may well believe it is dangerous."

Poor man! He had no notion of why Bartrum burst out laughing, and in my relief I laughed at the giant's expression. I saw that Bartrum was bound to have his way, like a stubborn child; so I said hopefully, "Yours appears to be the only shop on the island."

"Quite so, Signorina. Only I."

In triumph, I made the point to Bartrum, "You see? Sanson could not have been visiting this island. Unless it was to buy glass. The island is deserted, but for the shop."

The giant completed his change, throwing over himself an old-fashioned cloak of black worsted which looked, and undoubtedly felt very practical in the seeping dampness. He could not seem to comprehend the importance of our questions and treated them as though they were mere efforts at polite conversation.

He motioned us to join him as he left the shop and only then remarked calmly, "The place is a fair enough retreat. If one wishes the silence, the loneliness. There are two small villas. Little cottages. Even the remains of a palazzo. One sees the inhabitants upon occasion, but I believe there are less than a dozen. Perhaps but three or four during the season of mists and fog." He shrugged huge shoulders, looking like a gigantic bat in his black cloak. "I am not one to seek them out, if they have no love for me."

"Aha!" cried Bartrum. "You see, Anne? It's one of those. Mark me! He visits a . . . a secret."

"What is this?" the giant asked. "Who visits?"

I said hastily, "Nothing. It is a joke of the Signore. Is our gondolier still waiting?"

It was difficult to tell. Puffs of fog now enclosed the canal and its bordering path and though it was not yet twilight, the island itself was closed away from the great Venetian world of carnival and noise and lights.

"A moment, there," Bartrum exclaimed as the glassblower was about to lock and bolt his little shop. "May we have a light? Set it to my reckoning."

While I protested impatiently that the gondolier would leave at any minute, the glassblower obligingly got Bartrum a storm lantern and then, having bid us a jolly good night, he went striding off past the canal to some other place of anchorage further along the shore. He obviously had a private boat that got him back to Venice and the district of the Merceria. We could not see him after the first minute or so.

I moved in gingerly fashion to the edge of the canal, or what I conceived to be the edge, but was so near to walking into the misty, indistinct waters that I stopped and asked Bartrum if he would light my way to the gondola. Even the gondolier might have a little trouble making his way across the Lagoon and into the Grand Canal through this dripping fog. Bartrum had the grace to hesitate; since he was hoping to cozzen me into his way. He attempted to bolster his argument by pointing along the rugged, misty shoreline toward a vague shape slightly inland.

"Anne, this is an ideal time. We may not have another soon. Ten minutes. What is that?"

"Very much, if our gondolier leaves during those ten minutes. Do come along. And don't be tiresome."

"Oh, Anne! You are a complete hand! What if we were to find the grave of some poor victim of Sanson's? Wouldn't you want to know?"

"Definitely not!"

I started off with every show of confidence which was strictly superficial. But it was with considerable relief that I saw the light raised behind me. Then Bartrum strode rapidly along beside me with the glass packet in one hand and swinging the lamp with the other. He must be very cross with me, I thought. The canal sparkled beneath a layer of fog, looking deep and cold. I avoided it after that first glance and kept my gaze fixed upon the stony path beneath my feet.

It was a shock when Bartrum stopped abruptly. I looked up. Within sight of us, even through the fog, was the empty quai. Very dimly, out on the Lagoon, we could make out what I assumed was a little gondola light. Bartrum and I looked at each other in consternation.

"Good Lord!" he muttered. "What are we to say to that?"

"There go my four scudi."

That made him laugh. He swung his lamp around, briefly illuminating bits of the atmosphere, forming long, ragged shadows between the flickers of light. I stopped him quickly.

"Don't. You'll kill the light."

From this step it was not far to the next, which, in Bartrum's view, was that we must return to one of those villas on the island and borrow a boat of some sort.

"And will you play the gondolier, and row us back to the palazzo?" I asked ironically.

He grinned. "I rather thought *you* might—"

That made me laugh and I raised my hand as if to slap him, and we ended by agreeing that he had won. We must return to the island and seek help from the odd recluses who chose to live in this desolate place.

"There is sure to be a little sailing vessel somewhere along the shore, in one of the coves. A felucca, perhaps, like those across the Adriatic. You'll see them everywhere in the Turkish Empire. I've seen them when I went to the other islands of the Lagoon. We can borrow such a boat. Then neither of us need take the oar."

"And you will gain your wish," I reminded him as we made our way back toward the glass shop.

"That's as may be." His hesitant reply showed a doubt I had not thought existed.

He held up the lamp and peered into the gloomy dark. He should have been much happier. I could not but be aware that he had no real relish for wandering this desolate island in search of—what? He knew not. "A secret worth a life's competence." But what kind of secret neither he nor I had the remotest notion.

"I think we had best cut across here," I said, seeing that we could avoid the full walk to the glassblower's shop by following northward the grassy, broken cobbles that once had been a street. "If we hurry, we may be able to get a boat back to the Fundamenta or the Piazza before the evening crowds grow too great."

"Quite right. I've no taste to go crashing into one of the revelers on the Lagoon." He looked at me, tried to make a joke which had much truth in it. "Then, too, think of the scandal to us both if you were caught with me after dark and unmasked. My dear girl! You would be ruined."

I said tartly, "I hope I might live that down. Meanwhile, though, the light in that cottage or villa—whatever it is—has died out."

"No matter. Perhaps they go early to their beds."

Nevertheless, as we made our way, first over the broken Roman cobbles of the street, and after, across a dead, crackling field of nettle, I knew from the way Bartrum's hand nervously waved the light that he had lost his first taste for playing the Bow Street Runner and tracking down Sanson's secret. The villa he had counted upon was a broken cottage with scattered outhouses in which I heard the disturbed chickens making their little protest against our presence. Bartrum hurried his steps and mine too. He whispered,

"Shall we knock, or call out? We don't wish to frighten anyone. Besides, we must be cautious in asking them anything. They must not suspect."

I was beginning to believe he wanted to put off his inquisitive notions until daylight for fear any trouble tonight might prevent us from borrowing a boat and its owner.

A dog began to bark somewhere and I knew we could not stand debating. I raised my hand and knocked. There seemed nothing except dirt beneath our feet, but our shoes grated upon it. Probably, there were pebbles worn down and lost in the damp earth. The shutters of the house were tight-closed at all the windows and the wooden door had a little judas-hole through which an eye finally peered at us. It was unsettling, and before I could answer, Bartrum burst out, nervously,

"I say! May we come in? Only a minute, Sir. I would like to talk to you."

"In Italian," I whispered and he said the whole thing over in Italian, but the horrid eye, old and blood-shot by the look of it, merely stared and then, after blinking once, turned away and a pair of aged lips appeared at the judas-hole.

"Go away," said the lips in Italian. "Begone. I do not open after dark. I am not that great a fool."

I said quickly, but speaking in Italian, and as clear as I could, "Please, Signore, we must borrow a boat. I'll pay. You understand? *I will pay.*"

One might as well speak to the blind door itself. The lips disappeared and with them the tiny light which had come to us in a nimbus around the face of the old man. The judas-hole closed.

"Now, what's to be done?" Bartrum asked, ready to pound on the door and force an entry.

Being in no very cheerful temper myself, I said sarcastically, "At least, you have ample time now to seek out your father-in-law's secret. In fact, you may have until morning."

"I beg you, dear girl don't put me in mind of it." He made an elaborate pretense of shuddering, so elaborate I guessed it was only half a pretense. "Damme! What a predicament!" He set the packet of glasses down and flashed the lamp around at a very unpromising scene. The cottage proved to be a crumbling old villa, once a delicate pink form of stone, but now a dismal, weathered color impossible to distinguish from dust or fog. The cottage seemed to be the front, or added part of the villa and the villa's ground had been given over to small livestock.

"The old man is daft," I said. "There is no use in troubling with him. We had best go on. Throw the light along the road, where it curves inward beyond that little cove."

He did so and we began to make out another building or prominence, perhaps five minutes' walk from the man's place.

"There is no light in the place," he objected.

"No matter. The lights may be on the far side, or there may be an extra boat in the cove."

He glanced around and then followed me.

"There must be. The old man has no boat."

I did not think it necessary to disillusion him, but in all likelihood, the old man would ride into Venice in someone else's felucca. In any case, we were better off searching for another inhabited cottage than in frightening that old man. I found myself walking so rapidly I nearly ran. Bartrum was forced to take long strides to catch me up.

"It is an unhealthy place entirely," I said by way of explanation for my sudden haste which had almost been prompted by panic.

"That it is! Still, and all, we may serve both purposes if one of us keeps an eye to what is unusual, while the other inquires after the boat."

"Unusual! I should think the whole island is unusual. It is only the usual that looks out of place here." I had just stepped in a bed of nettles which stung through my skirts, and stung my temper as well. But my surly observation made Bartrum grin and his cheerfulness had its good effect upon me. This was no time to be impatient or bad-tempered. The truth is, we had need of each other.

Having crossed the narrow patch of ground with its long-untended vegetation run wild, we came upon the remains of a low stone wall, probably once a property line but now so well hidden, Bartrum stumbled over it and sprawled full-length across a pebbled road. I was sure he would be cross but he behaved remarkably well, laughing at his clumsiness and announcing that he was now entitled to have himself fitted for a new wardrobe, "Chargeable to my father-in-law, naturally, since it is his fault I am here."

This latter reasoning was round-about, though true, and while I dusted him off, I was reflecting that if I must be marooned on this Crusoe's Isle which was generally in full sight of Venice, I preferred to be with a person of easy disposition. As he got to his feet, however, looking ahead at our second fogbound villa, he caught sight of something that changed his cheerful look to one of keen concentration.

"What is it?" I whispered, suddenly tense again.

"Beyond the stone fence at the long, barred window on the side. You see?"

I caught a faint movement, or thought I did before the light within the villa was darkened. Even so, I was sure the heavy folds of a portiere were dropped down into place, and that very likely, this required a human hand, as did the darkening of the room itself. We moved closer to the villa.

"Perhaps it's someone frightened of us," I suggested hopefully. "The old man was afraid. And with this dreadful weather, we must look considerably more dangerous than whoever is hiding behind those portieres."

He was a bit rueful. "Sometime I wish I'd never heard of those infernal wine glasses."

"Glasses!" I looked down at his free arm. So did he. The packet was gone.

"Damn!" He swung around, looked back along the rocky path full of obstacles by which we had come this far, and remembered. "I left them at the old fellow's cottage."

I suggested that we try and rouse the frightened creature at the villa, and having gained consent to borrow a vessel, if any, we could go back and get the glasses before sailing back across the Lagoon. He agreed, but reluctantly, and he was ready to expect the worst when we reached the villa's garden which, in this case, was well cared for, with exquisite little wild flowers tucked away close against the stone foundations. By sunlight they must be purple and bright gold and some blue. Nothing well-known, but all showing signs of human care.

Bartrum whispered, "I've an idea. You rap at the door. I'll go along under the window on the side. If he's afraid of you, he may go to the window to watch you leave."

I nodded. He left the lamp with me. I waited a few seconds for him to get out of sight, and finding an old-fashioned but serviceable brass knocker, I put it to use. The sound seemed to carry in an eerie way through the misty fog. I felt a stronge urge to raise the lamp and peer behind me into that fog, like a child who imagines everything at her back is evil. I decided that if the villa's owner heard my voice, he would be more likely to open to a woman than to a man. I called out.

"Hello, in there! May I speak to you? I must get back to the Fundamenta. Hello, in there!"

I could hear nothing within the house, but there was

a curious noise somewhere in the fog, a rustling sound, and then, quite hideous, a sound like a human groan . . .

Trying not to panic, I swung the lamp around, saw nothing except the creeping fog, and banged very hard on the door.

"I know you are in there! Please help me."

And then, I remembered Bartrum off around the side of the building alone. He hadn't even the lamp with which to defend himself and I doubted if he was a man of leonine courage, despite his very commendable figure. I must have taken several steps when I trod on something that was partially sunk in the dirt and pebbles. It cut into the sole of my shoe and I reached over, mechanically, to pick it up. Of all curious things, it was the wooden frame of a mantel clock.

I am very vague as to what happened next. I know that I tossed the clock to one side, determined to join Bartrum and see if he had met with accident or foul play. I don't even recall the blow across the back of my skull, though I seem to remember blinding lights like little stars bursting before my eyes, as though all the heavens had exploded.

XV

I was told later that only the excessive play of my imagination could explain the extraordinary thing I saw when I came to myself some time deep in the night. Someone had taken me by the shoulder and was shaking me. I winced and complained so fretfully in my half-conscious state that I wakened myself.

"Glory be! My head! Don't be after touching me." Under considerable pressure from a headache, I opened my eyes.

Staring down at me was a masquerader, the curious, shadowy monk who had haunted my return to the palazzo a week previous. Somewhere close at hand was the lamp I had overturned in my fall, and still illuminated the ground about me, its light somewhat diluted by the fog and my own vague, though painful return to awareness. The face above me, in its protective, concealing cowl was unmasked and I saw the eyes, strangely familiar, gazing down at me. The rest of the face was in shadow; yet the eyes haunted me, both sad and terrible. I fancied I had seen them in a portrait somewhere but could not remember the circumstances. I thought of Michael Sanson at once, but what I could see of the face was younger, I thought, and bore not the least resemblance to the Frenchman, except the emotions of pity and fear it might arouse in the beholder.

"Help me!" I pleaded in a hoarse undervoice that even I could scarcely make out. "Help me and the gentleman with—"

My head ached abominably. I closed my eyes. I felt so thirsty I stood in great need of waters, of anything that would relieve the intolerable thirst...

Seconds later, or hours later, I never knew, I opened my eyes and began to pull my body together, to get on my feet. I was not surprised, oddly enough, when I did not find my strange nemesis, the ghostly monk, peering down at me. I was alone in the misty night. The fog had risen and through the mist, I made out the silhouettes of hummocks, broken walls, bushes that inhabited this strange, dead world. High overhead the stars were out, and as I stared at the scene, vaguely wondering what I was doing here, I saw the new moon rising.

I put out my hands flat to the ground, an act that cleared my mind by the pain of the sharp little pebbles which pressed into my palms. It was not until then that I asked myself where my mysterious monk had gone. He had either struck me down and bent over me to observe how well he succeeded, or he had come upon me as a witness, and fled for some reason. He was certainly not in sight now. Aside from the danger of the monk, I cared little for him now. I was desperately anxious to find out whether it was Bartrum who made that odd, sickening "groan" I heard before I lost consciousness.

With a little effort I got to my feet, swaying dizzily, and looked around. The lamp had gone out, but the moon and stars, cutting through the light fingers of fog, gave me enough light so that I made out the low, broken stone wall, the villa itself—now oddly, no longer dark—and the endless little shadowy points on the horizon which marked the obstacles over which Bartrum and I had stumbled on our way to this villa. My first instinct was to call to Master Bartrum, but if the watchful, or frightened person who stared at us from the villa was still listening, I preferred that he should not know where Bartrum was. To know, was to be a part of the attack upon him. There was one light at a front villa window.

I swayed, got my balance, and stumbled a few steps before I found my limbs working naturally. Then too, I was fearful that I might fall over the debris on the ground. One thing struck me clearly as I thought of that debris, turned and glanced back once at the place where I had fallen. No mistake: the clock frame which had puzzled me just before I fell unconscious, was now gone. Even if I had thrown it from me as I collapsed, I could not have thrown it beyond my present view of the scene. So my assailant, or the monkish-phantom, or both in one person, had removed the clock! For what reason I could not begin to imagine. It was perfectly empty, no thick wooden base, no secret compartment. The plain skeleton of a mantel clock. Perhaps the thief simply had a passion for clocks.

In that quick, almost ridiculous supposition, I was nearer right than I could have imagined.

I found the lamp where I had dropped it. The flame was out now, and I carried the lamp only for the sake of holding some sort of feeble weapon in my hand. It was not until I reached the corner of the villa, peering into the moonlit scene under the barred window that I had my worst fear of the night. I could not see any sign of Bartrum Huddle. I did not dare to call out, for fear that our attacker might come instead. My knees threatened to give away under me.

. . . What have they done with him? Who—or what —is it? Did we really come too close to the truth about Michael Sanson?

I leaned against the villa's rough stone wall, regaining strength, and, though I did not know it, listening. The late night was full of little sounds—tiny creatures in the dry grass; insects and birds disturbed. Something was here in the darkness with me. I swung around, whispered,

"Is it you, Master Bartrum?"

There was a sharp, metallic click behind me and afterward the door of the villa was opened in a gingerly way. An old, heavy-faced woman wearing a frilled night cap over her grizzled locks, looked out, not at me, but at the enormous night.

I hurried back to her, stumbling a little in my eagerness.

"We've been attacked, my employer and I. Could you help me—give me a light for my lamp? I can't find him."

"Eh?" said the old woman vaguely. "I cannot see you, Signora. I am blind. Usually the night is still, but tonight I hear things outside, and I am frightened."

I was feeling better by the second. Small wonder the woman was alarmed at all the disturbance! In her blindness she exaggerated all the dangers. Perhaps I too had exaggerated them. I myself was not dead, nor even badly hurt. Yes, but what of Master Bartrum?

"May I borrow a light to find the gentleman?" I asked. "And do you have a boat we may borrow? We will pay."

The woman gazed somewhere behind me but her head was cocked on one side as if she were listening to something only she could hear. It was unnerving to watch the strange, old woman.

"Who is there with you?" she asked.

"No one. I am searching for my employer."

"As you say, Signora. Come. I will find a light for your lamp." She felt of the lamp I placed in her hands and remarked as one who knows, "It is broken. The wick . . . I will find you another."

After a moment's hesitation and a brief look around into the starlit, shadowed night, I stepped into the old villa. The entry way and the rooms it opened into were very like the style of an ancient Roman house my husband once showed me. In the center of the house was an open loggia, very Roman, with a fountain and grass actually kept green. Low-burning lamps illuminated the lovely scene which seemed like such an anacronism on this forgotten island.

While I waited for the blind woman to fetch me another lamp, I started forward to get a better look at this unexpected beauty spot. To my surprise, the blind woman came shuffling back to me.

"No, no, Signora. You are not to leave the entry. You understand?"

"Of course. I am sorry."

Nevertheless, I was excessively intrigued by her secrecy, her anxiety that I go no further. What was hidden here? It even occurred to me that Bartrum himself might be a prisoner somewhere in the villa, particularly in that area, the garden and loggia, where I was forbidden to go. I stood there in the entry a few minutes, gazing around at the subdued elegance, hearing my own feet shift upon the rich tiles.

A light sound from the enclosed garden beyond the next room arrested me. It was a person, a man, I thought, clearing his throat. Or could it be Master Bartrum, trying to signal to me? An absurd and farfetched idea, but everything that had happened to us tonight had been farfetched; yet I was here, and Master Bartrum was unquestionably gone. I decided that it was my footsteps upon the tile which had informed the blind woman of my movements. I took great care not to set my heels to the tile as I stepped over to the archway leading to the loggia and garden. I remained in shadow which was not difficult, as the big lacquered case clock in the corner showed that the hour was nearly two in the morning, and the world was fairly well asleep. It was shocking to learn from the clock that I had been unconscious, or semi-conscious, several hours. Small wonder that I had this frightful headache. And as to Bartrum, anything might have happened during so long a time.

From a dark place behind one of the loggia pillars, I got a clearer view of the person I had briefly glimpsed in the rectangular garden. A man who appeared to be thirty, perhaps a trifle older, leaned forward in a high-backed chair, staring into the white, splashing foam of the fountain. His hands were pressed tightly together, palm to palm, as if he had been at his prayers, like a child, and only lowered his fingers a moment since. I could not see his full face, only his profile, and I felt at once that I had seen such a face before, though not, curiously enough, upon this strange and elegant man. A woman. Though the man was not effeminate, yet I associated the nose, even the arrogant curve of the lips, with a female.

Mother of Heaven! This could well be Julie Sanson's father, the one who was dead, "killed by Michael Sanson." Was this Michael's great secret, the dreadful knowledge, also, that had been so useful to Elvira Huddle.

Why was the man hiding away in this forsaken place? It was a strange business altogether, the man deserting his daughter, pretending to be dead, living his life out in this luxurious oasis, apparently intending never to reveal himself to the daughter who revered his memory. And worst of all, by his behavior, he allowed his daughter to make dreadful, false accusations against Michael.

The gentleman seemed to arouse from the study into which he had fallen, and to glance around. I was now so astonished by this scene that I remained where I was, fascinated, wondering who his companion might be; for he was obviously not alone. He spoke in French to someone beyond my vision.

"I am not ready now, but I think I may sleep later."

A harsh-featured, muscular man came into my vision. He was surprisingly kind to the gentleman whom I took to be Julie's father. The relationship between the men baffled me.

"Oui, Monsieur. As you say."

The hard-faced man was dressed, curiously enough, in a hunting costume with a deal of leather, including high boots. Very formidable. He put me in mind of the local police whom the Italian servants at the palazzo called the *sbirri*. But the gentleman treated the hard-faced man with scant courtesy; so my first theory, that the hard man was a jailer, could not be true, at least, in the eyes of the gentleman. I did not know what the man did or said that was annoying, but as he murmured something I couldn't hear and started to seat himself on a stone bench close to the fountain, the gentleman raised his head suddenly and said in a dreadful, cutting tone, "You dare! Watch yourself!"

I was so startled I moved away from the pillar, and only just in time. The two men looked toward the room in which I had been eavesdropping. The ugly, hard-featured man started toward me. I retreated so rapidly I almost walked into the blind woman who said sternly,

"You are not here when I come with lamp, Signora. You are not honest."

"I beg pardon," I said and snatched up the lantern from her hand. "Have you any notion where I may find the Signore Huddle?"

Behind me, I heard the harsh man's footsteps on the tiles. The old woman said in haste, "I cannot tell you. I do not see."

"What does the female want?" asked the man brusquely in French.

In the same language the old woman replied, "She comes searching for her man. He is lost."

"Lost? Now God be damned! We want no lost ones here prowling about to lose us our pay. Send her on her way."

"She asks for a boat."

I pretended ignorance of the conversation, but since they knew I had spoken in Italian, bad though it was, I went on in that language, to the man.

"Signore, may we borrow a boat? A sail boat. I can give you the name of the palazzo where I am employed."

The man scowled, said to the woman in French, "What does she talk about? A boat. And this—'we.' Where is the man? Who is he?"

Suddenly, I took a long chance. At least, I reasoned, there must be a reaction if Michael had anything to do with this villa and its curious residents. If not, then Michael's name might be known because he was reputed to have money and a position of sorts.

"I am persuaded the Signore Michele Sanson will thank you for giving us your assistance. I am employed in his household."

"What is this? What of Sanson?"

We were all startled. The gentleman with the arrogant mouth had come so silently to the entry, moving over the tiles with catlike grace. The movement, the silence, even his presence among us troubled me in a way I could not understand. I was terribly frightened and I did not know precisely why. The gentleman was handsome, elegant in every gesture, his voice low and melodious, carefully trained; yet, this moment of confrontation was one I prayed to end, and quickly. I kept to my Italian, explaining that I had come to the Ile Isola with Bartrum Huddle for glassware and needed a boat to get us back.

"Yes, but you mentioned Sanson," said the gentleman in French.

I was not to be caught so easily and asked that someone speak in Italian or English.

The hard-faced man exchanged a few words in French with the French gentleman. I listened while pretending to be confused. The French gentleman agreed: "Ah, well, if it is not Sanson she is searching for, she may take the small felucca. What harm in that?"

The old woman translated to me, eliminating the personal opinions expressed, and I accepted the offer, but pleaded, "May we at least make a bit of search for Master Huddle?"

"Now, that—no!" said the harsh man with decision. "We've no time. We are for bed soon." This he said in Italian.

"The young Signore went to the glass shop," put in the blind woman in French to the men. "I know it must be. I heard footsteps a few moments since, going toward the shop."

It would be like Bartrum to run off and leave me here, if he took a notion to rescue his packet of glassware. But still, I put up a fuss, because I was not at all certain they had told me the truth. After all is said, someone had struck me on the back of the head, and I was not like to forget it. Very probably, my assailant was one of these people. Or the monk . . .

The monk! Was that only part of my nightmare? Or had he actually existed in the flesh?

I knew I should remain, make difficulties, or if nothing else, I must pretend to leave and then return, perhaps search the villa for Master Bartrum. But my head ached, and these people, this household terrified me, in a way I had seldom experienced. It felt unnatural, as though I intruded upon the dead who, in some eerie way, were doomed to re-live their hours through all eternity.

I was not allowed to remain, even had I wished to. Almost at once, the old woman disappeared, and the French gentleman returned to his strange, mesmerized study of the fountain in the garden. I remained under the guard of the hard-faced man in the leather hunting jacket and boots. He said nothing to me. The blind woman returned with a sleepy, yawning boy about twelve, who, it was plain, had gotten hastily into breeches and a well-rubbed jerkin. He was barefooted.

"The boy speaks only in French," the man reminded me directly. "He will not understand you; so you are advised to say nothing to him, Signora."

I said I understood and with my knees still trembling, I went out of the villa in the wake of the boy who carried the lantern and beckoned me on with it. I had not asked for a cup of water which would have been exceedingly welcome. I had not even looked into the other rooms of that villa to be quite sure they were not holding Bartrum Huddle. I believe, upon reflection, that I was in something of a stupor, and intensely chilled, though the night was no longer foggy.

The French boy went surprisingly near the surly old man's cottage in order to reach a cove where I saw the graceful felucca with its triangular, striped blue-and-white sail loosely furled. The faint moonlight show on the mast and gave me some security at sight of this escape, at long last. At the same time, I could see the patch of ground this side of an uprooted cobblestone in front of the old man's cottage. It was in this place that Bartrum had left his packet of glasses. It would have been difficult for the old man to see the packet; yet it was gone.

"One moment," I said to the boy, remembering to speak in my bad Italian. Though he may or may not have spoken the language, he would understand my gesture as I motioned toward the area and then retraced my original steps to the uprooted cobblestone.

I thought I recognized the marks of Bartrum's rich and fashionable boots, but that might have been hours ago. A short distance away, I saw what was unquestionably the broken fob of Bartrum's expensive watch. All young gentlemen wore these, and if they were true dandies, at least in England, they wore "two clickers" as the watches were called in the *cant* phrase. I picked up the fob and held it up to the starlight. I knew it for Bartrum's property. He had not broken the watch and fob when we were together. There was an excellent possibility that he had returned here to pick up the glasses and at that time, broken the chain on the watch. I felt better about leaving the island, now that I found it very probable Bartrum was well and had left me without a second thought.

The boy helped me into the boat and I sank down, huddled in the center, hugging my shawl close around me and trying at the same time to keep my now tousled hair from lashing across my face in long snake-locks. I recall bits and pieces of the trip back to the palazzo. The Lagoon was full of ships from all parts of the Orient and the Near East, many of them with the odd, lateen sails common throughout the Turkish Empire, but they were anchored and remained only black hulks agaiist the wide, starlit sky. With great skill the boy maneuvered our little boat between these hulks and into the Grand Canal.

Shortly before dawn, we were wending our way through one of those narrow, intriguing canals toward the palazzo when the boy woke me from a half-doze to say in French,

"We arrive, Madame."

Confused, and with a bursting head, I looked up at the boy's abrupt voice. We were approaching the mooring pole in front of the cellar entrance to the palazzo. I sat up stiffly.

"No! Not this quai."

It would really be more than I was prepared to face at the moment, to make my way through the cellars and up into the house.

"Eh? No, Madame?"

"No. The other canal. The garden entrance."

He did as I asked and when I got out and offered him three scudi, the boy took the coins with a sudden, beaming countenance and pushed off happily. He was so pleased with what he had earned that he nearly steered into a garbage scow. My exceedingly unpleasant night had not yet ended. Although the garden was beginning to emerge from the deep night shadows, the household was still asleep. I hesitated to use the knocker on the garden door, but lost my hesitancy along with my temper when several raps produced nothing. It was perfectly true that I had no reason to expect the servants to be up and about, but I was in no case to be reasonable.

I pounded until my knuckles were sore, and when the door opened at last, I nearly struck Humphrey Cobb in the face with my upraised fist which had been readied for another assault on the door. Not a flicker marred the bland face he presented at the sight of me arriving at nearly four in the morning, disheveled, and looking as nearly like a hoyden as makes no matter. I looked even more disheveled before this little man who was fully and correctly dressed for his day's work.

"Good morning, Miss. Brisk weather out, I see. We may expect a variable day."

"I have *had* a variable day!" I announced as I passed him, hurrying in, only to find that Mrs. Huddle's miserly indifference to heating still obtained in the house. The small entrance beside the steps up to the first floor was very nearly as clammy as the out-of-doors. I went up the steps, shivering so badly I had to grip the balustrade. I scarcely heard Cobb following me.

The splendid first floor salon was cold and very still, giving me the fantastic idea that the Renaissance and baroque furnishings had a life of their own and were listening for me, waiting for me ... I thought suddenly of that strange secretive household on Ile Isola. What connection was there between that villa and Elvira Huddle's palazzo? But, of course, it was not Elvira's palace. It belonged to Michael Sanson, and the tie with the villa and its weird occupants was Michael himself!

I went on up to my bedchamber, recovering a little because I would not put myself to shame in Cobb's presence, and because, if I uncovered a secret of Michael Sanson's, I must banish it from my memory and my emotional viewpoint. Anything else would be unforgivable, until, at least, I discovered how Sanson was guilty. And that, he could never be!

I opened the door of my room, enormously relieved to be here, and took several steps inside before I knew that my "variable day" had not ended. From one end to the other and from shutters to worn carpet, the room had been ransacked, brutally torn apart. Even the wall paneling in several places had been pried off and lay scattered like sticks of firewood across the floor.

I wanted very much to burst into tears, but in the midst of my desolation a small, furry creature dashed out from under the bed where he had been cowering, and Puss leaped up onto me, fastening his claws with painful persistence, into my garments. He was clutching at me as though his life depended upon it. How frightened he must have been while the invader tore apart my room!

XVI

ALL MY inclination to weep and collapse went glimmering when this small creature with great, terrified, golden eyes, looked to me as his brave defender. I could not fail the one living thing in the house whom I still trusted. I took up Puss and closed the door behind me, shot the bolt, and went and sat down upon the tumbled sheets of the bed and exchanged a long, thoughtful stare with the cat.

Was a madman living in the palazzo? I almost hoped this would be the explanation. But I was sure the criminal who perpetrated this latest outrage had a very straightforward, far from insane reason for searching my room. Since arriving at the palazzo, I had come into possession of only one item which might arouse this fury: the bit of paper from the journal of the dead parlormaid. It seemed evident now that I was suspected of having made off with the rest of the journal; the supremely ironic fact being that I myself would very much like to know what that journal had contained.

I took a deep breath and looked around me. It was disheartening. I could scarcely lie down, or get an hour's rest while the room was so hideously torn up. I kept thinking of the savagery this search revealed, the long, gleaming knife that must have slashed the mattresses, the wall paneling, even the knobs off the four bed posts. While my hand absently caressed the frightened cat in my lap, I considered what I must do. Aside from the obvious and all-important task of cleaning the room, replacing the torn items of linen, personal clothing and the broken furniture, I must choose whether to confide the affairs of the past night to anyone in the house, and—

Mother of Heaven! I had not asked about Bartrum Huddle's safety. I must have been quite irrational when I entered the palazzo. I moved off the big bed and still carrying Puss, more or less unconsciously, I unbolted my door and went out into the silent and shadowed second story salon. Naturally, Cobb was nowhere in sight. Ever suspicious of him, I wondered if he had gone off about his business or was hanging around, watching me from some secret place in this ancient palace whose corners were still unknown to me.

The house felt unhealthy, closed in. I crossed the salon to the distant, long windows two stories above the mooring pole at the cellar steps. The first rim of light was visible now in the east, behind the needle towers and ancient rooftops of the city, beyond the snatches of canal and lagoon I could make out on the way to the horizon. I threw open one of the long windows and looked out. Despite the pre-dawn chill, the air was fresh, brisk with spring and I breathed deeply several times, until the cat in the crook of my left arm roused himself and pawed at my shawl plaintively. I was thus recalled to the present and about to step back into the room when the first morning light caught the side of the palazzo and a tiny gleam somewhere below, attracted me.

I looked out again, and down. The balacony near Elvira Huddle's apartments was immediately below me. Something just inside the low iron railing had reflected the light. Glass, obviously. A bit of broken glass. An odd bit, however; for what extraordinary thing could be that shape? It mattered so very little, of course, except that I had seen such a bit of glass more than once before in my life. My first employer, Miss Nutting, took laudanum drops upon occasion, in order to sleep, and their container was just such a glass phial.

I stood there staring down at the bit of glass, wondering why it should matter to me that a commonplace phial, one of a sort used every day for a dozen purposes, had been tossed away, onto that balcony. It was precisely the place where an emptied, useless phial would land if carelessly tossed away. Obviously, it had not quite gone over the iron rail into the canal below.

. . . The canal . . . or the stone quai at the head of the cellar steps.

I was too muddled and tired to think this through clearly.

Somewhere in the house I heard a crash of crockery. It must come from the kitchen or the scullery, both of which were also below these windows, though two stories down. The kitchen, in fact, had a window which opened out upon this canal. I cringed in sympathy with the breakers of the crockery, and thought: "That'll be my tray of morning tea!"

The sound, however, shook me out of my curious preoccupation with a silly bit of glass which probably meant nothing amid the evil I had stumbled upon in Carnival Venice. I started to set the cat down, telling him to "Run along to the pantry. Catch your breakfast." But he was either too frightened or too clever to fall in with my scheme to be rid of him and merely clung hard, with every claw, to my shawl. There was nothing for it but to take him with me or leave him in my badly damaged bedchamber. I felt that would not be humane. He had certainly been terrified when I came into the room.

So it was that I still had the cat when I passed the apartments in which Mrs. Huddle died. The rooms were occupied, until the wedding, by Michael Sanson, and I almost stopped, wondering what he would say if I challenged him with my discoveries at Ile Isola, and my suspicions about the identity of that gentleman who bore such a marked resemblance to Julie Sanson. But I knew that the truth was, I had rather not confirm those suspicions. Not unless I became convinced that he was responsible for the attacks on me, and upon my room.

Since my curiosity had now gotten the better of me, I went on past Mrs. Huddle's old apartments to the balcony doors, unbolted them and looked out. Surprisingly enough, I could not see the broken and discarded phial as I stood in the doorway. It was only when I stepped out upon the narrow balcony and studied the space under the iron railing that I caught sight of the broken phial. I glanced up at the windows on the story above and realized that only from that angle was the glass cylinder likely to be seen. Only from above.

Not that it mattered. I picked up the phial, found the upper half was missing and assumed the phial may have struck the iron, broken, and the upper half gone over into the canal far below. It still meant nothing. I supposed any member of the household might use laudanum. Captain Dandolo would know. And the phial may not even have contained laudanum.

It was all very confusing, and my head ached, enough already. I tucked the broken phial into my shawl and went down to the kitchen where Rosa and Angelo were on the floor, in the process of cleaning up what remained of my breakfast.

The girl looked up at me tearfully. "Not my fault, Signorina! *Per favore,* you no tell Madame D'Entragues. Is all Angelo. The fault. He make his foot in my way."

Angelo had his mouth open to issue an eloquent denial when they both stopped their mutual recriminations to stare at me. And well they might! I had not yet changed after my hectic ten hours. Nor could I have changed; since the open armoire had revealed my small wardrobe of gowns to be in as bad case as the gown I was wearing. I looked, in every way, plague-stricken and in rags.

The girl almost screamed. "Ah! *Madre Maria!* What happens to you, Signorina?"

"I had a—an accident," I explained briskly, trying to present a reasonably dignified front in spite of my most undignified appearance. While I was wondering how to broach the subject of my bedchamber, Angelo, looking especially ferret-faced, remarked wisely,

"It was wondered at in the household when you remained away all night. The Signorina Julie was very much— You imagine her feelings. She believed the Signore was with you, until he returned alone. And even then, it is said that she still believed."

I leaned wearily against the huge, warm hearth. "When . . . did Master Bartrum return, may I ask?"

Rosa and Angelo exchanged glances.

"I am asleep when it happens," Rosa put in with regret, seeing that her testimony might be of interest.

But with a smirk, Angelo managed to put worlds of meaning into his own observation, "The Signore Huddle arrived a time not too long before Cobb says you arrive. He was of some concern for you, and would have gone out again, but for the new master."

"Master Sanson knows I was gone?"

"But of course."

"Does he know where I went?"

"I hear the Signore Sanson, very angry, say things in French and the young Signore is very—ashamed . . . regretful. The young Signore says over and over that he believes you have returned before him, that he does not mean to desert you."

Feeling decidedly confused and weaker than I could ever remember, I moved away from the comforting warmth of the big hearth which had also mesmerized the cat in the crook of my arm. I had been hesitating far too long. I must have the matter settled now.

"Send Mr. Cobb to me in my room above, as soon as possible."

Rosa's dark eyebrows were raised in surprise at the boy and I saw that she was suggesting something disreputable above the way I had expressed my demand.

It annoyed me. I was too tired, and my head ached too much for me to regard her suspicions with any humor. But the astonishing thing was Angelo's attitude. Instead of playing upon the girl's suggestive expression about my seeing Cobb "alone, and in my room," Angelo ignored her and asked me almost incredulously,

"You wish Cobb in *that* room, Signorina? I mean, at the moment?"

"Certainly." I left the hearth and slowly crossed the kitchen. In the doorway I met D'Entragues, the cook, who bade me a polite good morning, adding with a bite to the words,

"I trust you had a pleasant jaunt last evening with the young Monsieur, Mademoiselle."

"Pleasant is scarcely the word for it," I said, and left abruptly. Let her and the others think what they liked. I was in no case or mood to argue.

The door closed slowly behind me and I heard Rosa chattering away, some rigamarole about me and Bartrum and Cobb which Angelo, curiously enough, silenced.

"A deal *you* know, Rosa. It's something else. Quite different."

And then my muddled senses cleared momentarily and I thought: "He knows. Angelo knows my room has been torn apart and yet he said nothing of it to me. Is he the one who is responsible? That boy?" It seemed highly unlikely; yet he knew something about the conspiracy which was closing around us.

I found it remarkably difficult to get up the dark servants' steps and at one point halfway up, I felt giddy enough to reach out to the clammy stone wall for aid. Puss meowed when I crushed him slightly, and I murmured with a sudden access of bad temper, "Oh, be still, you tiresome feline!"

It was evident that someone in the salon above had heard me. Footsteps stopped abruptly and as I began to climb again, Humphrey Cobb's voice called to me through the vague morning light.

"What, Miss Anne? Talking to that poor dead girl's cat? Beware. They'll have you in Bedlam." He laughed, a light, tittering sound that grated all up and down my spine, and I was dizzily trying to ignore that the while I broached the subject of the invasion of my room, when Puss suddenly made an end of Mr. Cobb's amusement. He leaped out of his warm, safe haven in my arm, scooted past Cobb and ran to earth under a splendid old sideboard. Cobb had certainly disturbed him.

"What an extraordinary thing!" I exclaimed, staring. "What can have made him take fright?"

Cobb was clearly not a cat-lover. "Who is to say? Cowardly creatures, so furtive. They are forever prowling where they should not be. But forgive me, you look—"

"Disheveled. Yes. It's been noticed by the rest of the household. I haven't had time to change since my appalling night. Not," I added curtly, "that there remains anything left to which I may change. You'll do me the honor of glancing in at my bedchamber? There's your Bedlam!"

He stared at me as if he actually suspected my sanity, but then, as Julie Sanson called to us across the big salon, he said, recovering a little, "It is Miss Anne. She says there is some problem with her bedchamber."

"What? That horrid creature! She may go to the Devil for all of me!"

At the same time, one of the doors of Elvira Huddle's apartment opened behind us. I knew without seeing him, that Michael Sanson had returned from his mission to "rescue me" and was observing our none too pleasant beginnings of a lively quarrel.

"I beg pardon, Miss Julie," I said, wondering what in the name of all the Saints was ailing her. "Have I offended you?"

"You and Bartrum! Don't imagine your escapade went unnoticed, Anne Wicklow!" In my confusion I felt that she was everywhere around me, stinging in her juvenile way.

I said nothing to all this, as I only understood the half of what she said, and my head was throbbing madly.

"Oh, Anne! How could you be so horrid! You thought you'd put my Bart in leading strings. But it's me he—"

"What is all this about?" came Michael's voice with

that sense of command which cut through Julie's light, shrill tones and shook both Cobb and me. "Julie! That will do. Cobb, if you are going somewhere—go!"

Julie flung around in a flutter of pale green muslin and went off to hide her fury in her own apartment and I raised my head with an effort and looked at Michael. His strong face was so concerned, so sympathetic, I wondered that I could ever have suspected him of any evil. He took my hands and I borrowed that obvious bloodstirring strength of his from his touch upon my flesh.

"My dear child, I've been over the half of Venice, searching for you," he murmured, gazing at me, seeing all my disheveled appearance with an expression so much opposite to the sneering, cold contempt of Cobb's stare. "Are you all right?"

I laughed half-heartedly, because it seemed rude and thoughtless to dismiss his care for me in any other way.

"I am persuaded, Sir, that you must know the whole of my night's adventure. I was concerned when I re--covered my senses and found no sight of Master Bartrum, but I take it that I need not worry on that score."

"No. Naturally not. His kind invariably save themselves and the Devil may take the rest." He was looking closely at me, as if he tried to divine what was at the back of my brief report, or what, indeed, that I might be concealing. "He says he fell unconscious . . . tripped upon some sort of overturned Roman stone or other, and when he came to himself, he found you had . . . 'fled in terror,' I believe he called it." From the way he quoted Bartrum I was sure he was contemptuous of the opinion of me expressed in that quarter, but all the same, the word inflamed my Irish temper.

"In terror, is it now? And what'll the gentleman be calling a good bash upon the head? Which is what came upon me, and me with no time nor notion of fleeing in terror!"

He laughed, but sympathetically, with a warmth I badly needed.

"Come now, Anne, do not be so angry. You are not looking yourself, you know. I don't like to see you so pale."

"It's the headache," I said quickly, anxious to be done with the bad things I had to tell him, the things that suggested a suspicion of his household and ultimately, of himself. "But, Sir, my room is torn apart. Someone has ruined the furnishings, my clothes— That is what I was discussing with Cobb when you came."

He was leading me to a chair but I did not want to sit down yet. There was too much to be done and to be unraveled.

"What was the vandal searching for; do you think?"

I started to mention the journal of Maria-Elisa. Then I looked up at him. "Why did you think the vandal was searching for something, Sir?"

"Well? Wasn't he?"

I wondered if the little pause before he spoke had been his reaction to the straight-about way I asked the question, or if it had taken him that second or two in order to recover himself.

"In any case," I said stiffly, "I will appreciate your circulating throughout the household the fact that I am hiding nothing. It might save me from future such nasty business."

"I shall certainly do that. Come. You need rest, and you can't very well rest in your chamber. Come into Elvira's rooms here. You'll find them surprisingly comfortable. I'll get something to calm your nerves. A few drops of somewhat."

Shocked at my own vehemence, I nearly screamed: "Please! No drops of—anything!"

Good God! Would I be poisoned like Elvira Huddle? And in her own apartments?

"Anne! What is it?" I felt myself shaken by strong hands and began, confusedly, to try and release myself. "Tell me. What happened on Isola? When you fell, where did you strike your head?"

"Don't!" I whispered through dry, trembling lips. "You know why it was done. I didn't fall. I was struck by someone. You know that."

"Never mind," his voice tried in vain to soothe me. "We'll talk of it later. Julie! Send one of the servants to the surgeon, Grassini. Julie!"

It was all rather vague, Julie's confused reply, and

my own irrational behavior, but I do recall the ease with which I was lifted into Sanson's arms, and, despite all my struggles and my terror, I knew there was no help for it. I was being taken to the room in which Elvira Huddle had been poisoned and died. I remembered the broken phial still caught in the threads of my shawl. Someone was sure to find it, and that would lead to further suspicions that I knew the secret of Mrs. Huddle's death. My present collapse made it doubly simple for Elvira's murderer to send me after her in that dark gondola of the dead.

I must not close my eyes. I must not sleep!

But all I found myself staring at was the room itself, with all its reminders of my long vigil with the dying woman, and the heavy curtains that had been pushed back from the bed, but whose folds recalled all the fears I had known that night, and knew now in force. Even if Michael Sanson was not the person to fear, I felt that I was helpless to defend myself, so long as I was a prisoner in this room. How easily I might be poisoned! With a glass of water, a bit of food, a few drops of a healing medicine. Even without thse accouterments of murder, I might be smothered by the pillows under my head ...

No. I must not sleep.

XVII

In spite of all my efforts, I found that in closing my eyes, I relieved the aching pressure at the back of my head. It was too painful, lying on my back, and I tried raising myself to a sitting position, which served me briefly, but not after Grassini, the surgeon, arrived.

"Not another overdose of powders or drops, I trust," was his cheerful comment as he began to consider my countenance, my heartbeat, and my exceedingly tender skull.

"Assuredly not," said Michael Sanson, standing beside Mrs. Huddle's big bed. He added with such conviction I wanted to strike out at him, "She was shopping for glassware and tripped over a rock or something of the sort."

"There's a lie on the face of it!" I came back, rousing myself to do so.

Michael smiled and gently eased me down against the pillows. "Say rather, on the back of it," he amended.

But Grassini ignored us both. He set about prodding my skull and making me wince.

"You fell backward, Signorina?"

I looked Michael full in the face while replying triumphantly, "No! I fell forward."

Grassini glanced at Michael and then at me. One could almost read his thoughts, that the familiarity between master and servant was suggested by our brusque contradictions of each other. I doubt if the surgeon had any idea of the undercurrents that were clear to me and undoubtedly as clear to Michael. He asked Michael to hold a cool compress to my head, an act I also fought, but which proved to be remarkably healing, as was the touch of Michael's hand. Although I resented his denying what I knew perfectly well had happened to me, and at moments, I even feared danger from him, I was as moved by his touch as though I loved him. As, indeed, I might!

The surgeon completed his examination, announced that I had sustained a slight, though undoubtedly painful bruise which "might not result in a perforation of the skull." This latter was so horrifying a diagnosis that I was very nearly willing to take the medicinal draught he ordered for me.

Julie brought it in the elegant wine glass which Michael put to my lips. I took two or three swallows and heard an all-too familiar voice in the small salon beyond the bedroom.

"The Devil you say! Lovely Anne in Mother's room? Isn't she afraid of the old girl's ghost?"

Someone silenced him and he tiptoed into the bedchamber, his fashionable champagne-glossed boots catching the candlelight so that, with some painful difficulty, I moved my head on a neck that felt like a broken stem, and glanced his way.

Sanson, however, made known one person's opinion of his presence, and with no uncertainty.

"Get out of here, you fool! Can't you see you are disturbing the girl?"

"I want to—let me see him . . . let me talk—" I tried to get up, to push myself up against the pillows, but I was held back by Michael and was too tired to struggle. Too tired . . .

At my broken words, Bartrum came across the bedchamber to look down at me. I felt sure he was fully conscious of his stunning good looks, his flashing charm, and all of it was at work now. He tried to take my free hand, but then it was in someone else's grasp. Confused, I looked down. Michael had caught my hand in his clasp and my fingers felt hot and dry and the sensation of his flesh imprisoning mine made me acutely aware of him.

But Bartrum too seemed to care for my predicament, in his easy, casual way. I was very nearly impressed.

"My dear girl! They didn't tell me it was this serious with you. The tumble you took must have been worse than mine."

"I didn't take a tumble! Will you be hearing me truly now? I was struck. And perhaps by one—" Michael was restraining me and I did not finish. Almost too late I caught back the end of the accusation: "—by one of you!" If I had spoken it aloud, I would very probably be receiving another rap on the head, and this time follow Mrs. Huddle into the grave. I raised to my lips the wine glass that I had drunk from. In my nervousness I drank the half of it, and remembered too late that Elvira Huddle had died in this bed and, undoubtedly, from laudanum drops.

I tried to stir around, to shake myself awake, but these actions only made my head begin to ache again. Besides, against Michael's strength, there was very little recourse. He looked over his shoulder at whoever was in the room.

"Get out. All of you. You are disturbing her."

I hoped this was not addressed to Grassini who had been excessively kind, but in any case, people shuffled out. For a minute Bartrum remained and looked down at me, with a very friendly smile that included his eyes. For once, I thought, he is being sincere.

"Annie dear, do believe me. I was sure you'd left the island. You weren't anywhere in sight. I wouldn't have deserted you."

"I know."

As Michael was pushing him away, with his elbow, Bartrum leaned over Michael's arm, adding, "We'll talk later, when you are feeling more the thing. We'll talk about—you know."

He was tugged out of the room by an angry Julie who, misunderstanding his last words to me, remarked in a very shrill undervoice, "How could you? And then to claim you two were innocent. Truly, Bart, you take me for a ninny!"

Michael and I caught each other's eye and he remarked to me with his dry humor, "There is the making of a typical happy marriage." He leaned over me and kissed me in the gentlest way.

It was surprising how his amusement and his warm concern for me combined to soothe my fears. Or perhaps it was the laudanum drops after all.

When I came to myself hours later, I felt so much better, I was of a very good mind to get up and go about my household tasks. The moment I stirred, however, I heard the swish of skirts and Julie Sanson stuck her golden head around the bedpost. She looked mutinous, her lower lip pouting, but she said sullenly,

"I am to apologize to you."

I sat up, leaning on my elbows. "Good Heavens! Why?"

Her very young face cleared slightly, as if my question had put her into a better mood.

"Well, I thought you and Bart—you know."

I believe I used the best argument possible, and it happened to be true. "What? That infantile young man?"

She giggled. "Do you truly think so? He said you didn't give a farthing for him. But— Oh, Anne! He is so excessively handsome."

"All of that," I agreed, so breezily I felt sure she accepted the fact that there was nothing between us.

She hesitated, tried in a polite and charming way to plump up my pillows and straighten the coverlet, and I suspected she wanted to say something shocking or secret and was fearful of broaching it.

"Anne, I ought to feel jealous of Princess Ketta. Bart and she were talking in greatest secrecy this morning, about what happened to Bart yesterday. He said he had to confide in someone, and the Princess was a good deal astonished. But he would not tell me. Isn't that horrid? It is something about Uncle. I mean Sanson. He is trying to discover something, or has discovered it. At any rate, Ketta said he was a very silly young man if he went off at a half-cock, as the saying is."

This was worse than I thought. To be telling all this to Her Highness! The woman might not be able to hold her tongue, and would doubtless only make matters worse. I did not help Julie in her halting questions. I said briefly, "I have no notion what it is about."

But she persisted. "Is it something about how Papa died?"

I hesitated, unsure of how much Bartrum had actually told her about the Ile Isola, or, indeed, how much he himself had discovered about the gentleman who lived at the villa with a blind woman, a boy who spoke only French, and a hard-faced man who could be a guard, or a jailer. Surely, if he had seen those strange inmates of the villa, he would even now be challenging Michael Sanson. Master Bartrum had been so sure that someone on that island was the key to his control of his future father-in-law's money. If he had discovered what I knew, the occupants of that villa, he would be much more sure of himself than he had appeared to be since our visit to the island. I decided that Bartrum had not been inside that villa, or seen its occupants.

I made a pretense that my hesitation was due to weakness and confusion.

"Miss Julie, you know a deal more about Master Sanson than I do. If I am not to trust him, then you must tell me why. I have no knowledge of your father and your mother, for example. If your guardian was guilty of some—crime against them, I might understand better what I have discovered about Master Sanson."

Julie peered over her shoulder. Mrs. Huddle's bedchamber looked very large, crossed with thick shadows in which a half dozen assassins might have hidden. The same thought must have occurred to her, because she stared a long time into every corner, shivering a little in her fashionable buttercup yellow gown which gave her somewhat the look of a small field flower, frail and easily broken. A touching and charming flower, perhaps, but quite unsuited to the harsh winds of the wind. It was only when she raised her haughty little chin that I perceived she was not as frail as she appeared.

"Well then, I did not know Mama well at all. I think I must have been a mere infant when I was taken from her to live with Papa and Sanson. It was at a great seaport, I remember. And Mama was . . . something dreadful. A barmaid. But she was used to tell me that I would never be one, that she would see that I had a deal of money. And then, one day, she never came home, and I waited and waited and I got so hungry! Anne, you could never credit how hungry I got."

Drawn to the girl in sympathy by an experience so near to my own, I said quietly, "Yes. I could credit it. Please do go on."

She sighed. "Then dear Papa came. I scarcely remembered him. Mother had brought him home to our little rooms only twice before. But I knew him when he came for me. He said Mama was dead, that some wicked person had killed her and now I was to live with him and the person he called Uncle Sanson. Papa was so kind to me! And he was dreadfully concerned when I cried. But then, Sanson came along and said we were taking too much time. We must go at once. So Papa took me, and Sanson took all my clothes and my toys and we went away from the city."

I cleared my throat. It was difficult to ask my next question.

"Was Monsieur Sanson cruel to you?"

She shrugged. "Not cruel. No. But indifferent. And often away. He was a smuggler with his own boat. I think he tried to be kind to me, but he was not elegant or beautiful or exquisitely mannered, and Papa was all of those things. And Sanson was always lurking about. Watching us. It made me take him in strong dislike. Once, when Papa and I were going out walking, he came and took Papa by the arm as if he would wrench it off, and he said in such a tone: 'Louis-Charles!' And I was terrified . . . Papa was terribly angry." She looked up at me, her unmarked forehead knit with the problem. "But Papa obeyed. He said, 'I cannot take my own child to walk.' And Sanson said, 'You dare not!' So you see, Sanson is a very wicked man, to keep Papa from walking out like that."

I looked at the mantel clock. It was half after eleven and as Miss Julie was wearing a day dress, I assumed it must certainly be half after eleven in the morning. I was feeling quite myself again and got out of bed while the girl looked at me curiously.

"Don't you wish to stay in bed and be cosseted by everyone? I love it!"

"I detest it! Mother of Mercy! I'll not have a thing to wear beyond this gown I wore yesterday, and the Saints only know it's in a sad state." I had been put to bed in the gown and felt unclean in it.

Julie grinned and clapped her hands. "No. The most famous thing happened. Princess Ketta came to breakfast with Sanson and Bart and me as I said, and when she heard of your horrid experience, and I said your clothes had been torn and slashed while you were gone, she sent to her palazzo for several day dresses that had quite gone out of the mode. She thought such things as fashion would be of no importance to you. Sanson was excessively grateful to her."

I did not know which I disliked the most, the notion of Michael being excessively grateful to the Princess da Rimini who might be plotting with Bartrum against his back, or the fact that everyone assumed I was so dead to what is proper that I cared nothing for the current mode. It is true. I did care nothing for the mode, but it is quite another thing to hear it boasted by a woman like Her Highness who was "all the crack" as the schoolgirls at Miss Nutting's were used to say.

I said stiffly, "It was most charitable of Her Highness,

but I am persuaded any dress she might wear would be highly unsuitable to a housekeeper."

"Nonsense, Anne. These are dresses she wears when she speaks to the gardeners, and when she visits the Hospital of the Poor Clares. Places like that."

This hardly raised my expectations, but by the time I laid eyes upon the four dresses after finishing my warm, scented sponge bath, I could hardly wait to see what these new petticoats and the rather too elegant sprigged green muslin gown looked upon me.

Miss Julie, after being refused the offer of her maid, Babette, to assist me, watched this process of my change with great interest. By the time I hoped she had forgotten, she said shrewdly, "You don't want to hear how Sanson murdered Papa, do you?"

I was trying to adjust the shoulders of the pretty gown, which were a trifle narrow, and the waist, which was too lose, and I pretended to be preoccupied, though the truth is, I was hoping she would forget her accusation against Michael. Seeing her eyes upon me in the mirror, I said finally, "No. No. Please do go on. How do you know he—as you say—murdered your Papa?"

"Well then, Papa came to me one morning very early, all dressed at hazard, not like himself at all. He was usually so very elegant you know. We were in Genoa. In any case, Papa was even wearing a cloak he wore only in the evenings, and his gloves were ball gloves. But you see, he was afraid of Sanson, and had dressed in such haste. He said we must run away. That Sanson would kill him. But it all came to nothing. Sanson found us and locked me in my chamber. I was but ten and far too silly to climb out of the window and escape."

By now I had forgotten my dislike of hearing such a tale and asked eagerly, "Well, Miss Julie, what then?"

"Then— Nothing!"

"What do you mean . . . nothing?"

"I never saw Papa again. The last thing he said to me was that Sanson would kill him. And," she ended triumphantly, "he did!"

I set this opinion aside momentarily. "What was your Papa like?"

"Oh, very handsome. Though I do have his nose. And his mouth. But no one notices. They think me very handsome, indeed."

I suppressed a smile at this artless conceit. "And so you are, Miss Julie. You look like a young queen, when you behave and are in good humor."

"When I am not, though, I am even more like a queen." This was a palpable truth, but I did not encourage it. She went on, "Papa was so elegant. An aristocrat. I am sure of it. And slender as a prince."

It had been my opinion, gained at third hand, it is true, that most princes were far from slender. No matter. Miss Julie had certainly described the gentleman on Ile Isola. I wondered again if the aristocratic gentleman was a prisoner, and if so, why? He was hardly the criminal sort. Perhaps he had run mad and was kept there so as not to harm himself or others. What would happen if Julie met the gentleman?

If only I knew what to do, or how much Master Bartrum had guessed! I was beginning to believe now that the secret which had killed Maria-Elisa, and very likely Mrs. Huddle, was in some way concerned with Julie's mysterious father. The corollary to this, however, was what I refused to admit, that Michael Sanson was responsible for the things that had happened during these nightmarish Carnival weeks. Besides, I thought, clinging to every possible assurance of this nature: if Michael was so dangerous, he would have ended my life with an overdose of those laudanum drops. No one had a greater opportunity.

Then, the devilish suspicion intruded. Perhaps he had not yet been informed that I was aware of his secret on the Ile Isola.

"Where are you going?" Miss Julie wanted to know, following me out of the depressing bedchamber that had seen Elvira Huddle's death.

"There'll be a thousand things that need doing, Miss. I've the household to care for."

"Oh, what fusty work!"

This was comprehensive enough. I saw her whirl around past me and go pattering out to the sunny balcony. That put me in mind of the glass phial I had found on the balcony, between the iron guard rails. I went back into the bedchamber and searched for my shawl. I found it just when I had given up hope. The shawl had dropped to the floor at the foot of the bed, and when I ran my fingers over it, I gave myself a little cut besides tearing the threads of the already dilapidated shawl. The broken phial had not been disturbed until this minute. And even now, I had not the vaguest idea of what to do with it, or whether it had any significance, but I meant to keep it.

Julie had found Bartrum Huddle on the balcony and they came in bickering. Bartrum was going out and his betrothed complained that she might as well be in a nunnery as to be always left alone "with some tiresome female." Like me, I thought, amused, and was on the way up to my room to see what must be done before it was habitable when the lovers' quarrel was drowned out by sounds at the garden door. To my surprise I recognized the Princess da Rimini's penetrating bell-like voice, and very much obscured by that sound, her companion, Captain Dandolo, speaking to Cobb. Knowing myself to be behaving like a typical eavesdropper, I retraced my steps to a place barely beyond the vision of the three at the foot of the steps.

Her Highness was saying, "Nothing could exceed my pleasure. The young woman is quite unexceptionable. I told you, Captain, how I first met her at the quai. Her improvement renders me easier in mind."

"I should think so, indeed, Highness." That would be the young Captain. "Far too many—deaths have occurred in this palazzo of late. For which there will be payment exacted one day soon."

Cobb said mildly, "The Captain has found nothing of great importance in the young woman's room, however. Doubtless, such matters as will help him to solve the nasty bit of vandalism will occur to him later."

This must have made the Captain blaze but he was discreet. I was happy to know that the dreadful destruction in my room had been considered and at least investigated. The Princess apparently soothed the Captain.

"Yes, yes. Such things give me an immovable disgust."

It was an odd way of expressing the matter, but she went on with a very curious idea that interested me at once. "Cobb, I would appreciate your occupying Bartrum's attention the while I am private with that so-capable Anne Wicklow. Will this satisfy you, Captain?"

Whether this indeed satisfied the conscientious Captain Dandolo, I did not wait to discover. I only hoped my cheeks were not as red as they felt while I crossed the salon and walked up the stairs toward my own quarters. By great good fortune, I was out of sight by the time Cobb came hurrying up after me, his steps light as always.

"Miss Anne! You will drop whatever you are about, and oblige Her Highness."

Feeling myself a complete hypocrite, but dying of curiosity, I turned around on the stairs and went back down. What under the sun must the Princess speak to me about, and in confidence? Above all else, why was Master Bartrum most particularly to be excluded?

With an attempt at a normal dignity, I curtsyed and followed Princess Ketta as she beckoned me into one of the bookrooms at the back of the salon, a neat little place we hoped to adapt for a withdrawing room where Miss Julie might entertain her feminine friends while Bartrum presided grandly over after-dinner port. The Princess put one long, slim, gloved finger to her lips and tilted her elegantly coifed head in the direction of the big salon and the balcony. I knew, of course, that the gesture indicated Bartrum and Julie, and I wondered again just what secrets the Princess and Bartrum might be anxious to keep from each other. Bartrum had been quick enough to confide in her this morning about our discovery on Ile Isola yesterday.

"May I thank you, Ma'am," I said hurriedly, "for your generosity." I indicated the gown I wore, but she frowned severely.

"No, cherie, that's of no account. I must tell you, your discoveries last night have been reported to me."

Before I could reply, though I'm sure I had nothing intelligent to say to that remark, she caught my hand and drew me across the room to a long, barred window over the canal. "He came back early this morning. Bartrum, you understand." I nodded as though I learned this for the first time. "And he docked there at the cellar quai. All very secretive, you note."

I stammered innocently, "But, Ma'am, the quai on this canal—it is, or was used to be a normal entry."

"For the servants, perhaps. And even they hesitate these days. Cobb tells me the cellars are avoided here below the palazzo. You yourself returned by means of the garden."

I was suspicious upon the instant. "How do you know that?"

"But from Cobb, naturally."

I should have known that. The only curious thing was what Cobb hoped to gain by his talebearing to a comparative stranger like the Princess. She went on confidentially, "I must tell you that I am aware of what you and Bartrum discovered upon Ile Isola. He was so good as to confide in me when I was here earlier to breakfast with Julie."

I took a deep breath. "And what was his purpose? I daresay he also confided in Miss Julie. And in his future father-in-law as well!"

"Hush!" She glanced around. I could have sworn she was uneasy, even frightened. "You must understand the significance of the prisoner on the island. Bartrum says he is the very image of Julie. You noticed, of course. What name did the gentleman answer to?"

I thought back. I was by no means positive, and a name kept popping into my head. I associated it with the man I saw last night on the island; yet I was not sure I had heard the name there.

"Louis-Charles, I believe."

"No, my dear. Chartier. That proves my theory. Louis Chartier was Julie's father's name. I am of the opinion—" She glanced over her shoulder and lowered her voice. "—Sanson is responsible for his imprisonment. For what reason I could not even conjecture. I encountered Captain Dandolo tied up below. I very nearly told him the whole of what I know. He seems so intent upon laying the blame at Bartrum's door."

I was extremely unnerved. "But then they would

think Monsieur Sanson had committed these crimes at the palazzo! And I know he did not. I know it!"

Very nearly laughing. she regarded me with that superior and light contempt I have received from my superiors. It is like a burn that one endures but feels in every nerve-end.

"But what passion, my dear! And if you know that, you must know something of which I am not aware. Surely, it will be carefully managed so that Julie's father is released, but without being able to ruin Sanson. It might even be put to Chartier that he will be aided only to his freedom, that we will not support him in any effort to bring Sanson down in revenge."

Still much agitated, I made objections. "Perhaps the man is imprisoned for good reason. As a friend of Sanson's he could scarcely be sent to one of those monstrous asylums. I have seen Bedlam's and one or two others. You would not believe the horrors there. And this man may be dangerous, or mad. We know nothing of this ourselves. It might be unsafe to have the man released."

"Perhaps. And it will not be easy. I have only just returned this moment from Isola, and I was unable to do more than approach the place. Naturally, it would be far better if we need not inform Captain Dandolo."

"Absolutely, Ma'am. I agree. We must proceed slowly. I was in the same room with the gentleman, Chartier, as you call him, and yet I was not permitted to speak with him. I do think we should move cautiously. After all, we know nothing of the prisoner."

"Hm . . . You may well be right. And it could be disastrous for Sanson. I should not care to entrust such a delicate matter to a creature like Dandolo. He is much too jealous of Bartrum because of Julie." She sighed and took up her reticule, presumably ending our strange little conspiracy. "So it seems you and I must depend upon our own good offices to protect Sanson from the just results of his acts: yet we must do what is right." She flashed a quick, flickering little smile. "I was once a prisoner myself, a political prisoner, and I have a natural affinity for opening doors."

I looked my surprise and she added with a graceful shrug, "Yes. I was foolish enough to have been invited to several of the Empress Marie-Louise's soirees at the Tuileries. You may imagine how popular that made me when fat Louis the Eighteenth climbed back on the throne. No matter. Let us hope we may relieve Julie's father, without involving Sanson. I should not, in any case, care to expose myself to his wrath. He can be quite formidable, I imagine."

"Who is this formidable creature whose wrath is so deadly?" Michael Sanson asked from the doorway behind the Princess.

XVIII

His voice suggested amusement, but I was ready to sink with embarrassment, and a little fear, too. The Princess turned as I did, gave the man in the doorway an enchanting smile, and chided him with a light, teasing manner I very much envied, "Now who else in this tiresome little Venetian World would arouse such feelings? Captain Dandolo, of course!"

This, in the circumstances, made me laugh, and Sanson smiled, much to my relief. Nevertheless, he surprised me by taking Her Highness' arm as though he had been given a silent command to escort her to the door. Princess Ketta laughed, a bit glassily.

"Yes. caro mio. I was on the point of departure. Now, you must not chide your pretty housekeeper. She is a charmer and we have been discussing the various problems of the wedding; for I shall naturally act in place of Julie's mother. Anne! Mind you now, not a word to the gentlemen about all our pretty arrangements."

I sank in a curtsey but as Sanson escorted her across the big salon, she turned and one carefully gloved finger summoned me to her.

What? More secrets?" Sanson asked with easy irony. But he stepped back and elaborately bowed me to the lady. I thought her frighteningly indiscreet and when she pinched my sleeve and made me descend several steps with her, I could only cast a helpless look at Michael Sanson standing, as I hoped, just out of hearing.

"Recall, my dear," said the Princess. "At all costs,

Bartrum must not be permitted to bleed poor Sanson, no matter what he may think he has learned."

"Quite so, Your Highness."

"We can put a hindrance in his way if we see that Julie's father is examined by a competent surgeon and freed. If he is truly ill, in some way, then of course, he must be put under constraint. But legally. Not through our dear Sanson."

"Come now," Michael called down to us. "That will do, Ketta. I need the girl. We've an entire household to organize."

I detest being "the girl" but I daresay it is better than being called sharply "Wicklow!" which is the alternative. I nodded to Her Highness, whose conduct to me had always been gracious, and hurried back upstairs. Sanson saw her to her gondola and I nearly walked into Captain Dandolo who wanted to know exactly how I had sustained the injury that caused me to collapse this morning.

"Shortly before your injury, the young Signore was your escort, I understand."

I agreed that he had been, but I reminded the Captain, to be scrupulously fair, "I am certain I heard him groan and fall . . . Well, perhaps not fall. But I did hear him make a sound of pain just before I was struck."

Bartrum and Julie heard this and Julie put in excitedly, "But Anne, you know you are not certain you were struck. You only fell unconscious. Isn't it so?"

"I—that is—" I hardly knew how to answer. I was inflexibly of the opinion that someone had struck me a blow, probably with a padded weapon, across the back of the skull.

Captain Dandolo's nervous, serious young face was a reproach to me. I felt he deserved my honesty and, in fact, that I should tell him the full details of the aristocratic gentleman called "Louis-Charles" or Chartier. I believed with Bartrum and Princess Ketta that he was in some way Sanson's prisoner. And certainly, an investigation ought to be made; yet I hesitated. I could not betray Sanson or Bartrum either, in spite of everything. I had no real proof that either of them was guilty of the crimes in the house, whatever they might have been capable of in other places.

"Yes, Signorina?" the Captain prompted me expectantly.

"N-nothing. I am not certain of what happened, except that Master Bartrum and I were perhaps both attacked, that we lost each other in the dark, and came back to the palazzo in different conveyances."

Bartrum eyed the young captain with a triumphant grin. "You see, Dandolo? Our stories are precisely the same. If you hoped to drag me off in chains, you are wide of the mark."

They would have gone on in this fashion but for Sanson's arrival, and the resultant hints on Bartrum's part that Captain Dandolo would do better to try and solve other and older mysteries in the Lagoon. I was sure he referred to the mystery of the strange gentleman on the Ile Isola and wondered at his callous hints in the presence, not only of Sanson, his prospective financial victim, but of the prisoner's daughter. Had Bartrum a heart at all, he would have some compunctions at performing so disgustingly in Julie's presence. Perhaps I had better tell everything I knew about him. But then, that would involve the reasons why he was capable of bleeding Michael Sanson. And I was back in doubts again.

"All the same," the Captain cut in finally, blushing under the influence of Julie's heavy scowl, "We have not discovered who is responsible for the cruel ravishment of the Signorina's garments and her bedchamber."

Julie was rather nastily proud of her own addition: "You can hardly lay that crime to Bart."

I was aware of this; since Bartrum had been with me during all the time in which my room had been searched. Yet he had reached the palazzo before me. I gasped and they all looked at me.

"Yes, Signorina?" the young Captain promoted.

Was it possible that Bartrum had time to tear my room apart in the hour or so before I arrived? It might be possible, but I did not think so. The job was so very thorough, it must have been performed by someone either very confident of my absence, or very knowledgeable about my room.

"I was going to suggest ... since it seems obvious that a search was made, perhaps Captain Dandolo has some idea of what was concealed there."

The Captain assured me, and by inference, the others present, that he was very close to discovering why my room was searched. I very much wanted to tell him what I knew, or suspected, of Maria-Elisa's death, that she had been playing a dangerous game with a person who possessed a secret terrible enough to kill for. And all that followed, including Mrs. Huddle's death, was a part of the first deadly secret.

I glanced surreptitiously at Michael Sanson but he was his cool, confident self. I let his attitude convince me momentarily that the murderer's secret had nothing to do with him. As for Bartrum, he caught my eye and tilted his head very slightly toward Sanson. I pretended not to understand and asked to be excused, on the plea of much work to do.

"I must see you when you have your first free minute," Sanson called.

I went down to the kitchen and stillroom at once, saw that a hot luncheon was in readiness for serving, and discovered that Madame D'Entragues and the servants were all incensed over stern questioning by Captain Dandolo. I did what I could to soothe them all, and pointed out with what I considered three-quarters honesty, that none of them were suspected of tearing my room apart.

"Just so," said D'Entragues tightly. "It is one of what the insufferable Cobb calls 'the gentry.' I have known that. Now, Mademoiselle, about the dinner menu."

We got through that very easily, there being but one problem: how many of the family would be home to dinner. While we were planning for all contingencies, Angelo came loping into the stillroom where the cook and I were writing out the menu.

"Exciting, I call it. The stupid Capitano. Out there sticking swords and knives into the garden urns. Hasn't found a thing." He shrugged his bony shoulders. "Cobb says the Capitano is a fool and blind to all but his silly, golden-haired—"

"That will do!" I said.

He subsided, but with a knowing smirk. A familiar smirk. It brought to my mind a similar expression very early this morning when I guessed that he knew about the damage to my room before he should have known. I said something casual to the cook and listened to her demands for greater food allowance, but I listened with only one ear. I was waiting for Angelo to forget the importance of what he must know, to go offguard, in fact. I had not long to wait. Rosa came in and Angelo began to tease her, to flirt and whisper doubtless shocking suggestions in her small ear.

I turned suddenly and said in a conversational tone, "You were more clever than I thought. You were lucky not to hurt yourself. All that tearing and destruction. He is a clever boy, Rosa. Truly."

Angelo raised his head and when Rosa's eyes got very big and she coaxed, "Oh, but you must tell me!" Angelo, tremendously impressed at his own brilliance, murmured modestly,

"Well then, I only obeyed orders. Cobb did most of—"

"The devil you say!" Madame exclaimed, shaking Angelo out of his pleasant dream of consequence.

I completed my business with D'Entragues who looked at me in an understanding way and left the kitchen as Angelo was trying to sneak out before me.

"Angelo, lad," I told him lightly. "I know. And Cobb knows I know. It is no longer important."

The boy stopped, glanced at Rosa who was still wide-eyed and impressed. He relaxed as I left. I heard him explaining his heroism to the girl. His own role in the destruction of my room was impressive indeed, according to his talented imagination. It had all been done for the best of reasons, which he could not, at that moment, divulge. I smiled somewhat grimly as I went out into the garden looking for Captain Dandolo.

He was gone and I found only one of his men, elderly, stout, with an Austrian moustache, reminding me of that Empire's long influence on Northern Italy. He was completing his investigation of the urns, having found nothing. I thought this whole search a trifle late and useless, but I asked only if the Captain had gone.

"Just gone, regrettably, Signorina."

"Could you please find him and tell him I have some news? The Signorina Wicklow. The Irish housekeeper ... you understand? Important news."

After a confused few seconds the stout man's moustaches moved up and down with excitement. "But yes, Signorina. Perfectly. I go. I trust he is not far."

When I had seen him off in his very odd and businesslike version of the usual gondola, I went back across the garden, acutely aware as I did so, that I was under the eye of anyone in the many windows of the palazzo. It was an eery feeling and when I looked up quickly, I was positive, for an instant, that I saw the afternoon sun gleam on Humphrey Cobb's spyglass at his high window. It was gone when I looked again. No matter. I trusted that Captain Dandolo would return before the ubiquitous Cobb was able to pay me off for my betrayal.

Bartrum and Julie were finishing a late luncheon in the delightful summer dining room when I went up to the first floor, but Sanson left the table and came out to the salon as soon as I passed the partially open doors.

"Anne, come and talk with me," he said, taking my two hands and looking down at me with such warmth in his dark eyes that my heart began to behave like a schoolgirl's at sight of her idol. I knew, even as the heat of his gaze swept over me, that he might be evil, murderous, but his emotional hold upon me had the effect of blinding me to all that commonsense should have revealed.

"Yes, Sir?"

"You, at least, are not afraid of me."

I looked at him frankly. "Should I be?"

He frowned and then smiled, a bit ruefully, I thought. "Not you. No. Nor anyone else. I am afraid you have been listening to my enemies." Before I could answer this by pouring out the truth of my fears, of the mysterious gentleman who was probably Julie's father, and all the rest, Michael lowered his head and I found myself trembling as his lips brushed my mouth. Then I was absorbed by his power over my senses.

Remembering now, and at this distance of time, that first kiss of passion between us, I am aware that I found my response quite beyond anything I had imagined, a product both of my maturity and of Michael's power over my emotions. And even as I felt myself drawn to him, enclosed in his love, a part of me was still tormented by suspicion.

"If I were free . . . if I could tell you—" he murmured, so low I scarcely heard it.

From the haven of his strength, I said softly, "Can you not try me? Confide in me? Perhaps then, I could share this burden of yours."

He shook his head and then, very lightly, touched my hair with a gentle kiss. "It is too late. You do not know. You cannot know. You are so innocent of the world's horrors, you couldn't even conceive what men must do in life. What they are born to do, and taught. And trained."

He is wrong, I thought. Nothing he can have done would shock me . . .

The sounds of altercation between two shouting male voices on the canal below the open windows made us draw apart. I wondered why the very young male voice sounded familiar, for the language he spoke was gutter French and the responses, in furious Italian, were no doubt equally violent, but too fast for me to understand.

"What the devil is it now!" Michael tried to retain his hold upon me as he turned and strode to the window but I broke away nervously, wondering if what was the arrival of Captain Dandolo again, to hear my story.

"I think it may be the Captain. I sent for him, Sir."

He paused, stared at me. "You? Now, in God's name, why?"

"Because . . ." Then I blurted out rapidly, "I believe I know who damaged my room. I have reason to think it may have been Cobb, with the help of the boy, Angelo."

He was at the window when I spoke, and asked, as

he looked down on the waters in their afternoon shadow, "Why would Cobb turn his hand to such destruction?"

"They were searching for the pages of a journal written by Maria-Elisa."

He scowled. "Who may that—ah! The missing chambermaid. Why would her journal be of such importance to the fellow?"

I had come to his side again, wondering what I would do if Dandolo asked me, upon oath, for the meaning I attached to the journal page I had originally seen. Michael's arm drew me to him.

"I could wish you had a little confidence in me."

. . . Or you in me, I thought. But I pretended not to understand this, though I warmed to his assurance.

We gazed down at the occupants of the two canal boats. I did not know whether to be sorry or glad that neither of the two in the gondolas was Captain Dandolo. Then Michael muttered, "Good God! What now?" and without even excusing himself, removed his arm from my waist.

"Send Cobb to me. No! I'll fetch him up myself as soon as I have handled this business below."

He went across the salon toward the steps, at a very fast pace.

I stared at the canal, seeing the boy who spoke French, and realizing where I had seen him before. Only this morning he took me to the palazzo from the Ile Isola. He seemed at that time remarkably composed for a boy of his age, but now he was close to frantic. When he had won his traffic argument with the other gondolier, he tied up at the mooring pole while the second gondola floated on and out of sight. Almost at once, Sanson appeared directly under the window, saying in anger, "What is it? What has happened?"

"Escaped, Monsieur!" the boy cried breathlessly in French.

I ducked back from the window barely in time. Michael had glanced up at the windows before pulling the boy into the shadow and probably onto the cellar steps.

I was sure almost at once that the boy's panic was

based on the escape of "the prisoner" on the Ile Isola. I had proof of the importance of the boy's message when Sanson got into the gondola with him almost at once, without even changing the casual black frock coat he had worn to luncheon.

As for my own suspicions, I had the sudden idea that the Princess Ketta was responsible for the disappearance, or the "escape" of the man I knew as Chartier. It was all mere conjecture on my part; since I was not even sure the escape involved the so-called prisoner on the Ile Isola, but if the man had escaped, then I thought Her Highness was just the sort of quick unthinking woman who would blunder into such a scheme unprepared and very unwise. I still retained enough faith in Michael to believe he had strong humanitarian reasons for keeping the gentleman safe and incommunicado on the island.

As I crossed the salon and went about the household business, I was prey to frightful doubts. The more I thought of this latest occurrence involving Michael and his prisoner—if the man was a prisoner—the more I knew I must tell everything to Captain Dandolo.

I went up to my bedchamber shortly after and saw, to my surprise, that an enormous amount of work had been done on the room, obviously at Michael's instructions. Though there was a deal of bare and ugly scarred wood remaining, all linens, the bed coverlet and the clothing given to me at the behest of the Princess Ketta were pleasantly unslashed. Even as I looked at the furniture and the thick, oriental carpet, all obviously borrowed from other chambers, I kept seeing the precise and proper, almost immobile face of Humphrey Cobb as he tore apart my room. I glanced around, hoping to see a weapon handy, just in case Cobb should attempt another such fiendish act, and against me physically.

Though the damage had been corrected as much as possible, the room depressed me and I hurried out, looking over my shoulder every few minutes under the distinct impression that Cobb was hiding in each dark corner and might leap out upon me with the very knife or poniard that had done so much damage to my room.

I gave orders to Barbarita to notify me upon the instant Captain Dandolo arrived, and then went into the long-unused servants' quarters at the front of the palazzo, on the ground floor. All the furniture had been protected long ago by material similar to the holland covers we used in Britain. The result was a ghostly array of creatures, any one of whom might be Humphrey Cobb disguised as a chair or cupboard or some other implausible thing. In order to alleviate some of the gloom, I went across each room, opened the windows, banged hard on the warped shutters and flung them outward into the stifling afternoon air.

Miss Julie gave me a start when she slipped up behind me, murmuring in her plaintive voice, "He won't take me to the Teatro Fenice, even though I'll be masked. Isn't it the horridest thing you ever heard of? And he's gone off now to San Marco to drink for the last time as a bachelor, he says, and he wouldn't take me!"

I could well imagine Bartrum's situation if any of his lady loves of the Fenice called him by some endearment in Julie's presence. I tried to make some reasonable excuse, the one I thought she would believe, that "La Fenice and much of San Marco are full of tiresome, stout old gentlemen who behave most improperly to young ladies."

"All of them are old?" she asked in some doubt.

"But my dear Miss Julie, you would not, surely, wish to have such creatures making shocking suggestions to you, or mistake you for a plaything."

"N-no . . ." But I suspected her young heart hesitated over the answer. It has been my experience that virginal young ladies are exceedingly curious about wickedness of the sensual sort.

"You would do much better, Miss, to go and have an ice, or even coffee at the Cafe Florian tomorrow when Master Bartrum will take you there in grand style, no doubt."

She wrinkled her nose, complained first of the boredom of "woman's fate" and then of the dust in the room in which we stood. As she was leaving, she said with one of her mercurial changes of mood, "Bart says I shall be revenged on Sanson very soon. I told you he would pay for killing Papa."

"You must not talk like that, Miss Julie. It is most improper. And unjust."

I did not know whether she was wrong in actuality, or only in degree. But she went out of the room and I had gone back to the work of uncovering and estimating the usefulness of the furniture when I was startled by an unmistakable scream. I dropped cloths and coverings onto a low tabaret and started after Julie, first in a rapid walk, then, as she screamed again, at a run.

I had gone down the passage past the garden door and toward the kitchens when I realized that Julie's voice seemed to echo in a peculiar way, against many walls and passages. I retracted my way and opened the door heading to the flight of steps that plunged downward into the front of the cellars. Like the rest of the household, I detested the cellars and went down there as seldom as possible. It seemed unlikely that the nervous and inexperienced girl who had not even ventured outside the house without an escort, would wander alone down into the labyrinth of damp, moldy cellars below the palazzo.

I looked down that sheer drop of steps that were chipped and cracked and fading into the general darkness of the cellars below. Chiding myself for my infantile cowardice, I moved down one step and called firmly into the darkness: "Miss Julie! Are you there?"

XIX

My voice seemed to circle the hollow dark and return to me, not so much echoing as haunted, collecting in its flight the sounds of all the voices that had gone before mine . . . the desperate cries of the servants buried alive here, smothering, drowning under the influx of mud and slime and wave upon wave of canal waters in flood.

After a minute or two of silence that followed, I heard the faint sound of sobbing, which must be Julie. I went rapidly down the steps calling to her as I went, and privately cursing the miserly tastes of Elvira Huddle who had never permitted lamps or candles to be burned in the cellars except in the hand of the servant going down after supplies. As a result, most of the household avoided the cellars and only added to the bad conditions here. Once the living quarters abovestairs were attended to, I meant to give my attention to cleaning out and reorganizing conditions here, perhaps ordering some walls to be knocked down if practicable, and above all, seeing that the Dry Cellar and the Wine Cellar were reached easily and promptly.

If Julie had not been so close to the foot of the steps I would never have found her without returning to the floor above for a lamp or candlestick. I saw her dress first, a bit of light looking very like a bundle of laundry, upon the stone floor. Fortunately, this part of the cellars was higher than the slimy sector on the other side, which was directly beneath the barred apertures opening onto the canal itself.

I knelt beside the girl. "Miss Julie, are you hurt?"

She sniffed and to my relief gazed up at me, her face a pale, dampish moon in all that darkness.

"I s-slipped."

"Yes, but whatever were you doing down here, and without a light? You might have been killed."

"The door was o-open, and I saw . . . something."

"Of course you did. But come now. Can you stand." I put my hands under her arms and tried to get her on her feet. She was obedient but kept muttering complaints.

"I've got to see Bartrum. I've got to tell him what I saw. He doesn't believe in ghosts or—or things like that."

"Later, Miss Julie. You can't go to San Marco now. You must wash and rest and change this torn gown."

She looked at me in that mulishly stubborn way I've learned to dread.

"I *will* go. If you think I'll stay in this house one

minute without my Bart! I was never so scared in my life."

"Here is the lowest step. Now, have a care. When you get to your chamber, you can tell me all about your fright."

The truth is, I wanted to get us both out of this labyrinth as quickly as possible. I was still in dread of meeting Cobb unexpectedly, a Cobb armed with the knife he had wielded to such frightening effect in my bedchamber. She began to climb obediently but she was still chattering away about ghostly apparitions, a subject I could well understand, after any time in these cellars.

"Well then, Miss, what did you see? Why did you go down into the cellars?"

She stopped and turned around on the step, looking me in the face.

"Anne, you will not credit it, but I was coming out of the old Servants' Parlor where I'd talked to you, and it was very gray and misty in that passage. There are no windows there, you know. And the most shocking thing! The door into the cellars was open and I thought I saw my father's face."

Mother of God! I thought . . . Is Sanson's prisoner wandering about this house then?

"You—saw your father?"

"Not really Father, of course. He's dead. It was his ghost. And I won't stay in this house one minute without Bart."

"Nonsense. You'll be perfectly safe in your apartments until either Master Bartrum or your guardian returns. Did you follow this ghostly apparition into the cellar here?"

"I hardly saw him. I just wandered blindly after this—face. There may have been a body, but I would not be sure. The passage is always so dark, and these steps . . . I think my ghost was afraid when he saw me. You see, I called out 'Papa!' Did you ever hear of a ghost being afraid?"

"Very rarely." I tried not to make my voice sound too dry, but it had not been bad enough that I should imagine a vicious knife-wielding Cobb hanging about in these cellars. Now, I peered around into the dark behind us, wondering if Sanson's prisoner was down here, watching us also.

"Do ghosts have bodies?" she asked. "Because if they do, I couldn't see Papa's body. Being dead, he probably was wearing a gray shroud."

I raised my head suddenly. Bits and pieces of what I had seen and experienced all fitted together.

"No," I said. "I think your ghost was wearing a monk's rob, like a Carnival masquer. I've seen him once or twice myself."

She gave a squeakly little scream, almost a yelp, and began to run up the steps ahead of me.

"Then I really saw it. It really is a ghost! I'll not stay in this house another minute without Bart. I'll go to him."

I was still trying to persuade her that there was nothing to fear in her own apartment when she reached the top step and passed the open door. She stumbled and caught the latch of the door to regain her balance as she cried, "You shan't make me stay in the house alone!" and the next second, as I reached up frantically, guessing her intent, she slammed the door shut almost in my face.

Furious with her, and with myself for having been outgeneraled by this little ninny, I gave the door a hard push, expecting the door to fly open with a great, racketing slam. But I only jarred my body painfully against what proved to be a locked door. The vixen had thrown the night bolt. I rattled the door angrily, in such a temper as I have seldom found myself, calling out at the same time, on the theory that someone of the household was sure to hear me.

I was an optimist on that score, however. The household servants invariably avoided the area of this floor nearest the cellars. I might have fared better had I been locked in at the far end of this labyrinth, near the Dry Cellar, which, at the least, was more often used than this end of the underground area.

I must have wasted ten minutes shouting, and banging on the door and receiving nothing but scraped knuckles and a nasty bump on the knee for my trouble.

It was excessively annoying. When I finally came to my senses, stopped expending valuable energy, and leaned against the door, taking deep breaths of the rank and noxious air, the silence which followed my noisy banging was even more unnerving.

I stared down through the darkness, trying to make out objects that I must avoid if I was to find my way to the canal door, or—horrid thought!—the full length of the intricate cellars to the back entrance above the Dry Cellar. There was some sort of dim light filtering in, probably from the barred openings that served as windows beside the canal steps, but it was impossible to identify any object distinctively. I would have to make the best of my other senses to avoid bruising my limbs as I hurried through the cellars.

I walked down the steps angrily, making a great, rackety noise as my flat-heeled day slippers slapped the stone, but at the foot of the steps, finding myself surrounded by the fetid dark, I was less anxious to announce my presence. Very likely somewhere in these cellars that dreadful, if unfortunate, monkish prisoner was hiding. How had he found the palazzo? But then, he must have followed Sanson here at one time or another. It was still conceivable that he had been the monkish creature who pursued me through the back alleys and over the canals of Venice that unforgotten night.

Michael . . . Michael . . . I thought—if only there were justice in what you do. If you could tell me, let me share whatever this horror is . . .

I worked myself into a furious anger at him. He had gone off to the Island to find his prisoner and very likely, the monk who had frightened his supposed daughter was still here where she had seen him vanish. I became inordinately still, moving along as near to the walls as I could, while I approached the gray streaks of light which must come from the barred windows opening onto the canal. Very soon, my low shoes were slipping in the muck of canal overflow and probably leakage around the rotting foundations. It was a dreadful, insecure feeling, this having the floor beneath slip out from under one, and I slowed to a careful walk, my fingers groping for support along the cracked and worn stones of the wall. When I stopped momentarily I heard faint, dripping sounds, more leakage, no doubt. It was hideously magnified down in these long, intricate passages.

By the time I stumbled over the bottom step of the flight leading up to the canal door, I was enormously relieved. I realized how very alarming a jaunt the full length of these cellars might be. Here, all was familiar. I could see the spot where Elvira Huddle's casket had rested before it was moved to the death gondola, and the place where Michael and Julie and Bartrum had stood. Signs of death everywhere, and somewhere amid this stench of death was the monk who had twice before terrified me. About him too there had been the stench of death.

I hurried up the steps feeling all the while the awful, sad, fetid breath of that monk blowing faintly upon the back of my neck. I reached the top step, put out my hand for the latch, and had a sudden, ghastly thought: What if this door too is locked?

So powerful was this thought that when I tried the latch, and the door failed to give, I was hardly surprised for a second or two. Then I tried harder. It was locked.

I leaned as far away from the door as possible without losing my balance, toward the nearest barred opening through which the last light of sunset came in, reflected off the windows of the palazzo across the canal. I could not reach the opening, but my voice might be heard on the canal by anyone passing in a barge or gondola. Though the canal was deserted, I called out, feeling foolish. I hoped my voice might be heard by someone in the kitchen or stillroom whose windows faced on the canal further along. I called out once more, speaking as clearly as I could, "D'Entragues! Rosa!" and hoping the echo of my voice would carry along the canal.

When no answer came, I thought, "This is absolutely the last sound I shall make! If I have to walk the entire length of these cellars, it will be in silence." Already I had made known every move of mine to anyone locked in here with me. But there was one door at which the servants would be certain to hear me, if I could locate that door above the Dry Cellar amid all the darkness that absorbed the rest of this moldy, foul-smelling world below me.

I sighed, recovered my temper somewhat, and this time hurried down into the dark, hoping that whatever eyes watched me here would find me equally obscure and well hidden when I myself dissolved in the thickness of night. It was from here on, I remembered, that Cobb and I had very nearly waded in the mud and muck of the overflow from the canal above the windows. I could feel it now oozing around the soles of my slippers and I was forced to test each movement before I took an entire step. Always, there was that sickening feeling that I would find nothing beneath my foot at all except the bottomless ooze, and if I ventured to make a sound, I would let the hidden man in his monkish masquerade know precisely where I was.

There were no sounds now except the sucking of my shoe leather as I drew it out of the muddy floor covering. I had to feel my way after the light from the canal openings faded. The seamed, leprous wall gave me little comfort. Where is he hiding? I wondered . . . or did he escape out of the canal door and bolt it from the outside?

I must have been considerably more than halfway, and just past the muddy, sinking floor when I was stopped by the cold breeze blowing at my side from off the wine cellar. I shivered and hurried now, as rapidly as I could feel my way. Suddenly, my eyes made out a face in the gloom ahead. Someone was seated directly in my path, doubtless on one of the lower steps leading up past the Dry Cellar; for the face was opposite and at a level with my own. I backed up hastily and betrayed my approach by the grating of my foot on the now dry stone floor.

There must be light sifting down from above. Perhaps the door up to the ground floor was ajar; for I could now see Humphrey Cobb's pale face staring at me in the thick gloom. I could not make out his hands, and I doubted if, from his seated position, he could suddenly leap up and do me mischief. I decided to brazen it out.

"Good evening, Mr. Cobb. You'll not be telling me you too are locked in down here?"

In his insolent, immobile way, Cobb continued to stare at me until I was almost upon him and could make out the faint outline of his body and the steps above and below where he sat waiting for me. I wondered if that fixed expression would yield in any way to a human look if I stepped around him. Extraordinary creature! Was he merely trying to frighten me? If so, he failed. Having come face to face with him, I regained my lost courage and wondered that the little man ever possessed the power to frighten me.

Before venturing onto the step, I tried one more effort at politeness.

"Will you be so kind as to let me pass?"

It was not until then that my skirts brushed against his shoulder, as I tried to mount the steps around the annoying fellow. The touch was so slight I did not feel it, and what followed was so rapid and so confusing in this half-dark that I did not scream or make a sound when Humphrey Cobb simply dropped away from me and fell, face down, upon the time-worn stones of the cellar floor.

My breath seemed to catch in my throat as I peered down into the cellar, trying to understand what had happened. Nothing about him had moved, or struggled or given any sign of life as he fell. I was very slow to realize the ghastly truth as I knelt by him and felt his face, listened for a heartbeat. He must have been dead before my skirts gave the small impetus that sent his body crumpling to the floor.

"Dear God, no!" I thought in horror. "He was dead when he stared at me out of the darkness!"

The discovery seemed to wash over me by degrees, leaving me so weak for a few minutes that I could only kneel there on the stones of the floor, my thoughts in turmoil.

A slight, crackling sound somewhere aroused me from my stupor. My hands, icy and shaking, covered with a sticky substance that smelled of blood, came away from their examination of the dead man. I looked over my shoulder, remembering the possible presence of my other nemesis, the man in the monk's robe and cowl. Seeing nothing, I heard the crackle again and raised my head. I was wildly relieved to hear it louder now, the heavy walk of a booted man on the floor overhead. I called out as loudly as I could, and then got to my feet and scrambled up the steps. This time, when I pounded on the door just above the Dry Cellar, I heard voices and the door opened with a resounding crash against the passage wall.

I was blinded by the light for a few seconds, but there was no mistaking the sharp voice of Madame D'Entragues, and the echoing tones, a trifle less imperious, of the Princess da Rimini.

"Mother of Heaven, child! Or should I say—the devil!" was Her Highness' startled greeting. "We have looked everywhere for you. That goodlooking Captain Dandolo says you were in haste to see him."

"If you please, Madame!" the cook interrupted. "Mademoiselle is pale as milk. Let her at least recover first."

The Princess' airy good nature was undisturbed by this setdown from a member of the servant class. "Yes, of course. Stupid of me." She led me with surprising gentleness, to a stool by the stillroom door, but by this time I had gathered my sense and protested vehemently.

"No. You don't understand! He is dead down there. His whole back . . . all blood!" I held out my shaking hands, the palms up, and both women gasped. D'Entragues drew back, with revulsion, but the Princess, after a sharp intake of breath, asked only a trifle shakily,

"Who is dead?"

"Cobb. I asked them to send for the Captain. I wanted to tell him that Cobb had vandalized my room . . . I learned of it from—please hurry! Captain!"

The Princess looked as if I had run mad, but when we suddenly became aware of the sound of heavy boots that I had heard overhead in the cellars, I pushed past her toward the young Captain Dandolo. While I tried to blurt out my discovery in good order, wedging in my original discovery, that Cobb had torn up my room, the Captain seemed to understand perfectly. He patted me on the shoulder, announced, all too sweetly, that he understood and that the important matter, at the moment, was the prisoner kept on the Ile Isola by persons acquainted with my employer, the Signore Sanson.

I looked from the Captain's young, earnest face to Princess Ketta. She had the grace to look ashamed.

"My dear Anne, what else was there to do? I took a little ride to Isola. The man was gone. Escaped. Everyone was in a frightful terror. I came here to warn Michael, and whom should I meet in the palazzo but the good Captain Dandolo. Since you have already found a dead man, Anne, you may see that we have not arrived nearly in time. Michael's prisoner has done his work." She shrugged lightly, with the odd charm I had noticed the first night I met her on the lonely quai. It was a bit out of place here, and in these circumstances, however. "Well, then, I do believe Michael's prisoner will have a deal to say on his own behalf. And it was only just to warn the good Captain before the rest of us are murdered in our beds . . . Or elsewhere," she added thoughtfully, with a glance at the floor and, by inference, the cellars beneath.

I had gotten hold of myself now, but all this talk was just a jumble. I could scarcely understand it. I wanted to wash my hands, but I wanted also to defend Michael. Since it was clearly not Michael who had killed that man down in the cellars, and since he had kept the prisoner confined, he could hardly be blamed, in any event. I said harshly, "For the matter of that, your precious prisoner very likely is escaping at this moment while we stand gabbling about it. Miss Julie saw him and chased him down into the cellars. And Cobb was murdered there. So we must ask Miss Julie if she saw him after she left the cellar."

"But—but that is impossible," put in Madame D'Entragues, sorely tried by all this.

We looked at her, for the first time, I think, aware that an outsider had heard bits of our secrets. The Princess was crisp and cool, having recovered her own easy command of herself and her aristocratic world.

"Truly, D'Entragues? May one ask why?"

The Frenchwoman glanced at each of us in turn. She was puzzled but triumphant too, at her moment of importance.

"Becasue Barbarita and I—we tried to stop the child, but she was so determined. Something about her father. She had seen her father. She must tell young Monsieur Bartrum. Or go to him. It was very confused. I think she fancied her father was on the little bridge at the back of the garden. Barbarita ran after young Mademoiselle, but lost her, naturally."

The Princess glanced at me. "Her father was believed dead, but she has evidently discovered that he is not."

"Her father killed Cobb down in the cellars, I've no doubt," I said sharply. "And we must find Miss Julie before she follows Cobb to her death."

XX

THIS WAS ALL of a piece with the rest of the events that had sorely tried the household in recent weeks.

"She must be found at once, of course," the Princess agreed, glancing from me to the Captain. "Does anyone have a notion which way she would be likely to take in order to reach Bartrum?"

The Captain had already opened the door to the cellars, clearly anxious to locate and examine the body of the unfortunate Cobb; yet his concern for Julie Sanson was probably even greater than ours. "But—by gondola, surely, Highness."

I reached for a clean kitchen cloth and scrubbed at my hands. This did not remove the faint, acrid odor of blood, and even as I made my protest to Princess Ketta and the Captain, I was washing my hands again in the bowl she had set aside in which to wash some fruit for dinner.

"Pardon," I blurted out quickly, "but I believe Miss Julie must have gone through the alleys to St. Mark's. It is quicker, and if she thought she saw her father on the bridge, then I am sure she took that route. I am slightly familiar with it. I came back that way one night."

"I understand, Signorina. Two of my men are on their way to fetch the gentleman. There seems to be evidence that he was wearing a masquer's robe and a cowl. If the Signorina Julie is in the vicinity, they will have her back safe, I trust. Much safer than in the hands of young Huddle."

We did not doubt it, but one look from the Princess to me informed us both that we trusted his intentions more than their fulfillment.

"Very well, Highness . . . Signorina. If you are to follow her. But I will send for my men to check in the other way as well. And I myself must see to the matter of Cobb at once. I trust this will not take more than a matter of minutes."

In the circumstances, Princess Ketta and I set out almost immediately by that memorable and sinister route through the now shadowed alleys of Venice. I was relieved to have the company of the brisk, vivacious woman who knew this city of canals so well and found nothing in them to fear. The Princess looked at me with brisk sympathy as we passed hurriedly over the bridge that spanned our easterly canal.

"I have taken these little back-alley passages for years, cherie, and no harm done. Mama would never walk a step. Sedan chairs for her. But I find that very slow going. We will be in San Marco before dark and they will be lighting all the little lamps in the cafes. Then we can hire a gondola and take those tiresome lovers safely back to the palazzo."

"And how safe will they be there?" I asked, glancing back over my shoulder at the great, gray mass of the house we had quitted.

She laughed abruptly and then was silent. It seemed to me she was very near to running, and while I sympathized with her for her haste, at this rate, we would be very unlikely to see Miss Julie or even the escaped prisoner in any of the long, tangled alleys already shadowed in twilight. I could not forget the first night when I outran that eerie monk and then found him still there at the edge of the garden, only the eyes seeming alive in that mask. Even now, I could feel that ancient fear as we passed other well-remembered corners, a bridge arching over an abruptly turning canal, a long, stone quai so narrow that deep night had already engulfed its splintered mooring poles, and always ahead, another series of high, forbidding palaces, built perhaps six hundred years before, and looking it. Between these windowless walls we scurried along. The Princess stumbled once as we climbed still another bridge, but fortunately, she had her hand out and caught my elbow in time to prevent what I imagined would be an unusual accident for the Princess Ketta da Rimini.

Just as she had predicted, we reached St. Mark's Square when the candles in all the little cafes were being lighted. It would have been an enchanting sight at any other time, but that evening we were too tense, too anxious to appreciate the beauties of Venice by night, so long extolled by the rich dandies on their Grand Tour. What is worse, the Square was full of Carnival masqueraders. As we walked rapidly past the first cafe, glancing in at the little red plush rooms crowded with gentlemen in masks and ladies in concealing black dominos, Her Highness murmured my own feeling aloud.

"We shall never find them behind those stupid masks. Look there! A dozen females in mask and bauta. Not one who might be in the least different, identifiable."

"They should be at the Cafe Florian; don't you think?" I suggested. "Master Bartrum is forever talking of that Cafe. We went there the afternoon that you and Michael . . . Master Sanson . . . brought Miss Julie to meet her betrothed. And I could swear Miss Julie meant to meet Master Bartrum there today."

She had glanced at me when I mentioned Sanson by his first name. But now she sighed and, being pushed by a black-cloaked crowd of celebrants, groaned and stopped to rub her ankle.

"Quite drunk, I see. And it's scarcely dark."

I did not commit the discourtesy of reminding her that within a week we should be in Lent, and tonight we must expect to encounter these noisy, drunken revelers. It made our task twice as hard, but what is worse,

I suspected now that Captain Dandolo's police would find it more difficult to capture Sanson's prisoner whose concealing domino was an ideal disguise tonight, being duplicated several hundred times in the Square alone.

I had been studying the shadowy creatures entering the cafes when the Princess sucked in her breath so tensely I too was shocked by the thing we saw advancing upon us through the ins and outs of the shadows that barred the center of the Square. So exactly did he resemble the "monk" who had pursued me on those other occasions that I too gasped.

"Do you think it may be the one?" she whispered.

Something about the creature, his large teeth flashing at us below the black eye-mask, gave me the dubious comfort of saying, "No. He appears a mere dandy and doubtless regards us as prospective companions for the evening."

"Good God!" the Princess exclaimed with a dry little laugh, "We should have been masked. How stupid of us! But are you sure he is not Sanson's prisoner of the Ile Isola?"

"Not wearing those dandified boots," I said and we avoided the gentleman with flashing teeth rather obviously.

I think Her Highness was as relieved as I to reach the Cafe Florian. It being a chilly spring night, most of Florian's patrons were warm and cozy within the cafe's red plush confines, and as we were entering, an elegant, unmasked gentleman bowed to us ever so slightly, barring our way.

"Pardon, Ladies . . ." The way his thin lips curled over the old fashioned Italian form of the title, told me that he clearly assumed we were not ladies. "There are no tables. I regret."

But the Princess was now on her mettle. "Paolo, do not be tiresome. Your manners are atrocious."

"Your Highness! And unescorted? But where are the eager gentlemen who usually make a push to join you?" The thin-lipped man stared around behind us, his olive face colored still darker by his awkward mistake, and with a strongly obsequious tone now, he tried to wave us inside one of the little jewel box dining rooms to

201

our left. "Please to take seat. No. A private parlor, of course."

"Never mind, Paolo. We have only come to fetch up young Bartrum Huddle and his betrothed."

"Ah, yes. I remember Your Highness' friendship with the young man's prospective father-in-law. But I regret, he left here some minutes ago."

"Alone?"

"Alone?" I asked, for the Princess began to look around as though doubting him.

"Quite alone," said the fellow, ignoring me in order to address all his remarks to Princess Ketta. "His pockets were to let, as he phrased it. There had been a bit of gaming. His friends went on to La Fenice, but it was his intention to return to the palazzo." The waiter leaned toward the Princess. "He wished to make a loan from the Signore Sanson."

"It is strange we did not meet him," Her Highness said to me. "Unless he took a gondola."

But Florian's waiter thought it not so strange, after all. "He said if he could find a gondolier to trust him he would ride to the palazzo. Otherwise, he would walk. But it is only a matter of minutes since he departed. You doubtless passed him as you crossed the Square."

"Now, what are we to do?" the Princess asked me impatiently. "Poor Julie is sure to arrive here at Florian's any moment, if she has not—"

"—encountered the monk," I finished, amazed at the sharpness of my tone; for I felt very much shaken within.

While the waiter looked from one to the other of us, positively aglow with curiosity, the Princess nodded. "Just so. Not to mention the police and perhaps Dandolo himself, who will be dashing to Florian's very likely too late. Poor Dandolo is such a stupid young man! And as for that little gudgeon, if she does reach here and we are gone, she will not know what to do."

I was peering out intently at the crowds that milled about in the Square, and the Princess looked over my shoulder, frowning. She understood my fear almost at once.

"Well, Anne, the child is perfectly capable of getting

herself lost in that shuffle. Shall we venture around the Square once, keeping an eye to the sight of a flaxen-haired little goose, doubtless being mauled by those masqueraders?"

I agreed without speaking. My throat was dry as dust. I could not but think of the terror that an ignorant, sheltered girl like Miss Julie would experience if some of these drunken dandies had the natural idea that she was seeking their company.

Princess Ketta gave a few orders to the waiter, reminding him that he must not let Miss Julie leave the Cafe alone and that he should explain our predicament to the police if they arrived.

I put in then, "For if we do not find her, we should hire the first gondola and return to the palazzo. Michael . . . that is, Signore Sanson will have returned by then, surely, and he will know exactly what to do."

She glanced at me, her rich, full-lipped mouth curved in a slow smile. "So that way lies the trail! I rather suspected I was behind the Fair."

I looked away, avoiding those wise, clever eyes of hers, and we went out under the arcades. And a bit of luck they were, those arcades, for the evening sky had clouded over it and it was beginning to sprinkle. We made our way with a businesslike air and a bad-mannered push, through loitering knots of lovers and would-be lovers, passing the Campanile where the mist began to blow in needle-like pricks at our uncovered faces. The Lagoon in the distance, rolling into the Grand Canal beyond the Piazzetta, looked chill and ink-black. I did not enjoy the thought of riding back to the palazzo over those deep waters which nightly washed out to sea the debris of a great city, including such bodies as had been rolled down the slime-covered steps into the canals.

I was now chillingly convinced that some evil must have come to silly young Julie Sanson and the sooner we asked Michael to take over the search, the better chance there would be of her rescue. I wanted to pour the whole, frightening problem into Michael's wonderfully capable hands. During the last hour I had become more and more convinced that the terrors we presently faced might be laid to our lack of faith and confidence in Michael. He had been right from the beginning. The man who was probably Julie's father had proved to be dangerous. His imprisonment would now prove to have been thoroughly justified.

Thanks to the crowd running from the rain, we had difficulty passing the corner of the fantastic Doge's Palace, which seemed to me a preposterously fragile edifice to have been the center of stern Venetian justice before the arrival of the even more stern General Bonaparte.

"Look!" The Princess whispered and nudged me. "The girl in front of the Cathedral. There! Those rogues with the lantern have waved the light in her face."

We could not see the girl's face. She was turned away from us, and her head was covered by a black bit of lace. I thought she must be about to enter the Cathedral and the Princess added a little doubtfully, "To be sure, her hair seems a trifle darker."

"I am afraid so." I myself had an eye to a rain-soaked blonde head across the Square. The young female, very lightly clad in a day dress, had just rushed under the arcades and crashed into a quartet of male masqueraders, who, as the Princess and I neared them, completely eclipsed the girl from our sight.

"Julie!" the Princess called in exasperation that also sounded very like relief. She began to run as I did, but I was faster and unfortunately, a pair of drunken dandies got between us.

By the time I reached the blonde girl, I found myself being pawed and clawed at by the masqueraders who had been flirting with the girl. One glance told me she was not Julie, that she enjoyed the familiarities, and that the masquers exuded a powerful odor of garlic and sour wine. It was enough to turn the stomach, and I had a frantic struggle to free myself from the clutches of one excessively amorous fellow who tried to kiss me and prowled over my bodice while stifling me with his breath.

We were separated by a rush of masqueraders trying to escape the pelting rain in the Square, and I took to my heels and ran, heading across the Square. I preferred the rain to the odious dandies of the Carnival crowd. Though I did glance around frequently to see if the lamps of evening glinted off any young and golden heads, I am frank to say I had given up hope of encountering Julie here in this crowd. I could only hope that Princess Ketta would eventually wend her way back to Florian's where I would persuade her either to remain there in wait, or return to the palazzo. Clearly, if Julie had even a grain of sense, she had done the same.

Pushed and shoved along as I tried to go counter to the crowd, it seemed to take me forever to reach the other end of the Square. Then, I found myself discouragingly far from Florian's, separated from the Cafe by the full length of a colonnade. I started to struggle in that direction but was suddenly swept by the happy throng, into a cobbled passage which led to the wind-swept Grand Canal beyond. In the great hubbub I heard my name called and thinking this only my fancy, I set myself to braving the crowd again. It seemed to me in those moments that every masquerader who surrounded me was glaring at me with that bright, terrible and sometime poignant look I had seen twice before in the shadowed face of the monk.

Then my forearms were seized and I saw Paolo, the waiter of Florian's. He was breathless and excited which I could well understand. He apologized for having taken me forcibly.

"But Signorina Wicklow, the Princess asks me to find you. Impossible task, but I am in luck. You must follow by gondola. There! You see?" He swung me around, barely in time to catch a glimpse of a gondola dissolving into the busy night traffic on the waters.

"I don't understand. Why? What has happened?" I had to shout to make myself heard.

"Her Highness has a message. Her Highness finds the young Signorina weeping and puts her in a gondola for the palazzo. You are to follow quickly, for your safety. She asks a gondolier to wait for you. She regrets not to wait, but the young Signorina demands to return to her lover. She is in strong hysterics."

Knowing Julie, I shouted in his ear, "I can imagine!"

I did not envy the Princess her task of handling the noisy, hysterical girl in an unsettling gondola on choppy waters. However, it was my own task now to return to the palazzo as rapidly as possible, and, I hoped, to the comfort of Michael Sanson's presence.

I was grateful for Paolo's escort to the canal where the rush of traffic took away all the gondolas nearby and I hurried on the run along the worn and crooked cobblestones to the last remaining boat, with only the silver trappings on the bow catching the misty light from the heavens. I had long since outrun the waiter of Florian's and a pair of lovers in twin masks and dominos when I reached the dark gondola. The gondolier, who had been away from the mooring pole, came along as I did, rearranging his own heavy cape and a wide-brimmed black hat against the spattering mist. He set the gondola's lantern where it was shielded from the rain, just under the covered bow and then put out a gloved hand for his pay.

"The palazzo at the Rio del Cavallo," I told him and put all the small coins from my reticule into his palm.

He nodded. "She said you would come soon."

The rain pelted between us, blurring the scene and making me huddle down in my thin spring coat which was now sodden, clinging to me and chilling me clear to the bone. After we left the mooring pole, the boat swayed, caught sideways by the current, and I looked up, surprised by the clumsiness of the gondolier. We headed out into the black waters that were rapidly spotting with raindrops. Getting a splash of water in the face, I slumped down again and did not raise my head until I was stung by a sharp object that grazed my shoulder and made me start nervously. We were far out of the populous sector of the canal by this time and I did not like the deserted look of the buildings facing on the canal into which we turned.

"What was that?" I demanded.

But I got no answer. The gondolier was busy making the awkward push with his sweep to avoid the shoreline where four-hundred year old palaces overhung the water, casting it in deeper shadow. I reached around behind me and tugged on the skirt of the fellow's cloak. For the first time, he looked down at me, his face dim and only half visible in the shade of that heavy-brimmed hat. But I knew those eyes, haunting me with their sadness, as if the glitter of unshed tears lay just within the lashes. As if what they looked out upon was Death itself. I had seen those eyes looking down at me in just this way, out of the monk's hood on the Ile Isola, when I came briefly to consciousness that night.

I caught myself before I could reveal my panic. My senses warned me that only calm and a pretense at understanding would save me. I smiled. It must have been a ghastly effort; for I knew my mouth quivered nervously and my hands trembled so much I kept them hidden against my skirts.

The effort, I thought, had been vain, and I remember wondering how cold the canal waters would be, and how deep, and if I could swim as I had in my Irish childhood; for the prisoner I had seen in the villa, and the glittering eyes of the monk were now one face, leaning down, close over me.

"I gave you audience at my villa, did I not?"

I tried to agree but no words came. The poor man was certainly mad, which would explain his crimes.

"Do you know, they will not let me see my small daughter? Forgive me if I have deceived you, but I was told you will arrange for me to take her away to safety."

"Yes. If you wish." That, at least, I could understand.

"You must not be disrespectful, Mademoiselle. You must always address me as befits my station. Sanson said I must deny it always because they want to kill me, but I am Louis-Charles, the King. Perhaps you were not aware. When I walk out, I must always go disguised. I am fortunate when we are in Carnival."

I edged away from the great, dangerous sweep in his hands, eyeing the shoreline as casually as possible. We were coming to the Rio del Cavallo. But the gentle, yet curiously proud planes of his face arrested me in the midst of my horrified conclusion that he was mad as Bedlam! I believed he had murdered three people, perhaps more, and no matter how I sympathized with his desire to see his child, Julie, my first thought must be to save myself.

"We must tie up at one of those quais, you know ... Sir."

"Monseigneur!"

I corrected myself hastily, while I glanced ashore It seemed to me that there was a drunken masquer staggering along the narrow, cobbled quai opposite us. If the man was only sober enough to understand my signal for help!

I must have moved too quickly. A hand came down hard upon my shoulder. Making an enormous effort, I relaxed and looked up innocently.

"We must put in at the—the quai ahead. Your daughter will be coming home from San Marco at any minute, over that bridge."

We could scarcely make out the humped silhouette of the bridge, but I knew that we were at last within a part of the canal I recognized. Though it was lonely, except for the drunken walker on the shore, and the only light came from the gondola lantern, I saw, even through the slanting mist, that I could run across that bridge, through a narrow alley between the buildings opposite the palazzo, and come out upon the bridge behind Mrs. Huddle's dying garden.

My suggestion about his daughter seemed to reach his poor, confused mind. He made a strong effort to imitate the ease of the experienced gondolier in bringing the surprisingly awkward gondola along the side of the quai. I pretended to listen for distant sounds and explained excitedly, "I believe I heard Miss Julie's footsteps. Beyond the bridge. From that alley near the ivy wall."

It was a cruel but necessary lie. It turned the madman's thoughts from me, and it was almost believable, since the rain had slackened to a faint mist which I scarcely felt. The second we touched the quai, rubbing alongside with an ominous crunch of metal against stone, I leaped to the cobblestones, twisting my foot painfully under me. The madman did not wait to tie up to the decayed mooring pole but jumped after me. I ran madly, faster than I had ever run in my sturdy girlhood. Ahead of me was the drunken masquerader. Even as I ran, crying "Help me! Please help me!" the masquerader seemed to throw off that drunken lope, and transform himself into something else. I knew not what. A watching, tense, yet inhuman thing, as sinister as the madman who was stumbling after me. The stance of the sinister fellow to whom I was running for help looking oddly familiar, yet unidentifiable in the curtain of mist that fell between us. He was not so tall as the madman, nor so heavy through the shoulders.

Again, as early in our gondola ride, something sped by me, so near my face as makes no matter. I winced and then swerved in my course. Plunging through the slackening mist, I saw that my rescuer still held a pistol aimed at the madman behind me, but the watery mist flashed on the barrel and I saw that its one charge had been fired, so nearly missing me.

I glanced over my shoulder and with curiously mixed emotions, saw that the dueling pistol had done its work. My poor madman, Julie's father, had been struck in the breast and was swaying perilously on the very edge of the canal.

"No!" I cried then, not understanding my own awful pity. "Don't let him drown. He is mad. He thinks he is the King of France."

"But of course, he is. That is why he must die. There cannot be two kings," said my rescuer in a voice I knew well. "What a pity you witnessed this! That greedy Cobb said it would end with our having to remove you. You were too curious by half. You cost Cobb his life as well. Did you know that? When he came bleating to me that you knew who searched your room, Cobb became a danger to me. He might talk to save himself ... so you see, you did cause his death."

XXI

WITH MY SENSES spinning I still knew this must be a twisted, hideous joke. Then, looking from the wounded, suffering man to my rescuer in the black domino, I began to wonder if I had misunderstood the whole of it.

I ventured in a cracked, hysterical voice I did not know for my own, "Don't joke, please, Your Highness. Is he truly hurt? We must help him. He is mad, you know. He isn't the least aware of what he says or does." As I scrambled to my feet, trying to reach the man doubled over in his agony, I called to the Princess, still stupefied by her conduct, "What have you done with Miss Julie?"

"Oh, in God's name, do not be so stupid!" the Princess called to me coldly. "How do I know? I have not seen that ridiculous child. Nor had that poor waiter. He saw me, and gave my instructions to you. That is enough. Julie is probably with her impossible Bartrum at this moment. And more luck to them! I've no grudge against idiots."

I ignored the half of this rambling because the wounded man had sunk to his knees. I got my hands under one of his shoulders to prevent him from dropping over the side of the quai into the canal, but the flickering gondola lantern showed him to be so pale, and he was breathing so raggedly, I knew he must be dying. I was busy trying to relieve him of the agony that twisted his elegant features quite out of all recognition, and did not look up for a minute or two.

Seeing the Princess' shadow cross the lantern light, I cried out, furious, "He can do us no harm now. Go for help. In Heaven's name!"

A slight sound, a kind of "click" made me look up. Princess Ketta had thrown off the all-concealing domino which was in the way of her fingers; for in her hand, and pointed this time clearly at me, was the dueling pistol. Its silver mounting caught the lantern glow, and I stared at the facets of light thrown off, recovering at last from the paralysis which had gripped my wits when the Princess made her first easy, almost friendly warning: "Remove you as well."

"Let the poor creature fall, cherie. The waters will give him a shroud. You were right in one matter. He is better dead than in a madhouse. And he is certainly an embarrassment to those near the French throne."

From this I assumed that the heirs to the present King of France had employed her and Cobb as assassins! I marveled that in such high places murder was still the weapon to win a throne, though I failed to understand who the dying man might be. My terror of the Unknown was diminished by this confrontation with the woman who must prove to be the real monster. All my Irish anger at her treachery came to give me courage in what might be the last minutes of my life. I cleared my throat, made my voice as loud as my tight throat would permit. "You'll not be shooting me with that pistol, you know."

The Princess' eyes looked lifeless as agate. Just for a second or two she hesitated, then flicked a glance down at the dueling pistol in her hand. I had hoped that my question would put her at a loss, shake her confidence. But her hand was perfectly steady. I stared at the barrel, and the deadly mouth of that pistol.

"You can't be shooting, Ma'am . . . you do not know that."

"You foolish child! Let him go. And you . . . to the edge. I've no time."

I took a short, cutting breath, hoping by any means to prolong life, my one chance. For beyond this little corner of the Rio del Cavallo there were Carnival lanterns, moving gondola lights, distant sounds of Venice at night. And surely . . . surely some of those lights were nearer now than five minutes ago. I raised my voice called loudly, still on that wager to myself about her dueling pistol and at the same time, hoping to make myself heard by the men who carried those approaching lights. I had been loud enough heretofore, and in all likelihood, it was my voice which had told them where we were.

"And I say you can't shoot. There's only one charge in that pistol."

She laughed. Excellent! I thought. It was a loud, vulgar, triumphant laugh and it would be heard, I devoutly prayed.

"Dueling pistols popularly come in pairs. He is dead in any case. You can do nothing. A little closer to him, cherie. There! One more step does for you, I think."

I said very carefully—surely there was a growing brightness beyond the bridge!—"Your Highness forgets.

You fired one shot at us in the gondola. And a second a few minutes ago."

This time she did look down, only a swift, apprehensive glance before her long, lean fingers closed more tightly over and under, entwining in their deadly strength around the hammer. She was saying in a fierce, angry whisper, "There is such a thing as re-loading."

I had that brief second when she had glanced down in hesitation, in which to thrust myself flat upon the wet cobbles as the shot resounded along the narrow canal.

She rushed at me, kicking at me, balancing on the edge of the quai, turning the pistol to use as a club. I got a hard, burning smack across the shoulder, and then the canal bridge was blinding bright, and I blinked and saw Michael Sanson's tall figure. Before the Princess Ketta could strike at me again, he called to her and she swung around, threw the pistol at him just as another shot rang through the canal from out of the darkness behind Michael.

Though she seemed to be only grazed across the cheek, the Princess tottered, clawing at the air. Losing her balance she fell forward, crashing against the vicious metal teeth decorating the prow of the gondola, and then she was lost in the murky night waters.

There were running steps across the rain-washed stones of the quai, and as I was getting to my feet in a daze, I found Michael's arms enfolding me to his warmth and strength.

"You have a surprisingly loud voice when you wish it so," he murmured over my head. "Are all the Irish such shrews?"

I was still too cold, too sickened by the events of the past hour to get a word out in reply or thanks, but I pointed to the unfortunate wounded man beside me, who was silent and motionless, and with Michael's arms still around me protectively, warmly, we moved closer to him. I was surprised and touched by Michael's deep compassion for his wounded prisoner. Around us, I saw vague figures, led by Captain Dandolo, making efforts to drag the body of the Princess da Rimini out of the canal waters.

Bartrum Huddle raised a lantern over the prisoner, whose head Michael was trying to cradle comfortably between us. The wounded man's eyelids fluttered. When he stared up at us I do not believe he saw us. He seemed beyond pain and even in the flaring light his face was gray as ashes. A nervous tic gave brief, grotesque life to his left cheek.

"Easy . . . be easy, my son," murmured Michael in French.

The lips of the dying man tried to form words. He too spoke in French.

"Not—my son. *My Seigneur* . . . Remember, Sanson."

"Pardon, Monseigneur . . . for many things."

I started at Michael's form of address and looked up at Bartrum with the lantern. But he plainly did not comprehend the language and was frowning as he tried to understand the deep emotions here.

The dying man attempted to raise his thin, graceful fingers. They were caught between our bodies and I lifted them for him. He made a great effort, closed them upon Michael's hand.

"I forgive you. For myself. And . . . for them."

His heavy eyelids flickered. He must have been dead some seconds before we realized. When I glanced at Michael, terribly shaken, I saw that he was weeping.

Many minutes later, when Michael took me away from there, Captain Dandolo's men were still working to restore life to the Princess Ketta who lay stretched on the quai, the handkerchief that had been thrown over her face rapidly growing sodden with blood.

I looked back as we crossed the bridge.

"I hope—I hope she is dead."

"Don't worry," Michael said grimly, pressing my face to him with the gentle strength I loved and needed. "She will never be allowed to hurt anyone again."

He did not understand. He believed it was only my cowardice speaking. "No. It would be dreadful for her to live . . . as she is. Her face!" I shuddered, wondering if I would ever forget that ghastly moment when she plunged forward, the silver teeth of the prow on the black gondola slashing across her face.

"My love, she deserves no pity. Everything she said

to you bears out the ugly truth. I knew there were agents sent to murder him, ever since Elvira discovered his identity and began to bleed me for her silence. Elvira was employed as my housekeeper in Genoa some years ago when I was sailing as a smuggler." He looked down at me. "Do I shock you?"

I shook my head. Surely, nothing else could shock me tonight!

"It was exceedingly profitable during our incessant wars when I was younger. But where there is one leech like Elvira, the news gets out. It seems to have reached Paris, probably through Cobb. But don't let us talk of it now. You are cold and wet and hungry, I've no doubt."

I thought he was wrong on one score. I wondered how I could ever eat again. My body had been pummeled and kicked and was still shaking within, and I felt far too nervous to want anything, now that I was safe with Michael. But he knew me better than I knew myself. When he sent a sheepish and subdued Angelo to my room with a hip bath, followed by the chambermaids with steaming hot water, I discovered an hour later that a long, restful soak in the warm water, and fresh clothing did revive me wonderfully.

Puss, the lean gray feline, was in my room through my change from the hag-ridden and haunted creature who stumbled in until I became slightly more human and stroked him as I left. First, he licked his chops, and then showed a lamentable tendency to yawn. He seemed to have been fed; so I was relieved that I need spare no worries for him tonight.

I started down the stairs and across the big salon on my way down to superintend dinner in the kitchen when I heard the rush of silk skirts and Julie's light, airy voice. I wondered if any calamity, any horror would ever erase that completely self-centered spirit of hers. So long as her own little world remained to give her luxuries, the pleasure and happiness she demanded, she quite obviously saw nothing to dampen her mood. She might have been the descendent of many kings, rather than the adopted daughter of a man of the people like Sanson.

"Anne! Isn't it the most famous thing? That horrid

Ketta actually is a murderess! You must go and see Sanson in the summer parlor. Bartrum is going to take me to the Teatro La Fenice, after all." As I turned uncertainly, only to see Michael crossing the salon to me, Julie bubbled on, "Bart and Sanson both insist I didn't see that silly ghost of my father today. I'm ever so glad. Well, I must run. Bart's waiting in the gondola and I'm late, as usual."

Over her head I caught Michael's warm glance and he was almost rude in giving her a little nudge out of the way. When she was no longer between us, he took my hands and led me across to the dining parlor whose elegant old Sixteenth Century table was set for two. It was all most improper, considering our stations in the household, but I made no complaint.

As we finished dinner Captain Dandolo sent up word that he wished to ask Michael some questions which might throw light upon the events of the past weeks in the palazzo as well as the Princess' murderous actions on the quai tonight. Over after-dinner port the two men discussed the crimes in my presence when Michael pointed out that I too had some knowledge I had not heretofore disclosed. I could see, however, that Michael was exceedingly careful in his reference to his dead "prisoner" whom he called merely "Charles."

The Captain sipped the ruby port, gazing at it as if its color reminded him only of the blood shed today.

"The Princess da Rimini's husband is not dead," he informed us presently. "The French Embassy tells me that he is a confidante of persons close to the French throne. Why an heir to the throne of France should send someone to Venice to assassinate a madman you have been keeping confined, Sanson, is something only you can answer. Who was that fellow who died in your arms?"

Without a blink, Michael said easily, "I once had a brief . . . acquaintance with a great lady in the court of the late Queen—Marie-Antoinette. Charles was that lady's—unacknowledged son."

"What lady?" asked Dandolo, avoiding my eyes.

"The—ah—duchess de Polignac."

"In short, this Charles was your bastard."

Michael shrugged. I was sure he lied, and so, I think was the Captain, but very deep and dangerous matters were involved here and he knew the necessity for discretion.

The Captain said, "Very well. I accept this. And the Rimini woman was sent to find him and see that he was assassinated. Why?"

"Perhaps you are not aware that before the Revolution the Royal Family hated the duchess de Polignac for her influence over Marie-Antoinette. Obviously, they wanted to destroy the Polignac's bastard son."

I cut in abruptly, for I felt that the baldness of Michael's story would be challenged. "Captain, Elvira Huddle was once Master Sanson's housekeeper. I believe she spoke of this Charles to Humphrey Cobb. It must have been Cobb who started the matter by notifying the Princess da Rimini in Paris. Cobb was working for the Princess.

"How do you know this?"

I explained the Princess' remark about Cobb's greed as she was about to kill me as well. I added, "I believed the girl, Maria-Elisa, was killed when she discovered why Elvira Huddle was demanding money from Master Sanson."

The Captain nodded. I think he knew nearly as much about the affair as Michael. His great problem seemed to be how little he need report in such a delicate international situation. He explained now, "I have questioned the boy, Angelo, and he tells me that Cobb was angry with the chambermaid, this Maria-Elisa. That he warned her about what is called—listening at keyholes. I believe the Signorina's room was torn apart to discover if she had found the dead chambermaid's journal. At all events, the journal has not been found."

"But—Cobb," I murmured, puzzled. "He was murdered by her. She admitted it to me."

Michael laughed abruptly. "He had certainly been her confederate in the death of Maria-Elisa, and considering the enormous importance of the secret, if Ketta had not been forced to silence him, her orders would have been to do so eventually."

The Captain said, "We are convinced it was a poniard

that performed the so-unpleasant task upon Cobb. And in the back, naturally." His eyes narrowed as he added, "Am I still to believe so much of what you call 'enormous importance' was attached to the life of a Polignac bastard?"

He and Michael looked at each other. The room was so still I could hear the faint, distant sounds of gondoliers calling their traffic signals across the dark waters. Then Michael said blandly, "I ask you to believe that."

"Yes," the Captain agreed. "I am afraid anything more shocking would arouse such an international storm as my small Venice has not known since Bonaparte."

Beyond the partially open doors I could see the balcony over the east canal and I remembered the broken phial I had found on that balcony. A gondolier at this moment, called out his warning and I suddenly thought of an odd event days ago, on the cracked stones of the little quai below the balcony. I caught my breath and the two men looked at me curiously.

"But that may have been the reason!" I cried. When the Captain's eyebrows went up, I explained in a rush, "Cobb was showing me the cellars and as he went up the steps to that little quai under the balcony, he behaved most peculiarly. I thought he had fallen, but I found him on his knees searching for something. I believe the Princess may have thrown the laudanum phial out over the balcony and he found bits of it. I found the rest. It is in my old shawl. Cobb was terrified that someone would see the Princess at that hour and in Mrs. Huddle's room; don't you think?"

The men considered me, and then each other. The Captain shrugged. "Since the Rimini female and Cobb are both dead, we can never be certain she gave the Signora the laudanum, but I think, during the diversion later in the night, when your servant, Rosa, tumbled down the steps, Cobb must have finished off the Signora. And we do have the testimony of the waiter at Florian's that he did not see the Signorina Julie with the Princess tonight himself. The hysterics and the story that put you, Signorina, into the gondola this evening, were merely the Princess' effort to kill off the—ah—gentleman in mid-canal without appearing to involve herself."

... And, I thought ironically, I was to die merely to make the prisoner's death look less like a political crime.

With Michael's signature on a very involved legal statement in Italian, the Captain added it to other papers and left. Michael offered to walk with him down to his gondola at the garden entrance and when I would have left them, Michael put his arm around my waist and said, "Come along. The air will do you good."

When the gondolier had taken the Captain away, Michael and I stood there staring at the misty night around us.

"Who are you?" I asked at last, looking up at his sad, stern face that I had learned to love in spite of all my doubts. "And who was the prisoner, really?"

The muscles of his arm tightened around me but he said after a little pause, "When I tell you, I will have lost you. I am ... or was ... what my father, his brother, and all their ancestors before them were. When I was five I was apprenticed to my uncle who was the head of our family and held the most honored French post of all those in our profession."

I began to dread this revelation, wondering for the first time if he had been right, if his story would set at an end every feeling I had for him. "What was your uncle's ... profession?"

He said abruptly, his voice so harsh I scarcely recognized it, "It was my Uncle Sanson who drove the tumbril of the Queen of France to the guillotine, the Queen ... and how many hundreds of others! He was the Chief Executioner of Paris."

God of Heaven! It was beyond anything I had imagined. He must have felt my withdrawal though it was less outward than inward, and his grip on me lessened, became gentler, almost slack. I wet my dry lips and asked without expression: "Did you participate?"

"At the beginning of the Terror I was sixteen, and I did what I was told to do. I bound the—condemned to the plank. What you might call ... odd jobs."

I wanted very much to scream. I gritted my teeth and moved away from him, reaching a stone bench barely in time before my knees gave way. "And did you enjoy your job? Did you feel that there was a ... a glorious future to it?"

"Don't!"

"Well, what am I to think? I never knew a headsman before. What do they feel? Do they go home at night and say to their wives and children, 'Excuse the stench of blood but I held up two dozen heads to the mob today and the gouts of blood would not wash off?'"

He came and shook me frantically and looked into my face then. I could not avoid the bitterness I read in his dark, luminous eyes.

"I hated it! That is why I—did what I did!" He must have known by my expression that the first horror was beginning to dim a little, that I wanted to understand, that I pitied him in spite of everything.

"What did you do?"

"I was sent on a message from my uncle to a man named Simon, in the Temple where the Royal Family had been imprisoned, before—"

"—their heads were severed."

He winced and I regretted my cold interruption almost before it was spoken.

"In any case, the boy, son of the Royal Family, remained in Simon's care. He was now the undoubted King of France, his father having died some ten months before. I grew attached to the boy . . . he had been put through a frightful emotional ordeal in order to make him denounce his mother at her trial. Simon and the others had persuaded him to say that the Queen used him . . . unnaturally."

I had heard something of this frightful event long ago and now I looked Michael full in the face. "You could not have approved this—this appalling thing. My husband said Marie-Antoinette was not the wisest of queens, but she was an excellent mother."

"Good God! Do you think me a complete devil? Of course, I did not approve. But the knowledge of how the little king had been ill-used, browbeaten, his mind and senses twisted in order to make him tell this frightful lie . . . well, in short, an orphaned little street urchin of about the same age was dying of the lung sickness. I tried in various ways to heighten the resemblance, the dying boy's hair . . . a small scar that the little king had from an accident with a knife when he was carving some clockworks in the Temple Prison—and when the poor urchin was dying, I introduced him into the Temple with the aid of Dr. Tellier, the physician, who, like me, wanted to save the royal child. We made the urchin's last days easier, and after having dipped into my uncle's fat savings, I fled from Paris with the little king. Dr. Tellier died last year. I suppose he must have finally betrayed our secret to someone of importance; for I have not been back in Paris or Northern France since that day."

I began to realize who the sad prisoner had been and why certain people in high places in France must be rid of him now. Sanson's prisoner was the nephew of the present King Louis the Eighteenth, and as Louis the Seventeenth, was the rightful King of France.

"I understand why you kept silence during the Terror, but later, why was the boy—the young man, kept prisoner? And surely, in 1815, after the fall of the Empire, he should have taken the throne."

Michael glanced upward, frowning. "The mist is turning to rain . . ." Then he looked into my eyes. "Have you not guessed? I tried not to myself, for many years. His oddness, his losses of memory, his obsession for repairing clocks— He knocked you on the head at Isola the other night because he thought you had taken one of the clocks he was working on."

"Clocks!"

"Oh, yes. His father, Louis the Sixteenth, would have made an excellent clockmaker. A pity he had to be king. And the boy's jailers gave him broken clockworks to repair, to keep him occupied. But when I had gotten him out of France, we moved from place to place, Louis-Charles and I. Mostly seaports, as I soon learned that smuggling would be most profitable during those long years of the British Blockade. I have done well in that regard. As you may imagine, though, it was exceedingly dangerous to divulge the boy's identity during Bonaparte's regime—"

"My husband was a friend of the Emperor Napoleon," I reminded him, but he only smiled faintly.

"You must take my word, the Emperor would not have been happy to meet the young man who could depose him! And afterward, of course, it would have been even more disastrous, if Louis-Charles had been placed upon the throne."

"But why?"

"Because the emotional problems inflicted upon him as a child in the Temple gradually began to cloud his mind. I knew at last, and too late, how dangerous he could be. He had formed a liaison with a barmaid in Genoa and Julie was born. I knew nothing of Julie for several years, until one night Louis-Charles came to me to confess he had strangled the barmaid in a jealous rage over some rival or other."

"Good God!" I remembered Julie's talk of her mother's disappearance, and of being taken away to live with her father and Sanson. I said to Michael, "And later, Miss Julie says she and her father tried to run away from you, but you stopped them."

"There was nothing else for it. By that time, his rational senses seemed to be drifting further away from reality. So I brought him here, in charge of people themselves too ill-informed and illiterate to understand who he was. But, of course, Elvira moved here too with her son, and the old bleeding for money continued. Then she had ambitions to marry her boy to Julie." He shrugged tiredly. "It matters very little to me. Let them marry. I wonder why I ever threw difficulties in their way. They are worthy of each other. Come along. It is raining harder. You will be soaked to the skin."

We said nothing as we crossed the garden together. When he had opened the door for me and we were going up the steps, I murmured with my thoughts still back in that long, sad past of his, "You have expiated your past, surely. Even your—even Louis-Charles said that when he died."

"I have done what I could," he agreed, and then added heavily, "It is never enough. Louis-Charles was haunted by the lies he was forced to tell against his mother, the lies that cost Marie-Antoinette her life. But believe this one thing of me, Anne, I too have been haunted."

I put my hand in his. "I know."

He glanced at me, his eyes catching the lamplight, their poignant plea cutting to my heart.

"Do you think you could ever forgive me for what I was born to, Anne; do you?"

"He forgave you," I reminded him. "With his dying breath he forgave you for what was done to his parents and to him. As for me," I added tenderly, "I never had anything to forgive you for."

The warmth and the happiness that suffused his hard features were rewards enough for me. We went on up the steps together.